S0-AZI-178

# Molly Moon, Micky Minus, & the Mind Machine

ALSO BY

Georgia Byng

Molly Moon's Incredible Book of Hypnotism

Molly Moon Stops the World

Molly Moon's Hypnotic Time Travel Adventure

Georgia Byng

# Molly Moon, Micky Minus, & the Mind Machine



HarperCollinsPublishers

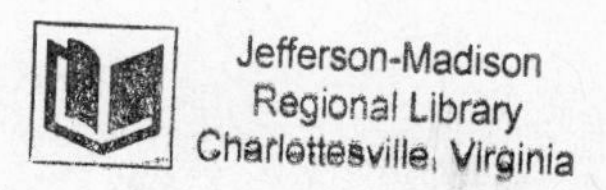

With a big thank-you to my clever and ever so helpful agent, Caradoc King, to my very conscientious editor, Sarah Dudman, to my very amusing American editor, Michael Stearns, and to Talya Baker, an unsung expert, without whom this book would be riddled with irritating mistakes.

Molly Moon, Micky Minus, & the Mind Machine

Molly Moon logo design by Andrew Biscomb
 For information address HarperCollins Children's Books, a division of HarperCollins Publishers, 1350 Avenue of the Americas, New York, NY 10019.
www.harpercollinschildrens.com

Library of Congress Catalog Card Number: 2007929413
ISBN 978-0-06-075036-7 (trade bdg.)
ISBN 978-0-06-075037-4 (lib. bdg.)

1 2 3 4 5 6 7 8 9 10
❖
First Edition

For Sky—our sweet baby

# Molly Moon, Micky Minus, & the Mind Machine

It was a brilliant, bright, hot morning. The sun was white in a cornflower-blue sky. And on a mountaintop, two children sat in a walled garden, on see-through reclining chairs. The eleven-year-old had a big green umbrella over him, obstructing the sun and blocking him from the six-year-old Chinese girl beside him. All she could see of the boy were his thin, white trousers and his turquoise suede slippers that soaked up the searing heat.

The small girl was wearing a silver dress with shiny shoes to match, and her hair was whipped up into the shape and texture of a pinecone. She wore rouge on her cheeks and solid gold bangles around her wrists. Her mouth was small and pinched, while her almond-shaped brown eyes were sharp and bright.

Sitting quietly at a table on the lawn in front of them were two men dressed in red, pom-pom-covered circus outfits. The table was laid with two lidded, clear plastic boxes that were full of wriggling orange centipedes.

"Your turn," the little girl insisted, sipping from a pink cocktail glass.

"All right. I ask your pawn this," the hidden boy replied. "Why were the experiments to make flies the size of *dogs* stopped?"

There was a pause as the pom-pomed man in front of the girl thought. Then he answered in a flat voice, "Because they concentrated on making vegetables grow bigger instead."

"WRONG!" shouted the tiny girl, hurling the contents of her glass so that it drenched him. "You are an IDIOT! You had ten hours on the machine yesterday! You should have picked that up! It serves you RIGHT! You're going to have to eat one!"

Obediently the man lifted the lid off his box of centipedes and picked one up, pinching it between his finger and thumb so that it didn't wriggle away. Then, without even a murmur of objection, he placed it at the back of his tongue and shut his mouth quickly. As he munched, the little centipede tried to escape. Briefly seeing the light enter the man's mouth, it saw a slim opportunity to dive for freedom. But the man felt it on his lip and, prodding it back into his mouth again, ruined its chances of ever getting away. Grimacing, he mashed it up with his teeth and swallowed.

"Yes, they are nasty, aren't they?" the little girl taunted. "Nasty and bitter! Well, you shouldn't have let me down. I'm four points behind now because of *you*!"

"Why don't we stop?" the boy under the umbrella said. "I think your player is feeling sick. That's his fourth centipede."

"Serves him right!" the little girl said vindictively. "And anyway, Micky, don't be so silly—it's only a game."

# One

It was a cold February evening and storm clouds were gathering. Drawn like gray curtains over the moon, they made the night sky even darker. And high up, forty thousand feet above the fields of the countryside, violent gale-force winds began to circle and play. Billions of raindrops plumped the blackening clouds, preparing to fall.

Far below, trees were tousled by the thickening wind that whistled through their branches. And in a grand country house called Briersville Park, lights twinkled at an upstairs window.

Molly Moon was sitting with her best friend, Rocky, on a Persian carpet in the TV room. Comfortable and leaning against red beanbags, they ignored the wind that was battering the windowpanes. Gusts sent down the chimney disturbed the flames of the wood burning in the hearth, but they didn't mind at all, for they were feeling cozy and warm. In their laps were brown Chinese-takeaway boxes with the remains of a meal of rice and wontons, and in front of them was the television, switched on.

"Ballroom dancing," Rocky said, tapping the TV controls and burping, "a history program, or gardening, or . . . or him?" As he spoke the screen changed channels, ending up with a suited man hosting a magic show.

"After the break," the magician was saying, "I will blow your minds, by reading your minds and *someone* from the audience here will be my . . . hmmm . . . victim!" The studio audience laughed. The showman winked at the camera. "So, see you later." And at once the commercials started.

"Looks good to me," Molly said. She stretched down to the black pug who lay quivering by her leg and scrunched its velvety ears. "Fancy some dumplings, Petula? Come on, don't be scared of the storm. We're all snug and safe in here." As Molly finished, a particularly aggressive gust banged at the window. Petula dived under Molly's legs. After a second or two the rattling subsided, and Petula looked up. On the television a very sleek pedigree Labrador dressed in a black dinner jacket and bow tie was eating his supper. Petula didn't understand about advertising. She didn't understand that this dog on the screen was there to persuade any dog owners watching to buy Champ to feed their pets. It looked like the Labrador was simply showing off and she thought that was funny.

Feeling better, Petula put her head in her paws and glanced fondly at her two human friends. Rocky, with his black skin and beautiful eyes, was definitely the most pedigreed-looking of the two. Molly was more of a mongrel creature. She was skinny with scraggly brown hair and closely set green eyes and a potato-shaped nose. The two of them had always been that way, right from when they lived in the orphanage together when they were little. Whatever Molly wore, she never looked well-groomed. To someone who didn't know her, Petula pondered, Molly really did look a most *un*remarkable person, which shows how deceiving looks can be. For the truth was, Molly Moon was the complete opposite.

Over the last year or so, Petula had witnessed massive changes in Molly. Only a short while ago, Molly, she knew, had thought of herself as useless. She hadn't been full of confidence like, for instance, a dog that could fetch the newspaper. But then Molly had found a book on hypnotism. Petula raised her hairy eyebrows as she thought of that amazing book. It had helped Molly reinvent herself. Molly had been like a caterpillar that turned into a butterfly. Not a beautiful butterfly, but she had certainly grown wings. For now she was a brilliant *hypnotist*, a *time stopper*, and a *time traveler*. And Petula had had first-paw experience of Molly doing all these things. She sighed and scratched at a tickle in her ear as she thought of what they had been through together. It had certainly been unusual.

Petula herself had once hypnotized some mice; and another time, using a time crystal, she had actually made time stand still. But that had been a fluke. Even Rocky could hypnotize using his voice, Petula knew. But he wasn't a *genius* at hypnotism like Molly. Petula stood up and dipped her nose into the cardboard box to nibble at a dumpling, and three mooing cows flew across the TV screen.

Rocky was now singing along to the commercial jingle.

"Choc-o-*late*!" he sang, with the xylophone music and the woman's voice on the television accompanying him.

*Choc-o-late!*
*Every day is a chocolate date!*

Molly reached her hand into the Yong takeaway bag. As she'd hoped, there were two small parcels in there, wrapped in crisp red paper. FORTUNE COOKIE read the black inked letters across the front of them.

"Here," Molly said, tossing one into Rocky's lap, and opening her own. Inside the packet was a brown sugary biscuit. Molly bit into it and, as she did, examined the fortune written on a strip of white paper that had fallen onto the floor.

"What does it say?" Rocky asked.

"It says," Molly replied, "'The leaf that clings to the branch will block new buds.'"

"Hmmm. Mine says, 'Travel and change of place impart new vigor to the mind.'"

"Who writes these things?" Molly wondered as she munched.

*"Well, that is the question,"* said Rocky in a strange eerie voice, pretending to be mysterious. *"Who, indeed, writes our fortunes in the book of time?"*

Molly laughed. Then a commercial on the television shattered her calm. A baby in a diaper was crawling through a jungle. He was dressed in a camouflage commando outfit. He crawled on determinedly, unaware that he'd narrowly escaped the jaws of a tiger. Intent on his baby mission, he crawled through the undergrowth, past an angry hippopotamus, under a venomous snake, and over a tarantula. Finally the baby arrived in the land of babies—a safe place, where the other babies were glad to see him. There, a deep voice boomed: "Use Podgeums diapers! Put your baby first—give him the support he needs!"

Rocky found it really funny. "I love that commercial," he chuckled.

But Molly felt sick. The gurgling baby commando had reminded her of another baby. The one she'd been born with—her own twin brother whom she had *never met*. She'd only found out about him *two weeks ago*. As the baby on the screen clapped his hands together, a feeling of peculiar longing rose up in Molly. Finding out that she had a brother had been like discovering a secret door in a house that led to a different country. She half wished that the door wasn't there, frightened to have to pluck up the courage to step through it, while the other part of her longed to fling it open and discover this place so near and yet so unknown.

Was her twin brother alive? If so, where was he? And what was he like? What was his name? He had been stolen from their mother just as Molly had been when she was a baby. But who had taken him? Had he been put in a cardboard box on a doorstep of an orphanage like Hardwick House as Molly had been?

Had the box been a Moon's Marshmallow box? Or had he grown up with a family? And wherever he was, did he know that Lucy Logan and Primo Cell were his *real* parents? Did he know that Lucy and Primo had been hypnotized for eleven years by Cornelius Logan, Lucy's *own* brother? Perhaps he even knew that Molly had freed them both with her hypnotism. Did he know about Molly?

As these questions jangled loudly through Molly's head, she caught them and, one by one, tried to put them into a box in her mind where she couldn't hear them shouting anymore.

She turned her thoughts back to the TV and hoped that the show would distract her.

Then there were steps in the passage outside and the door opened.

"What are you watching?" asked Primo as he and Lucy sat on the sofa. Their long-haired hippie friend, Forest, who had come in too, sat down on the floor cross-legged.

"It's a magic show," said Molly. "I expect this is the last commercial."

"Big storm brewing outside, isn't there?" Lucy said, glancing at the window.

"Seems to me it's already brewed," Forest replied as the wind buffeted the windowpane again.

Then Rocky turned up the volume and all conversation stopped. Applause pattered out from the television.

"Welcome back!" laughed the showman on the screen. A large clear plastic cube that had been wheeled onto the stage now stood beside him. It was filled with tiny colored balls that whizzed about inside it. "The time has come for me to find an assistant," he declared. "Look at these balls! Each has a number of an audience seat on it! Spotlights, please!" At once a bright beam shone out over the audience, dancing across rows of excited people. The showman clapped his hands and one of the balls shot out of a see-through pipe into a metal tray.

"M twenty-two!" The spotlight flittered across the seats, coming swiftly to rest on a plump woman with pigtails. She opened her eyes wide with alarm when she saw that she had been chosen. "What are you waiting for?" the showman cried. "Come on down!"

Uncertainly, the lady lifted her tubby body out of her chair, smoothed her red polka-dot dress and, her face twitching with a nervous smile, picked her way down the central studio steps to the stage. The showman welcomed her and shook her hand.

"Hello, hello. Don't be anxious. What's your name?"

"Irene Brody," the woman replied, starting to giggle.

"Well, Irene, are you ready to relax and help me read your mind?"

"I—I . . . suppose so." Irene tittered. "I've never been chosen from an audience before. It makes me feel a bit giddy."

"Well, don't you faint on us. Just sit yourself down on this chair." A black velvet chair was pushed toward her and she settled into it. The lights dimmed. "Now relax, Irene."

"Sounds like he's about to hypnotize her," said Lucy, narrowing her blue eyes.

"Irene, assure the audience that we have never met before!" the showman demanded.

"That's true," said Irene.

"Whom did you come here with today?"

"With my husband."

The spotlight searched the audience for Irene's empty seat and found her blushing husband.

"Mr. Brody, I presume," said the magician. The embarrassed man nodded. "Audience," said the showman, "just like everyone here, Irene Brody and her husband are strangers to me. Just like you, they bought their tickets and turned up. Irene's number has been picked at random." He paused for dramatic effect.

"Now I am going to read her mind. Irene will write down something she is going to think about, and I will *read* her thoughts. When the time is right, I will tell you all. Silence, please."

A lady in a blue-feathered gown passed Irene a pen and a pad of paper. Irene, with her tongue darting tensely from the side of her mouth, began to scribble something down.

Another gust of wind blew through the chimney. The picture on the TV flickered. Rocky threw a sock at it.

"This is rigged," he said. "Irene's an actress."

"I think you're right there," said Forest.

"Hmmm," agreed Molly. "But what if that show guy knows how to stop time? Think about it—he could just stop time, go over, and read her piece of paper, then go back to where he was standing and start time again. That would look like he'd just read her thoughts."

Rocky pressed pause on the TV controls to illustrate Molly's point.

"Yeah, like this," he agreed. The screen froze with the performer smiling and Irene holding her piece of paper in the air. "Except that you have to imagine that the magician guy is just nipping over now to read little old Irene's bit of paper. What a cheat!"

"Do you think he's a time stopper?" Primo asked.

"If he's a hypnotist who can stop time, he could be a time traveler too. But do you think a time traveler would waste his time being a showman? Hmm? I don't. I think time travelers have far more important things to do." Rocky released the pause button and the show continued. But before everyone could hear Irene's thoughts, the lights went out and the TV died.

"Power cut," Rocky said matter-of-factly.

Outside, the wind, howling now as it rushed around the parapets of the building, beat against the window again.

"I love power cuts," said Lucy, her face flickering orange in the glow from the fire. "It feels more exciting without electricity."

Primo stood up and lit an old-fashioned lamp on the desk. Molly got up too. "I've got a candle in my room," she said. And with Petula following her, she went to get it.

The passage outside the sitting room was dark. Its green carpet seemed black, and in the heavy gloom the tickings from the multitude of clocks that hung on the wall sounded like strange clicking insects. Molly hurried through the shadows. She didn't feel comfortable being reminded of time passing like this. As she walked, a wave of guilt swamped her.

For two weeks she had been relaxing at Briersville Park, having fun. She'd watched twelve films, read two books, made a home movie with Rocky and their new friend Ojas, and she'd learned to ride a horse. She'd mucked about with her friends in the pool, she'd scrambled on bikes with them in the fields of Briersville Park, and she'd even done an oil painting of Amrit, their pet elephant. She'd eaten scores of ketchup sandwiches—her favorite thing to eat—and drunk glasses and glasses of orange-squash concentrate—her favorite drink. She'd thrown hundreds of sticks for Petula and spent hours listening to music.

When Primo had talked about the man on TV she'd felt he was really saying, "Do you think a time traveler, Molly, should waste her time watching silly TV shows? Doesn't *this* time traveler have more important things to do *like finding her lost twin brother*?"

Molly had promised Primo and Lucy that she would go back in time and find their son. What had become of him was a complete mystery. At the hospital where they had been born, there was no record of him. Molly shivered as she passed a statue of a leaping hare. It looked so friendly in the daytime, as it jumped over a flower, but in the dark, and with this storm raging, it looked like a pouncing demon.

When Molly got to her bedroom she found the

candle in its stand and lit it. Then she lay down on the bed. Petula hopped up with her and Molly gave her a cuddle.

"What do you think, Petula?"

*Procrastinate* is a word that means to put off. Molly had been procrastinating and procrastinating and procrastinating ever since she'd promised her parents that she would track her brother down. She'd been putting off traveling back to the time when she and her brother were both babies because now, safe in her own time, Molly realized how scary and dangerous time traveling could be.

Since coming back from her adventures Molly had had nightmares about being stranded in the wrong time. She'd also had horrid dreams about other time travelers chasing her.

Molly sighed. "I suppose I really ought to just go and find him. Will you come with me?" Petula whined. "It probably won't be *all* that bad, you know. I think I've been working myself up about going. My imagination has gone wild and made me scared. It will probably be easy to find him, Petula. We'll tell him what it's like here, about Primo and Lucy and Forest and Amrit and Rocky and Ojas, and then he'll probably want to come back with us. Once we've found him, well, I can concentrate on life then. We'll set up that hypnotic hospital and begin curing people by hypnosis."

Petula looked at her mistress and tried to read her thoughts, but it was impossible. What perplexed her was why Molly smelled so worried.

Molly found her pajamas and put them on. It was late. If she was going to set off into the past tomorrow, she ought to get a good night's sleep. She blew the candle out and pushed her feet down under her duvet, curving her legs around Petula, who lay on the bed. As she drifted off, a buzz of excitement sparked inside her. Was it possible that by this time tomorrow she would have actually met her twin?

But as Molly slept, other things dampened and drowned her excitement—ripples of apprehension and fear. They took the form of dark dreams. These blew through her mind like the winds that encircled the grand house that she slept in.

In the worst dream, Molly was floating in a massive sievelike sphere. It was the Bubble of Light at the beginning of time, a place that really existed, for Molly had once been there—but in her dream the Bubble was different. Molly couldn't get out of it, and through the billions of little black holes in the Bubble, whining voices teased her.

"No, no, no, no," they whistled.

"Let me out!" Molly shouted.

She looked in a mirror. Her face was changing, becoming younger and younger because the light from the giant Bubble was shining on her.

This part of Molly's dream was true to life, as this was exactly what could happen in the special light at the beginning of time. So, although only a dream, it was terrifying.

"I HAVE TO LEAVE!" Molly screamed, her face and body now like a three-year-old's, "OR I'LL BE SO YOUNG I'LL BE NOTHING!"

And then there she was *outside* the Bubble, traveling through time with gale-force time winds blasting about her. And true to the nature of time winds, they were making her skin scaly—but it wasn't happening slowly like in her real adventures. A patch of scaly skin behind her ear was spreading like wildfire. It was racing across her cheek and down her arms. Now her whole face was old and wrinkled. Molly felt like a leaf that was turning brown and shriveling up.

Like a ball being bounced about by some careless child, Molly found herself back in the Bubble of Light at the beginning of time, with the miracle rays shining on her again. As they shone they rubbed away all the time travel scales.

So it went on, with Molly thrown from one terrifying moment to the next. Eventually, as though bored with her, the dream departed, and only then did Molly fall into deep, gentle sleep, where the winds in the park outside couldn't be heard.

# TWO

Molly woke up in the dark. A fox was barking outside and the drainpipe outside her window was gurgling as rainwater rushed down it. She rolled over, pulling the duvet over her shoulders, and tried to go back to sleep, but she couldn't so she stretched her hand out to press the light button on her alarm clock. A blackbird let out its first chirrup. Moments later another joined in. Molly lay back on her pillow and listened to the opening notes of the dawn chorus.

Outside, gusts of clouds raced across the sky, unveiling the moon. The park and Molly's bedroom were suddenly filled with silver light. She tipped herself out of bed and nudged her slippers on. Petula drowsily raised her head, then curled up into a tighter ball and shut her eyes again. Molly wondered what she was dreaming about. *Chasing sticks,* she supposed. She smiled as she imagined Petula's doggy dream. Then, yawning, and tripping on her clothes strewn all over the floor, she approached the window. Here, on a table glinting in the silver light, lay her clear crystal and her red-and-green time-traveling gems, threaded onto a piece of old string. She slipped the precious necklace over her head, realizing as she did that she wouldn't take it off again until she next went to bed at Briersville Park. For when she was in other time zones, the scarred colored gems were her only ticket home.

The clear crystal was simply for world stopping. To test herself, Molly stroked it now and prepared to stop time. She let her mind relax and looked out at the wet garden, focusing her hypnotic eyes on a rabbit that was nibbling the grass under a cedar tree. As she concentrated, the cold, tingling feeling that always accompanied world stopping filled her veins. Soon her mind was feeling fizzy. And then it was done.

The rabbit froze mid-hop. The world froze. Birds taking flight from the cedar tree hung in midair. The silhouettes of llamas in the far field were as statuesque as the animal-shaped bushes about them. Everywhere was as still as a picture. But not just in Briersville.

In New York, where it was half past midnight, night

traffic was silent. Nothing moved up or down or across the glittering streets. Partygoers leaving snazzy nightclubs and restaurants, ready to go home to bed, were suddenly rigid, frozen as they walked. Inside lofty skyscrapers the snores and dreams of sleeping people suddenly halted, replaced by hush and stillness. In Tokyo, Japan, where it was two thirty in the afternoon, chopsticks, pincering sushi, hung motionless in front of still, open mouths. In Sydney, Australia, where it was late afternoon, surfers were frozen as they rode motionless waves. All over the world raindrops paused. Waterfalls were suspended and hurricanes and winds were quiet. And at the center of the freeze was Molly, with her clear crystal, holding the world motionless with her will. The powerful feeling it gave her was dizzying. She released her concentration and in a snap the rabbit on the grass hopped away. She smiled. She was pleased to see she still had the knack.

Molly folded her arms. She wondered what the day held for her. For her today wasn't necessarily *this* day. No, her today was going to be a day from long ago—the day when she and her twin brother had been born. It would be a day full of detective work and hopefully lots of answers. Someone had kidnaped her twin brother—that was clear. Somehow they had removed his name from the hospital's records too. Molly had read in the papers of cases where babies had been abducted from hospitals. The thieves were usually sad, mad people who desperately wanted a child. If her brother's thief wasn't sad and mad, then it was someone very, very bad. Molly didn't relish the idea of meeting him or her *at all*. She clenched her fists. She suddenly felt enormously protective toward her unknown twin and furious with whoever had taken him. They had absolutely no right to him, just as Cornelius Logan had had no right to Molly when he'd stolen her. The difference between her and her brother was that she'd found out about her true roots. Right then and there Molly made a promise. Though she had been putting off finding her twin, now she would do whatever it took to track him down. Nerves bubbled up from the pit of her stomach, but still she was determined to get to the bottom of this mystery—for Lucy, for Primo, for herself, but mostly for him, her brother.

Molly opened the drawer of her rosewood cupboard and pulled out a pair of clean jeans. She found some underpants, two odd socks, a long-sleeved blue T-shirt, and a black sweater and put them on. Then she pulled her favorite red-and-white sneakers out from under the armchair. She went to the bathroom, brushed her teeth, and splashed some water over her face. Dabbing her nose dry, she ran her fingers through her hair and tried to untangle a few knots that had built up as she'd slept. Giving up, she stared at herself in the mirror. She was not a pretty girl, Molly knew, and today her hair looked as though it had been electrified. But she didn't mind.

"Good luck," she said to her reflection. Then she went to wake Petula.

Downstairs in the kitchen, to Molly's surprise, Rocky was dressed and opening a can of dog food for Petula's breakfast.

"What are you doing up?" Molly asked.

"What are *you* doing up?" he countered. Molly gave him a puzzled look.

"I had a feeling," he explained as he put Petula's bowl on the floor, "a feeling that you might try to find him today. It was that fortune from the Chinese cookie that did it." He pulled the small strip of paper from his pocket and read it again. "'Travel and change of place impart new vigor to the mind.' I hope you weren't thinking of going alone?"

"Well, Petula said she'd come."

"Any more space available?"

"There's always space for you, Rocky." Molly smiled. She hadn't asked Rocky because she hadn't wanted to make him feel like he *ought* to come with her.

She thought he'd be happier mucking about with Ojas and she wanted to spare him the scariness of the trip.

"Are you sure you want to come? I mean, you never know, it might be really difficult. Like last time—remember? I'm a bit nervous."

"What, so you think I'd let you go and do it alone, then? No way, Molly. If it's easy, that will be great; and if it's dangerous, then you'll need help."

Molly grinned. "Thanks, Rocky."

Molly went to the larder and got some sugar puffs and some milk. Then she and Rocky sat at the table and poured themselves each a bowlful of cereal.

"Aren't you going to wake them?" Rocky asked, munching and watching Molly write Primo and Lucy a note.

"It's better we just go. If we tell them, they'll only decide it's too dangerous and beg us not to. I know that deep down they really, really want to find him."

"You're right." Rocky sipped his apple juice thoughtfully.

From under the table where she was tucking into her chicken breakfast, Petula cocked her head and tried to sense what was happening. Her dog instinct gave her a nasty feeling that Molly and Rocky were about to embark on another one of the strange trips where they traveled down windy tunnels and arrived in different times and places. She hoped not. She'd planned to meet the postman's dog, Chomsky, today for a good chat and a tail wag. She'd have to miss that and keep an eye on Molly instead. Petula rested her chin on her paws and frowned. Last time Molly had been on one of her special trips things had gotten very hairy. Glancing up past the edge of the table, Petula could just make out the scar on Molly's neck, a souvenir of that adventure. She winced. Yes, Petula could sense something big was up. As she listened to them wolfing down cereal she knew that it was probably because they weren't sure when they were going to eat again.

*Please don't go, Molly,* Petula yearned, lifting her head up. *Let's stay here.* But her thoughts fell on an impervious mind.

Molly made herself a ketchup sandwich and wrapped it in cling wrap.

"Do you think we should bring back a *baby* or an eleven-year-old boy?"

"Let's just find him first," said Rocky.

Molly put on her anorak, and Rocky his sleeveless Puffa jacket and a rainproof slicker. Each stuffed his pockets with useful things; along with her sandwich Molly took a can of dog food for Petula and a bottle of water. They packed a compass, some money, a camera, and two bars of chocolate. Rocky took a flashlight from the back-door cupboard and Molly a rucksack that Petula would fit inside. Remembering their hats and scarves, and pulling their rainproof hoods up, Molly whistled quietly to Petula and they all crept out.

Soon they were on bicycles, pedaling along the drive toward the lodge gates. It had stopped raining, but the air was thick and oppressive. Thunder was coming.

Petula sat in the basket on Molly's bike, sucking on a stone, her ears flapping in the cold breeze. The morning smelled of wet fern and sodden grass, of mud and earthworms. The gravel under the bikes' wheels still held the scent of an elephant's footprints, and mixed up with all of this was the strange electricity in the air that made the tip of Petula's tongue taste metallic and signaled that lightning was on its way. Petula shivered. She hated thunder.

Black clouds hung above. The roads were dark and it was difficult to see where they were going, but Molly and Rocky cycled as fast as they could, eager not to get caught in the electric storm. As they passed the ONE MILE TO BRIERSVILLE sign, a distant roll of thunder rumbled in the sky. And then a bang of thunder directly overhead seemed to shake the very road they were on, and a terrifying flash of silver light forked across the sky.

"Stop the world!" Rocky shouted to Molly over the

wind, putting his hand on her shoulder. And so Molly did. When the next crack of thunder came, she froze time, making the world stand still just as a sheet of lightning was illuminating the sky. Rocky pedaled, touching Molly all the time, for that way he was able to stay out of the freeze. Petula, on the other hand, was as still as a stuffed toy.

So the two children sped toward Briersville with their way lit up and with raindrops hanging motionless in the air that popped and splashed as they cycled through them. But the town was eerie in the strange silver light of the storm. Molly was keen to switch the world back on again. As they came into Briersville, they saw that a few people were already up—a postman stood rigid in a doorway, sheltering from the rain, and a milkman sat in his milk float. Molly and Rocky biked down the High Street and followed the signs for the hospital where Molly had been born. Both Molly and Rocky had been there before. Molly's worst visit was when she'd fallen out of a tree and broken her leg. She'd been seven years old and hiding from the orphanage bully. Rocky had been admitted twice to St. Michael's Hospital for asthma attacks.

Now the speckled white building loomed up in front of them. They slotted the bikes' wheels into parking racks and locked them up. Molly picked Petula up, sending movement into her.

*Please don't go,* Petula whined to Molly, now desperate to stop this trip.

"Don't worry, Petula. It'll all be fine," Molly said, kissing her forehead and trying to feel brave. "Just stay really quiet." She carefully put her into the black rucksack and handed it to Rocky. Then Molly let the world move. The lightning exploded in the sky, and they walked through the hospital entrance.

Inside was a small shop selling newspapers, magazines, and flowers as well as stationery, puzzles, cards, and games for bored patients. To the right was a coffee shop. In the distance were the elevators and signs to different hospital departments. Petula poked her nose out through the top of the rucksack and sniffed. The place didn't smell too good. The air was clinical and filled with disinfectant. And under that was the odor of blood and illness and boiled cabbage. She snuffled and whined and then popped her head back inside the rucksack.

"'The Maternity Ward,'" said Molly, reading a sign. "'St. Mary's Wing'—that's where we go." She tied her soggy anorak around her waist. Rocky kept his sleeveless Puffa jacket on but wound up his slicker. Molly brought a bunch of daffodils. As the man in the kiosk turned to sort her change she whispered, "Better look like we're visitors." Then they walked along an olive-green passage, following the arrowed signs.

As they approached the maternity wing, Petula could make out the smell of babies galore and milk and diapers. Molly pushed a white swing door and they slipped through to find themselves in a door-lined passage. Outside there was another bang of thunder, then a huge flash of lightning, and from one of the bedrooms a baby began to cry. Molly and Rocky quickly stepped sideways into a small waiting room. Even though they were there to do good, both felt as guilty as creeping thieves.

"Go back in time now," whispered Rocky urgently, "before anyone comes." He put his hand on Molly's shoulder again so that he and Petula could be transported through time with her. Molly nodded and reached for her string of gems. She held the three crystals in her right hand and stared at the scarred green gem. That crystal would take them back in time. And if she made the scar on it open, it would follow very precise instructions and take them to *exactly* where they wanted to go. She relaxed her mind and bored her gaze into the scar. Molly steeped her thoughts with goodness, for that was the way she'd learned how to open the scar, and as she thought, the scar blinked wide. At once it was a swirling circle of greens, spiraling away into itself. They were ready. Molly's hands began to sweat, as they always did when nerves gripped her. Then she took a deep breath and thought an instruction to the gem. She asked it to take them back eleven years and two hundred days—her precise age. And as soon as the request had been made, Molly, Rocky, and Petula were plunged back in time. A BOOM filled the hospital waiting room as they disappeared.

The room around Molly and Rocky purred with pale light, bright light, and darkness as they moved backward through four thousand, two hundred and fifteen days and nights. Finally the light settled.

Molly put them into a time hover. By doing this, and not properly landing in the time, Molly and Rocky were able to see their surroundings and yet were invisible to anyone in that time.

In this strange, not-quite-there dimension, they stepped into the passage to check that the coast was clear. Then Molly released the time hover and they properly arrived.

It was eleven and a half years earlier, but the peculiar thing that both Molly and Rocky noticed straight away was that there was a storm outside there too. Rain was pelting down on the skylights above them and a blast of thunder rattled the windows. Molly gulped and shot a puzzled look at Rocky. Then she stroked Petula's nose and, keeping her grip on Rocky's arm just in case they had to time travel again suddenly, the two friends ventured down the passage, inspecting the names on the hospital bedroom doors.

Neither Molly nor Rocky said a word. They knew what they were here to do. And Petula sensed that she should be quiet too. She sniffed the air. It was still full of baby smells. Then a whiff of a baby that smelled like Molly hit her nostrils. Petula wrinkled her nose and wondered what was going on.

Molly and Rocky read the doors' labels. The first read C. YO, the next, M. BURTON, the third, D. A. LOWEY. Then they saw what they wanted—a sign that read L. LOGAN.

The door to this bedroom was open. In her last adventure Molly had met several of her younger selves, but still she felt a quiver of anticipation as she realized that she was about to see herself as a newborn baby. And equally as amazing, she was about to see her twin brother for the first time. Hot with curiosity, Molly tilted her head around the door.

In front of her was a white and yellow room with a metal bed in the center of it. Sitting up under sheets and blankets and in a pink nightdress was a much younger Lucy Logan. She was staring fondly down at a baby in her arms.

A nurse stood with her back to the door giving Lucy advice.

"When you've fed her, you can burp her and then she'll drop off, I'm sure. The lad's still asleep, but no doubt he'll wake up soon. Yes, twins are hard work, my dear."

Outside there was another roll of thunder.

Lucy Logan lifted the baby to rest her head on her shoulder and she began patting its back. She glanced at Molly, standing in the doorway, and smiled, completely unaware that this girl was this same child from the future.

"Have you got a name for her yet?" the nurse asked.

"No name yet," Lucy said. On the floor Molly noticed a rectangular Moon's Marshmallows box with bags of pink-and-white marshmallows in it. Three empty packets lay on the bedside table. Molly nudged Rocky and they sidestepped past the room.

"Where do you think my brother is?" whispered Molly.

Just then, double doors farther down opened, and a cot on wheels was pushed out to the passage and into another room.

"I bet there's a big nursery place where they keep all the babies," said Rocky. "I've seen them in films. Maybe that's where he is."

They crept toward the double doors. Through its glass windows they could see four wheeled cots, each with a swaddled baby inside. A dressing-gowned mother came out. She was so tired she didn't notice Rocky and Molly. When she'd drifted back to her room they stepped inside. Petula whined from inside the rucksack. She could suddenly smell the saltiness of an aggressive man. He was in the building—and coming closer.

"Shh, Petula," hushed Molly, completely oblivious to her pet's warning.

The first crib held a dark baby with tight corkscrew curls of black hair. The second held a Chinese baby. In the third and fourth slept two babies, either of which could be Molly's twin brother.

"Which one do you think he is?" Molly asked. Rocky pointed down at the distinct potato-shaped nose that was very like Molly's own.

"That's him, I reckon," Rocky whispered. "I mean, those noses don't grow on trees."

Molly's mouth fell open. Until this moment it had been hard to *truly* believe that she had a brother, but now, here was the living, breathing proof. "That is him, isn't it!" she yelped. "And he looks just like me."

"Two munchkins," agreed Rocky.

The baby was wrapped up in a white cotton knitted

blanket; his cheeks were soft and pink and his ears the shape of tiny tangerine segments. He sighed peacefully. Molly glanced around the room. There was a cabinet at one end with bottles and diapers on it.

"Let's hide," she whispered. "It's time to find out who took him."

Rocky nodded and soon they were crouched behind the piece of furniture.

Molly shuffled the gems on their string around in her hand until the red forward-traveling gem was between her finger and thumb. She stared down at the scar on it and, shivering with anticipation, bid it open. At once a red swirl, like the inside of a volcano, spiraled away to its stem.

"This is it, Rocky."

Molly beamed thoughts at the gem, asking it to lift them into a time hover and then to carry them slowly into the future. Through the time-hover mist, she and Rocky poked their heads over the cabinet and watched as the world reeled forward. People walked swiftly in and out of the nursery, their movements quick and jiggly as though they were in a film that had been fast-forwarded. Nurses and mothers flashed into the room and out again, pushing cots on wheels, holding babies. Molly saw her twin brother's cot wheeled out and whizzed back in with her own. It was like rush hour. A nurse zoomed around the room, dabbing at the babies, adjusting their blankets, and changing diapers. And then, just after a flash of lightning, a doctor with his hair gelled into a stiff quiff entered. He studied the babies in the cots as though they were interesting specimens and stopped to look at Molly's brother and then the baby next to him. He tugged at the blankets of both of the babies to look at the bands around their wrists. And finally, with the movement of a heron catching a fish, he plucked the baby boy from his cot and, astonishingly, *vanished into thin air*.

Molly took them out of the time hover and the mist vanished. The clock on the wall read four.

"Normal doctors don't disappear like that. Or have hairstyles like that," she said.

"I know," Rocky whispered. "He looked like some sort of rock 'n' roll pensioner."

Molly nodded. "He was a time traveler. He just popped out of this time."

Petula gave a small bark. Another rumble of thunder over the building seemed to reply.

"Rewind?" suggested Rocky. Molly suddenly felt incredibly nervous. The idea that the baby thief was a time traveler and therefore a hypnotist made the situation a lot more complicated and scary than she'd expected. He was obviously powerful and, she now suspected, nasty too. For a moment she wanted to leave the hospital and run back to safe Briersville Park. Then she thought of her defenseless baby brother, and anger eclipsed her fear.

"Rewind," she agreed. Carefully she concentrated on the green gem and lifted herself and Rocky up and back in time. Again they passed the moment when the doctor entered, although this time his movements were back to front. Then the room was empty, save the line of cots and the babies sleeping peacefully. Molly stopped. The mist cleared. Three minutes to four, the clock said.

"What shall we do? Just wait for him?" asked Rocky.

"I suppose so. And when he vanishes, when he disappears from this time, well, we'll have to jump too and follow him to exactly where he's going."

"Aren't you going to hypnotize him?"

"No. He must be a good hypnotist himself. Plus, who knows where he comes from? Maybe he has time-traveling friends, other hypnotists. We have to find out where he's from before we can decide whether we can get away with hypnotizing him."

"Do you think you can follow him?" asked Rocky doubtfully. "I mean, you don't even know whether he was traveling forward or backward in time."

"I'll get both gems active, so we can go either way,

and I'll do that lasso thing—remember that trick?" Once before, Molly had found that she could bring someone time traveling with her by sending out a sort of mind lasso that swung around the other person and carried him along too. This was the other way around. She'd never lassoed someone in order to follow him or her. She hoped it would work.

Soon both her gems' eyes were open. Molly and Rocky knew there were probably mere seconds to go now before the mysterious doctor walked in.

"Keep out of sight," Molly whispered, her heart beating furiously. "If he sees us, who knows what might happen to my brother's future . . . or mine?"

There was a flash of lightning that whitened the hospital room and the door opened. An elderly man entered. His face was wrinkled and his gray hair was styled into a strange quiff that bobbed over his head like a silver duck's tail. He wore a white doctor's coat and, underneath it, black shiny trousers. His shoes were muddy. Like an interested baby specialist, he inspected the first three infants before stopping at the cot next to Molly's brother's and leaning down to peer at the baby Molly. He prodded at her and read her wristband, and then undid her brother's blanket to read his hospital band too.

"Ah, so there're two of you," he muttered in a deep

voice, enunciating his words carefully. "Twins—a girl and a boy. Which is best? The girl? Maybe I'll take the girl. Or the boy? Hmm. Actually . . . Yes, I'll take him."

Molly couldn't believe what she was hearing. It seemed that she, the baby Molly, had almost been chosen for kidnaping. Outside, the crashing thunder sounded like giant marbles cracking together. Molly and Rocky got ready for the man's vanishing act. As he bent to gather her brother's blanket and put his hands about him, she gritted her teeth and sent an instruction to her gems to lasso the snatcher so they could tag him. At once her instructions hung in the air like static electricity. He picked the child up. Then he put his hand to a gem that hung around his neck. In the next second Molly and Rocky felt themselves being tugged. As the stranger sped away through time they found themselves following him.

In the room there was a BOOM as the space (once filled with the man, the baby, Molly, Petula, and Rocky) was replaced with air. Two babies woke up and began to cry.

A minute later the same blue-and-white-uniformed nurse who had talked so kindly to Lucy Logan walked in. She had no questioning look on her face, wondering what the loud noise had been. She was calm, as if nothing odd had happened. She stepped toward the now empty Logan baby boy's crib and pushed it to the wall. Her next job was to remove the baby's name from the hospital register and destroy all documents with his name on it.

The nurse wasn't acting maliciously. She was behaving unknowingly. For already, in her own mind, memories of the baby boy had been wiped out.

Someone had gotten to her. She had been hypnotized. Hypnotized to erase all evidence of Molly's twin brother. No one even knew that a baby Logan boy had existed.

# Three

Molly and Rocky found themselves shooting forward through time at a terrific speed. A warm time wind ruffled their hair. Around them the blurred room flashed with colors. The years flicked by.

Molly and Rocky sat very still so that the child snatcher, whoever he was, wouldn't see them. As time whisked past him too he was tucking the baby under his coat. Molly was in shock. She'd thought that she and Rocky would be tracking down an ordinary person—a batty old woman who wanted something to love or a dodgy criminal who was taking the baby to sell. She had never expected a time traveler. What did a master hypnotist from another time want with Molly's twin? And to think that he had almost taken Molly! The thought of that made her shiver.

They were well beyond their own time now. She could feel it. They were a hundred years farther on. And suddenly the time winds stopped.

The room was no longer full of baby cots. Instead there were modern glass display cases containing steel frames and surgical instruments. The walls were hung with photographs of hospital doctors and nurses. The room now seemed to be a hospital *museum*. The cabinet that Molly and Rocky had been hiding behind had disappeared, but various tables still blocked them from the man's view. He had already turned to leave. Molly pulled Rocky's arm and they followed, pausing at the door to open it a chink. The clip of the snatcher's footsteps receded into the distant passage.

"We—we have to keep up with him, without him seeing us," Molly stammered, clutching her necklace of time-travel crystals. "My gems are still lassoing him, but we must stay as close as possible so that they don't lose contact." Rocky nodded.

They darted past the room where Molly's mother had been and saw two women inspecting the exhibits. But Molly didn't have time to stop and see how people from the future looked. It was vital that she and Rocky follow the kidnaper to wherever he was going.

They slowed down to a fast walk, not wanting the

sound of their running to attract the man's attention. Outside the building it was very hot. Molly breathed in and filled her lungs with warm, dry air. They looked about. A palm tree grew in the center of a parking lot full of small podlike vehicles. And the hospital walls were thick with vines and clusters of red grapes.

"Weird." Molly sighed. "It's Briersville, but its so much *hotter* then Briersville should be. We'll definitely dry out here."

"Don't you remember seeing those TV programs about global warming?" said Rocky, removing his sleeveless Puffa jacket. "You know, where scientists warned that people's pollution and stuff was heating up the atmosphere."

"The atmosphere?" Molly whispered. She was carefully watching the man as he crossed the car park.

"Yeah. You know, the air that surrounds the world?"

Molly nodded.

Rocky continued, "Well, I guess those scientists were right. People obviously didn't do enough about pollution . . . kept their heating on full and kept driving smelly cars and running smelly factories. Phew! It's hot!"

The man stopped and wiped some sweat from his forehead, running his hand along the side of his gray quiff. Then he pulled a small bottle of water out from a pocket, which, after drinking, he chucked on the tarmac. With difficulty, because he was holding the baby, he loosened his white doctor's coat and dropped that onto the ground too.

He now stood in a black shiny suit with a reflective white T-shirt underneath it. He tucked the baby under his suit jacket. Behind him Molly recognized the copper-green pepper pot roof of the Briersville guild hall. Beside it were two new buildings, both made of steel and glass.

"He can't have come from here," Molly murmured. "His shoes are muddy. There's no mud here. Where's he going?" The man stepped toward what looked like a bus stop where a digital sign showing the date and time twinkled:

16.03.2108. 14.30. NEXT FLOAT 38 SECONDS

Molly and Rocky edged as close as they could without being noticed. They weren't sure whether people would wear jeans and T-shirts a hundred years in the future and they didn't want to be conspicuous.

"Poor thing," Molly whispered to Petula in the rucksack on Rocky's back. She ruffled her ears. "You can get out later, but not yet."

Petula sniffed the air and was very confused. This place had a base scent that belonged to Briersville. It had the crusty smell of the Briersville earth but the odor was less moist. The building behind no longer emanated its antiseptic quality. And it had lost the lovely scent of new babies and milk. The only baby Petula could smell now was ahead of them. The baby ahead smelled like a very young version of Molly. It was the fresh heart of the lettuce to Molly's more dark green, outer-leaf smell. The baby snatcher was sweating a little in the heat. His paws emitted a gingery scent mixed with the pepper of impatience. Under that he didn't seem too healthy. Petula detected the whiff of thickening blood and dry, wrinkly, oilless skin. She hoped that Molly and Rocky knew what they were letting themselves in for.

*Molly, don't follow him. He's dangerous. Go back!* she urged, looking up at her mistress.

But Molly was unaware of Petula's thoughts. Instead she was turning toward a swishing noise. A bullet-shaped, buslike vehicle with HYDROGEN POWER written on its side was pulling toward the sun shelter where the black-suited man stood. Its door slid open and he stepped inside. While he was distracted paying, Molly and Rocky ran around to the back of the bus. On the outside was a small metal ledge with a bar above. They lodged themselves onto the ledge and held on tight.

"How fast do you think this thing goes?" Molly asked.

"We'll be fine if we hold on," said Rocky uncertainly. "I read in the paper once about a toddler who climbed onto the back of his mum's Jeep and she drove all the way to town without realizing he was there. He just clung on."

"Hold the rucksack tight," Molly warned, concerned about Petula.

Then the vehicle let out a squeaky puff of air, and at once, smooth as butter, they were off. Within a few moments it was clear that the ride wasn't going to be a speedy one, and Molly had a moment to absorb the new face of Briersville. There were many buildings that she recognized, although all were much more crumbly looking then when she'd last seen them. Many of the new structures were covered in blue glass.

"Those are solar panels," said Rocky, "getting electric power from the sun. This bus float is powered by hydrogen, and that's really amazing, Molly. They are starting to invent hydrogen power in our time, because oil and coal and petrol are beginning to run out. They obviously did it."

"Why is it amazing?"

"Well, it's really clean. In our time they're trying to work out how to make tons of hydrogen gas that they can turn into liquid hydrogen, and then use that liquid instead of petrol. The cool thing is, when you burn hydrogen to run a car, instead of churning out smelly exhaust fumes, it just makes water." He pointed to the trail of water that was coming out of the back of the float. "Cool, eh?" On the street around them, small vans and pod cars all moved quietly, water squirting out from their exhaust pipes; some were collecting it in little detachable containers.

The float stopped at the end of Briersville High Street. A set of tanned triplets all dressed in yellow buttonless dungarees began laughing and pointing at Molly and Rocky. Their mother tutted and pulled them away. Rocky bent his head around the float to see whether the man was getting off. He wasn't. A woman in a short sleeveless denim dress walked past and gave him a wink.

"Looks like jeans are timeless," said Rocky and he laughed. "I'd love to go into that shoe shop and check out the sneakers of the future!"

But Molly wasn't listening. She was frowning with worry as she considered the time-traveling baby snatcher. For the more she thought about his sinister crime, the more complicated she realized it was. Had he known that she and her brother had been born? If so, why had he gone to all the trouble of fetching one of them? Did he need a *twin* for something? For an experiment? How long had it taken him to trawl through time and find them? Maybe he had just chanced upon them. Maybe he'd just popped into the hospital to get the first baby he could. But even if any old baby would have done, why did this man with his peculiar quiff of gray hair want a baby *at all*?

The float's route now curved, and they began heading out of town. It was far more built up than in their time, and the whole place felt foreign. This was mainly down to all the exotic colorful flowers growing in planters and because of the intense heat. Before long they were in the open countryside—a landscape that was browner and drier than it had ever been before, with olive trees growing in lines into the distance. The float stopped. They were at some sort of station.

"Watch Dr. Elvis now," said Rocky, peering around. "He's getting off."

Molly clutched her gems and checked to see that the red and green scars were still open and swirling.

"Quick," she said, pushing Rocky off the ledge and holding his arm at the same time. "We need to keep up with him, remember. He might be planning to hop to another time." They hid behind a bush.

The snatcher, meanwhile, had sat down on a metal bench. He reached inside his jacket and fiddled with something, then, pulling his hand out, dropped a plastic tag on the ground. From inside his jacket the baby began to cry, except that it sounded like more of a miaowing than a crying—so much so that a straw-hatted woman walking past exclaimed, "You need to get that kitten some milk."

As she spoke a gust of warm wind blew about the station, making her cotton skirt flap and whisking up the snatcher's discarded tag. Along with some other pieces of litter, the breeze danced them in a whirl of air before depositing the tag near Molly's feet. She picked it up. It was her twin brother's hospital band—well, half of it. The snatcher had torn it from the baby's wrist, so that the L and O of LOGAN were missing. GAN TWIN, the remainder of the hospital bracelet's letters read. Molly showed it to Rocky, then put it in her pocket and continued watching the snatcher.

He had ignored the straw-hatted woman completely, for he was distracted by something else. He was concentrating on pressing buttons on some gadget embedded on his sleeve. Then suddenly, his black tailored jacket swelled up. Like a smooth bud flowering into a puff of blossom, it changed. Instead of being sleek and shiny, it was now shaggy and heavy.

"I think he knows something that we don't," said Rocky, putting on his Puffa jacket and scarf. The man tucked the baby, who had now stopped crying, deeper inside his jacket and pulled up a hood from the back of his collar. He looked at the crystal in his hand. Molly concentrated on her gems.

"Here we go." She let her gems throw out a new invisible lasso. And just as she did, she, Rocky, and Petula were tugged out of the moment and transported forward in time.

Once again warm time winds caressed their cheeks and the world became a blur. Above them the sky flitted through its costumes of colors. The sun and moon streaked across its vista like comets as the days and nights flashed by. Storms of rain rattled over their safe bubble, and then the canopy above seemed darker for longer. The bush in front of them shot up, becoming a colossal wave of leaves, only to disappear and be replaced by a tree that grew and grew, its trunk thickening every second. Then the world materialized.

And what a different world it was! Molly roughly calculated that they had stopped about another hundred and fifty years into the future. Gone was the hot weather. It had been replaced by *wet* and *freezing cold*.

Shivering, Molly untied her anorak from around her waist and put it on. Inside the rucksack, Petula's fur bristled.

The station in front of them had changed dramatically. The building was now egg shaped. Pines and wintry conifers grew in its forecourt. The fields stretching away were muddy and icy. The grapevines and olive trees were gone. In their place grew low, bristly, hardy plants.

"It's like a different country," Molly whispered, her teeth chattering. "What happened to the heat wave?"

"I don't know. It's weird—but quick! He's moving."

The two friends hurriedly followed the man with the quiff past pale-faced people in long thick coats.

"Where 'r' yawer thick cots?" said an old woman in a heavy Chinese accent. She tugged at her own green fuzzy cape. "You catch flu in fancy dress. And you know how dangerous flu can be! We don't want more epidemic, do we?"

Molly nodded at her, watching the snatcher as he stepped into the egg-shaped building. "You're completely right," she said distractedly. "But eggs will be eggs," she added nonsensically. She and Rocky swiftly followed the kidnaper.

Inside, it was bright and spacious. Warm air blasted through rusty grilles in the floor, and strange music, like Chinese notes mixed with country and western, came from tinny-sounding speakers in the ceiling. In a metal box near the entrance a stall called Wangs advertised its wares.

Glittering electronic numbers and words flickered on black screens high up on the walls. The man inspected a timetable and then turned to look at another. Worried that he might look directly at *them* next, Molly and Rocky quickly slipped into the station's glass-walled waiting room. Shrinking down on seats, they hoped they were invisible.

Molly reached into Rocky's rucksack and put her hands around Petula's neck to give her a stroke. "I'm so sorry, Petula. This is so boring for you, isn't it? Maybe you should have stayed at home." Petula licked her hand. Then she gave a growl.

Molly looked up. Two teenage girls were sitting on the bench opposite. Each was dressed in a waterproof velvety coat and in pointed boots that were seamlessly joined to the bottom of their drainpipe trousers. They looked like vampires as they were all in black, although the fatter girl had green hair and a gold tooth; the other had pink hair. They began to snigger.

"Raided your granny and grandpa's wardrobes?" they asked, smiling snidely. "Think you'll start a retro trend? Think 'old-fashioned' is cool?"

Molly gave them a cold stare. It was amazing, she thought. Rudeness was rudeness, whatever century you were in.

"Is it so bad to look different?" she countered. "Maybe you're scared to look different."

Rocky glanced out of the window. "Still waiting," he said.

"Oooh! We've got a hard nut here!" laughed the teenager with the metal tooth. "What have you got to say for yourself then, Bog Eyes?"

Bog Eyes was a name Molly had been called when she was younger by bullies in the orphanage. They'd said her closely set green eyes were the color of a bog. Hearing the nickname again, Molly saw red.

"Hmm," sighed Rocky, raising his eyebrow to the teenager. "You know, you shouldn't have said that."

At once Molly summoned her hypnotic power. Her hypnotism was like a volcano that lay dormant inside her, but when she called on it, it could rise and erupt. She didn't need the full force of it this minute. A small vent of hypnotic lava would sort this person out. Molly's body warmed and tingled as her hypnotic powers flowed through her blood and surged up toward her eyes. Then she let the teenager have it. She bored her hypnotic gaze straight at the girl's pupils. At once it was as if the girl had received an electric charge. Her head swung bolt upright.

"Sassy, what you doin'?" her friend said, waving a hand in front of the first teenager's face. Then she looked at Molly too. Both now sat stiffly like robots.

"You are now under my power," Molly began. "Take off your coats and give them to us." The two girls dumbly undid their strange plastic-cum-velvet coats. Underneath, one wore a rubbery vest, the other a metallic shirt. "You," continued Molly, "will sit quietly in this waiting room for three hours, speaking to no one." Then Molly and Rocky put on the futuristic coats.

"They're much too big for us," Rocky said, "and they're too thin for this freezing weather."

"Maybe, but they'll be good disguises," Molly replied.

Transferring the bottle of water and the various bits and pieces that they'd brought with them into these big coats, Molly passed her anorak and Rocky's sleeveless Puffa and his slicker to the girls.

"Wear these," she said. The two teenagers obeyed.

"You shouldn't be afraid of looking different," Molly advised. "Variety is the spice of life."

"Molly," said Rocky, "Dr. Elvis has gone."

# Four

Molly and Rocky burst out of the waiting room and scanned the station. There was no sign of the baby snatcher. A shrill voice filled the dome of the egg building.

"Magnifloat for Vector Three. Two minutes until departure time."

"Do you think he's on that?" Rocky read the signs for directions. "It's over there!" They ran toward a set of stairs and hurtled down them three steps at a time. Petula bounced around in her bag. At the bottom was an indoor platform where a tatty white bullet-shaped train had pulled up.

"He's gone!" hissed Rocky, panicking.

"He'll be in first class," Molly replied.

Rapidly but calmly, so as not to draw attention to

themselves, they picked their way along the platform, dodging the bustling crowd buying wonton dumplings at a kiosk and stealing quick looks inside the train.

"There he is!" Molly nodded subtly toward a seat. "I'd recognize that weird hair anywhere. Now we should get inside a different carriage." With a swish the grubby white doors of the magnifloat opened.

"It's got no wheels," Rocky observed as Molly stepped inside, "which is probably how it got its name. I wonder what *magni* stands for—*magnificent* or *magnet*? When you put two magnets together they either stick or they move apart—they kind of hover away from each other. Maybe it's kept up by magnets."

Molly looked to the left, where people sat in single or double egg-shaped spaces. Some had screens pulled down in front of their faces and were watching TV. Others were staring out of the window or reading from palm-sized electronic gadgets. Most had removed their coats and wore clothes made of strange plastics or shiny nylon. Lots had muddy shoes, but Molly noticed that this didn't make the floor dirty. For strangely the floor of the magnifloat was sucking up the dirt. She and Rocky sat down in a two-seater egg.

"What's this thing with eggs?" Rocky wondered.

"Maybe they worship chickens," Molly replied quietly. Then she reached into the rucksack and pulled

Petula out. While she was giving her a good cuddle, there was a hiss and the magnifloat rose up off the ground.

"Prepare for depar-ture!" the loudspeaker announced in a Chinese accent. The magnifloat purred, then started to move. It glided out of the covered station into the cold. Molly marveled at the futuristic snow-proof chalets that flashed past the window. She wondered what had happened to their home, Briersville Park.

Within seconds they had picked up speed and their surroundings became a blur. Molly and Rocky sat back in their egg seat and inspected the colored control panel. Rocky pressed a button. At once a screen flapped down in front of his eyes, displaying a choice of red squares with numbers on them. Rocky pressed number one.

USING YOUR CONTROL DISC, PRESS NUMBER OF DESIRED CHANNEL, read the screen. Finding a detachable keyboard in his left armrest, Rocky pressed number four, and at once a newsreader's face shone out from a circle.

"Now for the weather," said a healthy-faced woman. "It will be warmer tomorrow with temperatures of minus ten degrees Celcius, dropping to minus fifteen at night."

"Crumbs!" said Molly. "We need to get Petula a

coat. I wonder why it's so cold here now. I mean, it's mad—a century after our time it got boiling hot, and then a hundred and fifty years after *that* it's the complete opposite."

"Look, in the corner there's a question box," said Rocky. He began tapping the keypad.

The screen flashed and then answered:

The period around 2100 was hot, due to massive global warming. The same global warming brought the temperatures of Africa, southern Europe, and South America to such heights that there were massive droughts. This heat melted the polar ice caps and warmed up the seas. The sea, when warm, could no longer keep the Gulf Stream running. This was a current that brought warm Caribbean seawater and good weather to northern Europe. Once the Gulf Stream stopped, northern Europe received no more warm water from the south. Instead, it got the weather it should always really have had, that of other countries with a latitude 45° North. This is how, by 2250, northern Europe has cold, cold winters and more extreme weather conditions than before. Meanwhile, the rest of Europe was not affected. Southern Europe has become so hot that it is now practically uninhabitable. Africa is a complete desert.

"Oh that's horrible," said Molly. "Ask it a fun question, Rocky."

"Okay." Rocky tapped in a question, the answer pinging up instantly.

Toilets in the year 2250 look like this. A picture of a toilet not dissimilar in shape to those in Molly and Rocky's time appeared on the screen.
There are many variations on this design. The modern toilet will weigh and analyze a person's excretions and give a diagnosis of the person's health, including recommendations on what fuel food that person should be eating and what fluids they should be drinking. Waste is carried to sewer power plants to convert into electricity.

"Wow!" said Molly. "A toilet that weighs your poo and tells you whether you're eating the right food!"

"Cool," said Rocky. "Can't wait to try one."

At that moment there was a bleeping noise by Molly's leg. She jumped, then looked down and saw a low metal vacuum-cleaner-type object by her feet. The top of it suddenly lit up with the words: **Magnifloat tokens, please.**

"Uh-oh, I think it wants us to pay," said Molly. She glanced about the carriage and then felt inside her new coat pocket. She pulled out a handful of glassy disks. "Whoops!" she whispered. "We took those girls' money." She investigated another pocket to see what else the coats held. There she found some hard disks with MAGNIFLOAT TOKEN embossed on them.

*Beep, beep, beep!* the little robot now beeped as if impatient. Molly held up the biggest token and, hoping it was the correct slot on the machine, pushed it in.

**Destination?** the screen now read.

Molly wasn't sure. "Err. Wherever this will take us, please," she said.

The robot whirred and then, where its tongue might have been, spat out two shiny triangular tickets. **Arrival time—ten minutes. Have a good trip.** Swiveling its metal frame and extending three silver aerials on its lid, the robot whizzed off to the next passenger.

Molly looked at her hard glassy ticket. **Return. London Sheng,** it read.

"Dr. Elvis might not be going there," Molly said. "We'll have to check on him at every station."

"Definitely," said Rocky. "Oh, wow, now that is what I call crazy!" he added in a whisper. Molly looked up and saw what Rocky was talking about. A woman in a turquoise jumpsuit was walking past, and trotting behind her on a lead was a dog, or was it a cat? The creature had the body of a dog but the tail and head of a cat, and it was blue.

Petula tilted her head and tried to understand its smell.

"That thing's been genetically engineered," Rocky said.

"Wow," Molly exclaimed. Then a silver object outside the train caught her attention. "And how about *that*?" She pointed. A small machine with a woman and two children inside it was flying alongside the train. The two kids smiled and waved at Molly.

"That must be bad when they have accidents in the air!" Rocky observed. "But I wouldn't mind having one."

Molly and Rocky grilled the computer. They found out that the population of their country, the total number of people living there, was one *quarter* the size it had been in their time.

"That's amazing," Rocky commented. "I wonder why it shrunk." He tapped in this question and in a millisecond had his answer. "Ah, so people had fewer babies, that's why, and— Oh no!"

"What?"

"There was a flu plague that wiped out millions and millions of people!"

"Crumbs!"

Rocky asked the screen more.

"And look . . ." he said. "Look how much of the rain forest has been wiped out! It says," Rocky continued, "'Since the destruction of the rain forest, thousands of miles of green algae are now grown on all the seas to make oxygen for humans to breathe.' Not very nice for swimming."

"But nice for breathing," Molly pointed out.

They also found out that the language in their country had changed. It now had lots of Chinese words in it because Chinese people and their culture had spread all over the globe.

"'Dishes like bird's nest soup and bamboo shoots, bean curd, and noodles are very popular,'" Rocky read. "'The knife and fork are things of the past. People eat with chopsticks.'"

"I'm useless with chopsticks," said Molly. "I can never get the food to my mouth."

"So you'd be even skinnier if you lived now."

Petula smelled the catty-doggy creature and felt very disoriented. She didn't understand the scents of this place. So many were the same and yet slightly different. She was still getting whiffs of the sinister man, two carriages in front, holding the Molly-smelling baby. The sourness coming from him made her feel very uneasy. Again she desperately tried to send a message to Molly to take them all home.

*Please let's go back,* she begged with a quiet bark.

Molly stroked Petula's forehead. "Don't worry," she said, giving her dog a squeeze.

Ten minutes later the magnifloat was nearing

another station—a city station. They approached a mass of tall, ice-crusted buildings surrounding frozen lakes. Molly put Petula back into the rucksack. "Sorry," she apologized, giving the pug's ears a gentle rub.

The magnifloat doors opened and Molly and Rocky stepped out into the freezing city. As they did, there was a hissing noise and their new coats did a miraculous thing: Each puffed up so that the smooth velvet was now a mass of thick, bristly fur.

"Whoa! Cool design," Rocky exclaimed, patting his chest. But they didn't stop to marvel at the coats for long, because the snatcher, instead of walking toward the escalators with all the other passengers, began heading toward an orange robotic station cleaner that was scrubbing the floor.

"Grab my arm, Rocky, if you don't want to get left behind." Instinctively Molly reached for her gems. In the next second the man with the quiff reached for his. Quickly, Molly sent out another time-travel lasso to follow him. With another BOOM, Molly, Rocky, and Petula were whipped out of that time, and the platform was suddenly left bare.

On the other side of the magnifloat tracks, a shriveled hundred-and-sixty-year-old man saw them go. He smiled and shook his head. Science was amazing, he thought. Next time he traveled he would buy whatever ticket those children had bought.

"Where's he going?" Molly exclaimed in a whisper. The world whisked past them, billions of its seconds flitting by in a moment. "Feels like two hundred years have passed!" she declared with horror. "Two hundred and fifty!" And then they stopped, half a millennium away from their own time. "We've gone forward *five hundred years*!"

Molly and Rocky were stunned. The station had metamorphosed into some kind of airport. Sleek jet planes parked in neat lines stretched away into the distance. The snatcher made his way toward an aircraft that bore a resemblance to a fly. He was climbing its steps and nodding at the pilot.

Molly quickly lifted herself, Rocky, and Petula, into a time hover. In this state they were just a few seconds behind the man's time, and although they could easily see their surroundings, no one could see them.

They ran to the insectlike plane. Hurriedly they mounted the stairs and walked straight through the man, who was speaking into some sort of device on his sleeve.

"This is so weird," said Molly. "Where *is* he going? And why?"

Rocky shrugged, shook his head, and looked about the aircraft.

An air hostess in a tailored purple uniform and a purple and white skullcap stood in the plane's aisle. Her hair was short and functional. Her eyes were vacant, as if there was nobody in. Molly instantly recognized the signs—she had been hypnotized. Her purple outfit, with its tailored cropped top, elbow-length sleeves, and tight purple skirt showed her belly button. To the left, in the fly's eye part of the plane, was a pilot also in purple. Still in their time-hover bubble, Molly and Rocky stepped past a round-faced elderly Chinese woman with blue eyes.

"Where shall we hide?" Molly whispered, her heart pounding. "I think we should materialize soon, as I'm not sure I'll be able to time-hover on board a fast-moving object."

Rocky nodded. "How about that luggage cubicle? Shall we risk it?"

So the two got as comfortable as they could behind a suitcase and Molly brought them into the moment. Immediately their ears were bombarded with the noises of the airport and the hum of the aircraft's air-conditioning. Molly kept a tight hold on both her crystals and on Rocky's arm, in case they needed to disappear again in a hurry. The man appeared in the entrance to the aircraft.

Through a gap between the seats, Molly saw the

Chinese woman leaping to attention. The snatcher passed her the baby.

"It's a boy," he said. "Could have been a girl—there were two of them. You're in charge of it now."

"What a sweet little dumpling you are. What an angel," the woman gushed.

"Hope you're not talking to me," the man with the quiff replied with a conceited laugh. Then he settled into a large reclining seat in front of hers and pressed a button to make it flat. Slipping a blackout visor over his eyes, he lay down.

The woman bent over the baby boy and smiled and cooed at him even though he was still asleep. "I'm so pleased to meet you," she said fondly. "Now, you'd better go in this cot."

Molly gave Rocky a perplexed look. The woman had evidently been expecting the baby. She seemed to be some sort of nanny. Where were they all going? Molly didn't like it. Things were getting more and more mysterious.

Now a sign at the front of the plane flashed: BUCKLE UP SEATBELTS, and the flight attendant with the empty eyes checked that all passengers were secure before she sat down too. The engine started. When it reached a peak of whirring the aircraft pivoted on its wheels and headed toward a runway. There, the engines picked up more speed, until they made a zinging noise.

Takeoff was like going up in a fast elevator. Like a jack released from its box, the flying machine shot up in the air. Molly's stomach felt as though she'd left it on the runway. She nearly screamed. Squashed in their cubicle, she and Rocky looked out the window at the twenty-sixth century world below. It was a scene of pine trees and snow and frozen lakes. Molly could hardly believe how her country had changed. People living here now would ski and skate and sledge. As they flew over domes and skyscrapers they passed other buglike aircraft. Below them were tiny flying machines that seemed to be coasting at the height of houses. Then they came to the sea. The flycopter tilted upward, and a red light on the seat displays read: `Propellers folding. Wings unfolding.` There was a loud *kerrrchank* noise on either side of the aircraft. And then, with the red signs warning `Upward thrust`, a huge jet engine sound whooshed from the back of the plane, and they shot up into the sky. When they were high above the clouds the plane leveled out and accelerated. They were heading somewhere very, very fast.

"We're heading southeast," Rocky said, examining his compass.

After fifteen minutes, the clouds cleared and the

earth below became visible again. It was now snowless, and they were whizzing over mountains. The pilot's voice came over the loudspeaker: "Mont Blanc approaching. Five minutes till landing." The red signs flashed: `Downward motion`, and on time the aircraft tipped its nose to start circling toward the ground.

"Mont Blanc?" Rocky whispered. "If that's Mont Blanc, this is Switzerland and those mountains are the Alps. But they've usually got snow on them, even in summer, and in winter they should look like white meringues and should be *covered* in skiers and snow-boarders." Molly peered out of the window. They were approaching a vast, gray mountain range with a huge, moatlike lake around the bottom of the biggest mountain. Rocky went on. "And that lake must be Lake Geneva. But I don't remember it being nearly as big as that in my atlas."

`Propellers up`, the warning signs declared. Again there was a *kerrrchank* as the aircraft converted itself from plane to helicopter.

Now they were closer to Mont Blanc, Molly saw it was no ordinary mountain. Fantastic silver buildings with turrets were jutting out of the top of it, and its side bore holes through which flycopters were entering and exiting, looking like bees buzzing to and from a hive. But the aircraft they were in wasn't going to the grand mountaintop city. Instead, it approached the lake at the foot of it, where there was another sparkling city. Some of the houses were palatial, surrounded by beautiful gardens with pools and tall trees. Around these smart houses were lush green fields dissected by small roads, paths, and canals and punctuated with tiny ponds and a few simple buildings. But this expanse of greenness wasn't everywhere. Beyond the massive lake was another town, a scruffy place with colored houses and bare, arid scrubland stretching away into the distance.

The flycopter buzzed toward the biggest of all the palaces, bringing them directly over a circular target-like landing pad. Then it descended.

"At last," said the man with the quiff, slipping off his eye visor. "Hope Her Little Highness appreciates this."

# Five

The door of the aircraft slid open and its steps unfolded. Molly's heart thumped against the inside of her rib cage like some bass percussion instrument. She was suddenly horribly nervous. She touched the scar on the side of her neck—the scar that had been the result of another time-travel adventure. Perhaps this trip would scar her too. But going home wasn't an option now. She had to finish what she'd set out to do. Her own brother's future lay in her hands.

She brought Rocky, Petula, and herself into a time hover and, in the mist that hid them, they followed her baby brother's party into the hot sun outside.

Before them was a garden filled with palm trees and flowering bushes. From a tall cypress hung a swing on long ropes, and behind it Molly could see what looked like the top of a red spiral slide. As she and Rocky turned to follow the other passengers they saw that the house they'd come to was spectacular. It was made up of a series of giant silver igloos with small ones attached. These nestled around it like chicks about a mother hen. Some igloos had vertical slits of glass in them, others large fish-eye windows. All had tall aerial-like flagpoles on top giving them the appearance of massive silver fruits with stems.

The man with the quiff stepped toward the largest building and was immediately met by a guard. The guard, who was dressed in red and white like a toy soldier nodded and waved his hand over a pad on the wall. The igloo's door slid up, opening like an eyelid, and the man ushered the nanny with the baby through. Molly and Rocky hurried after, safely invisible in their time-hover veil.

Inside the dome was a high, curved room with a pink marble floor. At its center hung another long-roped swing. This one was moving backward and forward with a young girl sitting on it. Molly reckoned she was about six. She was wearing a pink plastic dress and, on her feet, high-heeled cartoony boots. Her hair was sprayed into a beehive style so that it towered above her Oriental features. Unlike ordinary beehives, it then curled on top like a question mark. Her mouth was small and mean, and her expression was one of grim determination as she urged the swing as high as it would go. Around her stood five other children, of varying ages from about six to twelve—three girls and two boys. One girl looked Mongolian, another was black, and the third was white. The first boy was black and the second, Asian. All were dressed in brand-new-looking, brightly colored clothes, and each had a peculiar hairstyle, ranging from jagged Mohawks to ponytails set so that they wiggled upward. And beside them stood three suited adults: two women in black suits and a man dressed in dark maroon. They looked as though they were teachers—or guards.

Seeing the new arrivals, the little girl's face lit up and she clapped her hands. A butler, in an embroidered gold waistcoat, a white shirt, and tailored gold trousers, caught the swing to stop it. The girl's legs dangled as she slowed down, and the butler, bowing, passed her a saucer-sized swirly lollipop.

The child snatched it and gave it a lick.

Molly quickly led Rocky behind a lime-green, banana-shaped sofa at the edge of the room. Around the side of it they could see some of the action without being noticed themselves. And here Molly could release the time hover to hear what was being said.

Molly stroked Petula to keep her quiet, then let them join the six-year-old's time. At once a conversation became audible.

". . . dat de one?" the girl was saying in a squeaky, bossy voice.

"Without a doubt, Your Majesty," said the man with the quiff. "There were in fact two of them—twins. I could have chosen a girl."

The child hopped off the swing and walked toward the nurse, her sharp heels clipping the pink stone floor. "I must say this trip was rather exciting," the man continued, "I went the long way, via the year 2250, and I had a ride on a magnifloat!" Ignoring him, the girl clicked her fingers and pointed to the ground. A servant brought her a stool to stand on. Tottering on it, she peered at Molly's brother. The other children gathered around too.

"Urrgh! He's so ugly!" she snorted. "You *know* I fink ugly fings are weee-volting. Shall we give him to de surgeons to make pwettier?" She laughed. The man with the quiff looked puzzled.

"Don't be ridiculous, Qingling," he said. "You can't give children or babies plastic surgery to make them more beautiful—their faces are still growing."

"Oh, Wedhorn!" The girl giggled, waggling her lollipop at him. "You *never* can take a joke, can you? But he *is* disgustingly ugly. Almost as ugly as a mutant!" Around her the other children tittered. "I just hope he impwooves." Molly noticed a star-shaped birthmark on her wrist.

"Don't be too rude about him," Redhorn said, stroking his quiff. "Don't forget, we need him if our endeavors are going to be successful." He smiled nastily. "And, remember, he is one of my relations."

"Wemind me again how de family twee goes."

"Well, his mother was my great-great-great-goodness-knows-how-many-greats grandmother's *cousin*. It took me quite a bit of hunting about in the past to find him. I hypnotized all the hospital staff to wipe his details from the records and to forget he ever existed."

"Hmm, vewy *un*interesting. The good fing is, he's here. Well done." Then, tossing her lollipop into the air and catching it again like some expert juggler, the girl let out a screech that woke the baby.

"Miss Cwibbins!"

A tall, thin woman in a gray tunic, with a strangely beautiful face smooth as porcelain and golden hair scraped into a bun, stepped in through a side door. Her face was powdered white and her cheeks were tinted with circles of rouge. Above her left cheekbone there was a dense black beauty spot. Like an officer presenting herself, she stamped her foot and slapped her hands behind her back.

"Yes, Madame Fen Fang Feng Yang Yong Yin Ying Kai-Ying?" she drawled. As she spoke something poked its head over her shoulder. It was a pink cat with yellow eyes. Then in the next moment Molly saw that it wasn't a cat. Only its head was catlike. Its eight furry legs were those of a spider.

"Dis is de infant," the girl said.

The skinny woman sniffed at the crying child and wiped her thin nose with a gray hanky. "Seems healthy enough."

"You won't need to attend to its education for a few years," the girl elaborated, "so don't look so alarmed. Nurse Meekles will see to its needs now. Won't you, nurse?" The Chinese woman, who was rocking Molly's brother to quiet him, smiled.

"Take de baby." The girl dismissed her. "Luckily we won't need to see it until it's gwown up."

"It will be my pleasure, Fen Fang Feng Fing—er, no, Yang Yong Ying Qin—"

"STOP!" the small girl shouted. "If you can't get it right, don't say it at all. Maybe if you could wemember what my name *means*, you might be able to say it!"

"I can remember what it means, Your Majesty," the nurse replied calmly. "It's just my tongue gets tied around all the Yings and Yongs."

"Oh, so what *does* it all mean, den?" the little girl asked, looking around smugly to make sure that everyone was paying attention to the nurse's humiliation.

"What, you want me to tell you now?"

"Yes, let's see if you can wemember. It'll be a nice game. I wouldn't be supwised if looking after babies and toddlers has wotted your bwain!"

The nurse looked at the floor and then began. "Well, *Fen Fang* means 'fragrant,' and *Feng* means 'phoenix.'"

The little girl interrupted her. "Phoenix—de bird dat gwows old and den dies and den is born again. Dat suits me, doesn't it, Wedhorn?" The man with the quiff smiled and nodded.

The nurse continued. "*Yang* means 'beautiful,' *Yong* means 'forever brave,' *Yin* means 'silver,' *Ying* means 'cherry flower,' and *Kai-Ying* means 'exceptionally bright.'"

"Exceptionally bwight! Well, dat is most definitely me!"

Molly nudged Rocky. "Exceptionally nasty and pleased with herself too," she whispered in his ear. "I wonder what *that* is in Chinese."

"Poo *Pong*," Rocky replied quietly. The little girl had now been given a silver rope and was skipping.

"And *Qingling*," the nurse finished, "means 'celebration of understanding.'"

"Well, all wight, so you do know de meaning!" the girl said, out of breath as she jumped. "But, as I've said before, I WON'T have people twipping up on my name as dey say it, so if *any* of you"—she stopped and pointed the handle of her skipping rope at each person in the room in turn—"are in any doubt about my name, just call me . . ." She walked over to the tall man standing behind the other children. "Just call me what?"

"Just call you *Princess*, Your Majesty."

The small girl laughed. "YES!" she shouted. She consulted a flower on her dress. "Half an hour until our satellite meeting with Japan, Wedhorn. Are you wedy?"

The quiffed man nodded. "But don't hurry me. Remember, I've traveled to the twentieth century and back again to fetch this brat for us today. It's tiring, Qingling, and a strain on my heart too. You sometimes act as though you think time traveling is as easy as yo-yoing or hula-hooping or skipping. Give me ten minutes in the relaxation chamber and I'll meet you in the communication room." With that, the girl, her entourage of children, and the grim adults, followed by Redhorn, Miss Cribbins, and the servants, filed out through a door at the back of the room. The nurse, still cuddling Molly's brother, was the last to leave.

Soon the domed entrance hall was empty and Rocky, Molly, and Petula were left alone.

"Phew! It's so hot," gasped Molly, taking off her coat. Rocky ripped his off too. "Who was that kid?" Molly said. "I've never seen a kid so . . . so . . ."

"So bossy?"

"So advanced," Molly concluded. "She's a spoiled princess. Do you think those other children are her brothers and sisters?"

Rocky shook his head. "They can't be," he said. "They were all so different. One looked Mongolian. The tall girl was black, Molly. Forget them. What do we do now?"

"I don't know, Rocky. I mean, I'd love it if we could just take the baby back now, back home. I really don't like it here—it gives me the heebie-jeebies. But if we took him back . . . well, first of all, they obviously want him for something special and so they'd soon send that man Redhorn to find him. And in the meantime, Redhorn would definitely sort you and me out. Plus, if I take the baby and put him back in his cot, maybe *my* whole life will change because of it, and yours too. And if that happened, then Lucy and Primo might still be hypnotized by Cornelius!"

Rocky winced as he considered the situation. Molly

flicked her tooth with her nail and thought.

"I know what we have to do," she finally said. "We have to go forward in time to when the baby is the same age as I am now. Then we can start to interfere. I don't know what we'll do with that Redhorn man. Urrgh, I can't believe that Micky and I are related to him!" Suddenly a look of panic crossed her face. "Maybe there are *other* time travelers too, other hypnotists like Redhorn."

"Molly, I hope I can be useful on this trip," Rocky said. "I'm not exactly the world's best voice hypnotist. I always feel like you're doing all the work."

"Don't say that, Rocky. I couldn't do this without your help. You know so much and you're good at thinking things through logically."

Rocky smiled. "Okay. Anyway, how are the skin scales?"

Molly touched the dry patch behind her ear. It had definitely grown a bit. "It's fine," she said. "Anyway, it's just part of the deal."

Rocky scrunched Petula's ears. "Well, let's go and meet your brother then."

"Shall we stop on the way and see how he's growing up?" Molly pondered.

"If we do, we risk being seen." Rocky rolled up the coat he'd been wearing. "We'll need to borrow some clothes from those kids so we can blend in."

"If they live here," said Molly.

"And we'll have to keep our eyes open for security cameras, as I bet this place is crawling with them."

Molly cast her eyes down at her gem and thought hard for it to take them slowly forward to two years farther into the future. Rocky held her arm and gripped the rucksack that Petula was in. Time skittered by. Occasionally Molly slowed them down to a time hover to see how things were turning out. She and Rocky felt like flies on walls as they watched unseen. They saw the princess on the swing—always dressed in outlandishly frilly or sparkling outfits. They saw the bigger children come and go with the stern-looking, beautiful Miss Cribbins, as well as some other very serious adults. Occasionally there were seats in the room—seats that were hidden in the floor and that rose up when they were needed. The princess would sit on one, holding court, entertaining or arguing with smartly suited grown-ups. Molly couldn't understand it at all—these adults didn't look like the princess. Molly wondered where her parents were.

And then there were long periods when only servants visited the room. Molly stopped in one of these times. The room was warmer than it had been when they arrived because an even hotter sun was beaming through the windows.

"Phew!" Rocky panted. "It must be scorching out there!"

"Doesn't seem to be anyone about," said Molly, listening for signs of people. "Shall we have a look around?" Shivering with trepidation, she lifted Petula out of her rucksack. Petula shook herself and licked her lips. Molly poured some of the water she'd brought with her into Rocky's cupped hands, and Petula lapped it up. She wondered why her mistress smelled so fearful.

Then quietly they approached the door at the far end of the enormous room. At a slight touch to its yellow control pad it glided open.

Beyond, a honeycomb of silent passages led to the other igloos and other rooms. Straight ahead were some stairs. There didn't seem to be any cameras spying on them, and so Molly and Rocky tiptoed up. At the top was a giant, curved, bug-eye window with a view of the vast mountain above. On a table beneath the window was a long screen showing live pictures of the surrounding countryside and the lake.

"There must be a rotating camera on the roof of this building," Rocky decided. "It's turning three hundred and sixty degrees—that's how this view shows what is all around."

Molly and Rocky quickly studied this strange

world. They saw aerials and the silver tops of other spherical buildings peeping over the crowning branches of flowering trees. It seemed that other, similar igloo cluster estates were nearby. And, not far away, water glittered in the harsh sunlight, with a few white boats sailing on it.

"Seems there's a breeze out there," Rocky observed. "But it's quiet, isn't it? Look, there's no air traffic in the sky here. This place is a ghost town." In contrast, they saw that up at the *top* of the mountain it was very busy. Light aircraft buzzed in and out of its cavelike entrances. Molly snapped into action mode.

"Let's make the most of this," she said. "Come on!"

They crept along a maze of deserted passages, darting past cameras that were trained on the corridors and quietly opening doors. Petula kept close to them, her claws quietly clipping the smooth, shiny floor. Eventually they found a series of bedrooms. One, with its blinds closed, was a tall room with a curved ceiling. Its bed was quilted in pink and gold with big, flower-shaped pillows to match. Huge stuffed toys lined the walls, and sitting on chairs were sophisticated dolls whose eyes stared accusingly at the intruders.

"Her *Ladyship's* room, I suppose," said Rocky. "Some of her toys aren't toys at all. Look at that camera thing . . ."

"And that fancy jewelry," Molly added. "She must be about eight by now." She touched a yellow-haired doll. The doll's eyes opened and it grabbed Molly's wrist.

"Aaargh!" Molly yelled.

"Aararhah," the doll snarled.

Rocky pulled the toy's hand away, and it was still. "Programmed to be nasty," he said, grimacing.

Molly rubbed her wrist. "Imagine what dolls' tea parties are like around here."

Next door was a games room full of crazy-looking futuristic games. Its monitors and computers were all switched off. On a table was a flat black box with the words CAT AND MOUSE on it. Rocky picked up the controls. He couldn't resist switching it on. Immediately a very realistic hologram of a cat rose up from the box, and then a mouse. Petula growled. Rocky swiveled the joystick on the controls. The mouse began to move toward the cat. At once the cat swiped at it. Quickly Rocky moved the mouse away, but no sooner had he done this than the cat pounced. What followed was revolting. The hologram cat ate the hologram mouse.

"What a horrid game!" said Molly. Petula whined at the odorless cat.

"Yuck," agreed Rocky and switched it off.

The adjacent room was also full of toys and games.

"At least there'll be lots for your brother to play with," Rocky said, loitering at the door. "But come on, Molly—I'm starting to get nervous. This place is suspiciously quiet. I'm getting spooked."

After a dividing corridor, three more bedrooms with bathrooms attached, and three more spacious living rooms, they came to a wall with a door in it. This led to a small apartment. They found themselves in a sitting room with views of the gardens behind. The furniture was all upholstered in floral material, making inside feel as gardenlike as outside. On a shelf stood a photograph in a silver frame. Unlike a regular photograph, this one moved. In it was the nurse, holding up a two-year-old boy. He squeezed her nose as if it was a horn on a bike and she laughed, though there was no sound. The screen went blank. Then another short sequence commenced. This time the boy was at a table, feeding himself. His face was plastered with porridge. He shook his spoon and blew a raspberry, spraying half-chewed porridge at the camera. His hair was fair and curly. His eyes were closely set and the same green as Molly's.

"He looks so like you," said Rocky.

Petula sniffed about the carpet and at the paintings of animals on the walls, and then made her way into the next room. This one was simple with colored shapes and mobiles hanging from the ceiling.

"Where is he right now, I wonder?" said Molly, glancing out of the window to the mountain city above.

"Seems like everyone's there," said Rocky. "It's like every so often they move up there."

"For special occasions," suggested Molly, "or to avoid this heat? Look how hot it is outside. The heat's making shimmery lines come off the earth. This palace garden is only green and flowering because it gets watered. I bet the countryside around the lake is dryer than a bone, dryer than a desert dinosaur bone."

Petula's ears pricked up, but seeing no bone materialize she went back to sniffing the floor. There was a strange Molly-like smell. It was as if someone like Molly lived in this room.

"Mont Blanc," said Rocky, "means 'white mountain.' White because it used to be covered in snow. Obviously, five hundred years from our time, Molly, this place has heated up. I expect in the winter it probably still gets a bit cold up at the top of the mountain because it's higher. So in the *winter* it's better for people down *here* because its warmer, but in the *summer*, when it's boiling hot—sweltering hot down here—it's cooler up *there*."

Molly was too busy trying to find a disguise for them to wear so she only half listened to Rocky's theories.

"Wow. Nothing to fit us here. Come on, let's try another part of the building."

And so they continued, dodging cameras and exploring. At the other end of the corridor was a bridgelike passage that took them into another igloo. This one housed an apartment for the thin Cribbins woman. They could tell, because in a wardrobe near the bathroom were rows of her distinct, austere outfits. Each was a slightly different shade of gray. On the walls were mahogany-framed display cases full of dull-colored, dusty dead butterflies, pinned and lifeless. The carpet was black, as was the bed, and the room was sparsely furnished, without belongings, as though everything had been hoovered up. All except for a door-sized glass box that stood in the corner.

Inside this was a beautiful silvery-white spiderweb. And on its floor, a black velvet cushion. This was, Molly realized, where Miss Cribbins kept her strange cat-cum-spider pet. Petula sniffed at the cobwebby, feline smell. She didn't like spiders and she loathed most cats. She wrinkled her nose in disgust. Then she smelled something else. A person was coming who smelled of vinegar and something feathery too. She growled.

"I just heard something," said Rocky, lingering by the door. "Someone's coming. Quick!" But it was too late. In the next moment, a cleaner dressed in a strange Little Bo-peep outfit entered. Instead of a crook she carried a feather duster. In her other hand were a cloth and a container of some sort of cleaning fluid. When she saw the two children she stopped dead in her tracks.

"Can I help you?" she said in a monotone.

"Um, we're friends of, erm . . . the princess," Molly lied, thinking quickly. "She said we could come down here and look at the kennel that the spider-cat is kept in. We're both getting spider-cats ourselves too, you see, um, this Christmas." The Bo-peep woman narrowed her eyes.

"They are called 'cat-spiders' and they are very rare. Only elderly royal court members are permitted to own them," she said.

"Ah. Well, that *was* true," Molly explained, trying to dig herself out of the hole she'd obviously fallen into. "They changed the rules yesterday!"

"And Christmas?" the woman asked. "Where will you be celebrating that?"

"Oh, up at the palace," Molly continued. "There's going to be turkey and everything." As Molly said this she realized that her lies had not worked one jot. The woman was frowning. "But we must get going now. Nice to meet you."

"Christmas is not celebrated here. It hasn't been for hundreds of years," said Little Bo-peep. Molly nodded. And as she did, she prepared her eyes.

The woman looked as though she was about to sound the alarm. And so Molly let her have it.

In three seconds flat the Bo-peep woman's eyeballs were twitching in their sockets and she was completely hypnotized.

"Are there any other people in the building today?" Molly asked.

The woman shook her head.

"Good," said Molly. "Now you will completely forget that you've ever seen us. Okay?"

The Bo-peep woman nodded her head of curls. "Please get on with your business, but before you do, I lock these instructions in with the password 'Petula.'" The lady left.

In the next igloo was a set of rooms inhabited by children—though judging by their belongings they weren't ordinary children. Their shelves contained old leather-bound books, antiques now, originally from Molly's time and before, with titles like *The New Elements of Geology* and *Space Programs for the Millennium*. On shelves were stacked complicated puzzles and scientific instruments. Large desks with sophisticated computer keyboards built into them stood in every room. The cupboards in these rooms were stuffed full of children's clothes that were a perfect size for Molly and Rocky. Molly pulled out a stiff white cottonlike jumpsuit covered in zips and pockets. The shoes she found were fabulously sleek and modern looking.

"Sneakers of the future," Molly said, admiringly. "But too small. I'll have to stick to mine." Rocky chose an olive-green suit. It was slightly heavier than Molly's but of the same design.

"Lucky we don't have to dress up like poor Miss Bopeep," he said.

Soon both were ready, their own clothes and their bits and pieces stuffed into the rucksack with Petula. The big coats they'd taken from the teenage girls at the magnifloat station were now a burden.

"What shall we do with them?"

"Find a bin?" Rocky suggested quietly. "But we don't want to leave clues for that Redhorn man."

Molly glanced at the moving photograph of the room's owner. The boy's hair was scraped back and slicked with some sort of gel. In another picture the Mongolian girl had a question-mark-shaped hairstyle that was similar to the beehive hairdo of the six-year-old princess on the swing.

Molly pointed to them. "We've got to look a

hundred percent right."

Rocky curled his lip. "Do we have to?"

"Yes."

They went to the bathroom and opened a cabinet. Here there were lots of bottles and jars with perfumes and creams, as well as packets of multicolored pills. There was a section full of hair products. Molly made Rocky sit down and she squirted a large amount of a see-through purple gel into her hand.

"Hold still." She wiped the gel into Rocky's curly black hair, adding more until it was saturated; then she scraped it all back with a comb.

"Uurrrghh. Feels cold and slimy, like mashed slugs," he complained in a whisper. "*Thanks.* Now your turn."

Molly's stringy hair was more difficult to set, but eventually, after using the rest of the gel and a lot of hair-fixing foam too, Rocky managed to get it up on top of her head. Her question mark looked more like an exclamation mark, but it was just about right.

Petula cocked her head and wondered what Rocky and Molly were up to. She hoped they weren't going to rub the fruity, synthetic-smelling stuff on her. Molly's pointed pixielike hair reminded Petula of when Molly had lathered up her hair at bath times in Briersville. Thinking of home now made Petula want to go back. She didn't like this place at all. It had a bad feeling. She whined again, trying to beam her thoughts up to Molly. *Please, Molly, can't we go home?*

Molly turned and smiled down at her. "I agree, Petula. It's a really stupid hairstyle. Smelly and sticky." Molly stuffed the empty canister into the bag with their clothes. Then silently they checked the bathroom was spotless and went back to the bedroom. "Okay, Rocky, we're ready. Mind you, there is a problem."

"I'd say we've got a few," said Rocky, tweaking her hair. "Which one in particular are you thinking of?"

"Well, we want to go forward in time until my brother is the same age as me—so that's nine and a half years from now."

Rocky nodded.

"But when he got here as a two-day-old baby it was winter."

*"Yeeees,"* said Rocky slowly, seeing what Molly was coming to, "so everyone was down here and not up there in the mountain."

"Exactly," said Molly. "Let's say it was January or something. Well, eleven years on, it's January, but eleven *and a half* years on it's July. So he'll be up there!" Molly pointed to the city above.

"True. We'll just have to hitch an elevator up to the mountaintop."

"At least now we look the part."

"Um . . . sort of," said Rocky, worriedly eyeing Molly's hair.

# Six

Outside the igloo house it was so hot that Petula's soft paws couldn't stand on the tarmac. Molly picked her up and with the other hand cupped her gem necklace. Rocky dumped the two coats into a bin beside the flycopter landing pad and then put his hand on Molly's shoulder.

"Hope no one can see us," he said, glancing about.

With a BOOM they were off, hurtling into the future. Molly counted four years whizzing by and then brought their time travel to a very slow pace. From the protection of a time hover they watched the world about them. Various aircraft landed and took off, and people moved at very high speed as though on a film that had been fast-forwarded. Then Molly spotted the flying machine they had arrived in. They saw Nurse

Meekles holding the hand of a curly-haired little boy and leading him toward the flycopter. A servant dressed like Dick Whittington, in puffed-up shorts and over-the-knee boots, was loading cases onboard. The sky was speckled with aircraft, both above them and beside the mountain. It looked like some sort of rush hour. Molly pulled Rocky toward the steps and, invisible to all there, they went aboard.

Miss Cribbins, the smooth-faced beauty with icy eyes, whose hair was now fire-engine red, sat in the seat behind the pilot with her pink cat-spider crouched on her shoulder. Nurse Meekles and the boy were in seats across the aisle.

Molly and Rocky hid in the same cubicle space as before, then they materialized. They listened to the nurse's kind tones as she talked to the boy and to Miss Cribbins as she scolded him.

"No, you can't play with that in the flycopter," said Miss Cribbins harshly. "In fact, I'm confiscating it." A large squashy dinosaur flew over the seat and landed in the cubicle on Molly.

"MMMWWEEERGHHHH!" it roared as though sounding the alarm. Rocky pulled a face at it.

"But he'll be lonely in the back!" the boy cried.

"Oh, stop sniveling," Miss Cribbins replied. Then her words were muddied by the sounds of the engines.

"Oooh my tummy!" the small boy screeched as they soared upward through the air toward the city at the top of the mountain. Molly peered out the window.

Nearer the mountain's craggy top, she saw that the cloud-kissed city was far more lavish than she had realized. Its buildings were turreted with silver and glass and copper, and behind walls were marvelous gardens with fountains and trees and sculptures. The flycopter ascended higher and higher, up to the lofty peaks of Mont Blanc. They were approaching a palace far bigger than any of the other residences around it. It had ten or fifteen metal turrets and many ornamental gardens. Below was a cliff-side entrance. The flycopter flew in.

As the engines died down and the machine parked, the little boy clapped his hands.

"I'm so excited," he shouted. "This is going to be so much fun!"

Miss Cribbins, Molly could see through a crack in the chair, had turned to face him. "Not now that you are four," she said harshly. "This summer you are going to work hard, Micky Minus. Your *lessons* start with me. You won't be lolling about with Nurse Meekles anymore." She smiled, her strangely beautiful face made ugly by her malicious eyes, and then she chuckled. "You're going to be *so* tired from work, young man, that you won't have the energy to play. And you'd better work hard, because you know how the princess hates ugly things. You're not the world's most handsome child, are you now? You'd better make up for it by working, because if you don't please Her Highness, she might send you to live with the mutants!"

Molly shot Rocky a look of horror, then mouthed the boy's name. *"Minus?"* she questioned silently. Rocky shrugged as if to agree that it was a weird surname. Then Molly lifted them into a time hover and, feeling safe, she, Rocky, and Petula followed the party out.

They walked through a cavernlike aircraft hangar to a tall door and up a slope into a courtyard. Here Micky Minus clutched Nurse Meekles, hugging her leg. Only when Miss Cribbins had gone did he relax. As an entourage of servants brought their suitcases, the little boy charged down covered walkways and skipped through the gardens. He sprinted down paths, hopped past ponds, and galloped over tiny bridges. He stopped once to inspect a rainbow-colored parrot sitting in a tree. Then he ran on until he came to a tall green door. Beyond this was the courtyard nursery. He shot toward a pool there and peered in. Silver fish flashed in the water. Molly led Rocky and Petula behind a bush and let them all arrive in the time. The air here was cool and the sunlight a perfect brightness.

"I think the big furry fish has had babies," Micky

was saying. Then as the nurse came over to look, he confided, "Ai Mu, I don't want to have lessons with Miss Cribbins."

"You have to," the Chinese woman said reluctantly. "I've told you, little Ping—it's part of growing up."

"I don't want to go and live over there."

"But they need you, dumpling. You've got a very important job to do. And you'll be able to come and visit me. Look how near I am. And that stuff Miss Cribbins said about the mutants—well, that's nonsense."

"I don't want to go!" wailed the small boy, and he began to cry.

Molly bit her finger. "I wish we'd gone straight to when he's eleven," she whispered. "This is horrible. I want to take him back right now, but we can't. They'll only send that Redhorn man to get him again."

There was a BOOM as Molly took them into the future again. Nurse Meekles looked up.

"What was that noise?" Micky Minus asked.

"Don't you worry, my little sugar."

With elegant accuracy Molly's red gem thrust her, Rocky, and Petula forward to the time when Molly would be the exact same age as Micky Minus. They came to an abrupt halt. A silvery, bright sun shone down. Molly placed Petula on the ground.

"Poor Petula! You've probably had enough of this. Go on—go and have a good sniff about." Petula looked up at Molly gratefully, then cautiously began investigating the garden. She found a smooth stone on the gravel. She picked it up in her mouth and began sucking it.

"I'll just have to hypnotize anyone who comes along," Molly said. "We can't keep carrying her."

"I agree," said Rocky. He was trying to sound relaxed, but Molly knew he was worried because he still gripped her arm tightly. "I hope," he said, pointing to a camera attached to a small tree, "that the palace guards aren't paying too much attention today."

"We'll sort this out now and then we'll just zip back to the twenty-first century," Molly said, sounding more confident than she felt.

Rocky nodded. His eyes ran around the windows of the nurse's quarters. "Micky must be living in another part of the palace by now. Let's go and find him."

Molly whistled quietly for Petula. "Wonder why he's called Micky *Minus*?" she whispered as they walked past the nurse's rose beds into other colonnaded gardens. Treading quietly, the friends kept to the shadowy cloisters. Then they heard a noise.

It was Miss Cribbins's cool snarl and it was coming from an open window nearby. Petula's ears pricked up as she smelled the horrid stench of the cat-spider. Molly and Rocky crouched down and, commando style, crept to the window. Then, carefully and slowly, they raised their heads and peered in.

Miss Cribbins stood in front of a T-shaped stand. On this her cat-spider lay curled up, and beside it was a computer that Cribbins tapped with a spiky finger. Behind her, a screen showed the image of a human body. It showed the brain, intestines, heart, liver, spleen, lungs—the bits and pieces that chug away inside each and every one of us.

"As I hope you remember," the tight-lipped woman was saying, knocking a fluorescent green sack-like shape on the screen with a baton, "this is your stomach. Well, not *your* stomach. These are *healthy* intestines. *Your* insides are more like this . . ." The sack on the screen, an empty, deflated balloon-type thing with pipes going in and out of it, now turned into something else. It became covered with red spots and growths and lumps.

"Looks painful," said a thin voice. Molly lifted her head higher to see who had spoken. She saw the back of a boy. His hair was brown and curly. But he wasn't sitting—he was *reclining* on a piece of furniture that was part stretcher, part chair.

"Of course it looks painful," Miss Cribbins retorted.

"It *is* painful, as you well know. Don't try to wriggle out of it and deny it. THIS IS WHAT YOUR STOMACH LOOKS LIKE!"

The intestines on the screen became a moving picture, and the pustules and lumps on it oozed yellow slime. The boy said nothing.

"Which is one of the reasons," continued his nightmare teacher, "why you are so WEAK."

The picture changed so that now the model of the boy on the screen showed his muscles.

"These are healthy muscles," said the horrible governess. "But these are yours." Instead of thick biceps flexing in the moving image, now there were thin, puny fibers. Miss Cribbins switched the computer off. Her cat-spider rapidly awoke, sprang off the pedestal, and scuttled up her arm to perch on her shoulder. "It is tea now," she said. "As usual, the food will make you feel ill. It's pathetic that you are so allergic. What kind of human are you?" Under her breath she muttered to her pet, "I don't think he will ever get better. Do you, Taramasalata?"

"Thank you," answered the weak voice, "and excuse me." With that, as if on invisible ropes, the boy's chair levitated and, humming, transported him through a door at the end of the classroom. Molly and Rocky saw his face as he turned the corner. It was the unmistakable face of Micky Minus.

Miss Cribbins stood alone. Her pet cat-spider picked its way down her arm.

"Keep him down," she said, chuffing her sharp-toothed creature under its chin. "Reduce him, knock him, worry his dreams. Don't destroy him, but keep him down." The cat-spider began to purr.

Molly and Rocky dropped to their knees and exchanged a quizzical look. Molly put her forefinger to her head and, as if turning an invisible dial, circled it around twice. Rocky nodded and mouthed the word "nutter."

Molly wondered what had happened to Micky. Had he been in a terrible accident? Then she, Rocky, and Petula wriggled away from under the window and followed the wall around.

The first door they came to was a tall white one and it too was open. Inside was a gargantuan playroom with a giant curling slide that spaghettied around and down the room. Across the space, from a high platform down to a lower mat, was a tight nylon rope.

"That's a pulley," Rocky whispered. "You get on that thing with the seat on it at the top and you shoot down to the bottom. It's good fun."

"Not for my brother," said Molly. "He probably couldn't even get up on it."

Just then the far door opened and Micky buzzed in on his floating divan. Molly put her fingers to her mouth to give him a low whistle, but Rocky karate-chopped her hand to silence her.

"Not yet," he whispered. "We need to know more about him."

The boy silently drifted by into the next room, from where a thumping noise was coming. Molly, Rocky, and Petula edged sideways, crouched below the open window, and looked inside. There, they saw a sunken trampoline, and bouncing up and down on this as though her life depended on it was a little girl. She was wearing a mustard-colored dress with silver petticoats underneath. Bracelets jangled on her wrists while, amazingly, the girl's hair, piled on top of her head in the shape of whipped ice cream, stayed rigidly in place.

"Lots of gel," Molly whispered. Her own hair was now collapsing, and sticky strands of it fell about her face.

"Bet she's a princess too," said Rocky. "She must be the sister of the girl we saw before. She's got exactly the same eyes."

"Where are the parents in this place?"

The child's high-heeled yellow shoes lay neatly on the floor beside the trampoline, and next to them was a pile of books. Molly noticed their titles. *Astrophysics*—volumes one, two, and three. Behind was a grand indoor swimming pool with pink lights glittering under the water.

"Tea," Micky Minus said nonchalantly, his floating divan heading straight out over the water toward the far door. The small girl jumped very high, did a somersault, and then pounced onto a wheelless scooter. Without a noise it rose up in the air. The girl drove it on two airborne circuits of the room and then waterskied it over the pool before disappearing through the door too.

"Bwing my fings!" she shouted behind her. A hollow-faced servant in a medieval jester costume, who had been standing as discreet as a pillar, obediently trudged over to the yellow shoes and the books. The bells at the ends of his red felt hat jangled in the echoing room. His eyes were gray and empty.

"He looks hypnotized," Molly said, her voice barely audible.

"Not a good sign *at all*," said Rocky, checking behind them. "That creepy Redhorn guy must still be about." Molly nodded. Hearing footsteps coming closer, they were both suddenly filled with alarm.

"Quick. Get in!" Molly grabbed Petula, and they all tumbled through the window. A soft pile of toys squeaked and jingled, squashing as they broke their fall.

In a room reserved for guards at the other side of the building, twenty small screens showed what the spy cameras about the palace were scanning. Each was a monitor for ten cameras, so the views flitted from one view of the palace grounds to another.

Three tall, handsome men sat with earphones on, their eyes trained on the screens. All were silent, their heads occasionally nodding forward because of the boredom of watching and listening to the predictable monitors. There hadn't been any intruders at the palace since a wild bird had become trapped in the dining room six months ago. They had darted the bird. It had been interesting to see the strategically positioned, poisonous darts work.

The man on monitor one suddenly perked up. In room nine, two people—children, it seemed—had just entered through the window. The girl was carrying a bag of some sort. Now they were walking past the swimming pool.

"Impostors—Room nine," he announced in a monotone.

Immediately the man beside him got up and inspected the screen. Making the decision not to fire poisonous darts at them, since an interrogation would be necessary, he ordered: "Intercept—Number Twelve and Number Thirteen. Keep in contact."

Number Twelve, for that was the name of the tall, strong guard on monitor one, and Number Thirteen immediately got up. They removed their headphones and replaced them with walkie-talkie receivers that they plugged into their ears. Taking two gunlike weapons from a shelf, they left.

Molly and Rocky hurried toward the door at the end of the room. Beyond it was another garden—this one square and surrounded by sparkling walls. They began to move toward a silver door on the right, but just as they approached it, it made a bleeping noise. Molly and Rocky leaped for cover behind a bush. The jester servant they'd seen earlier walked past them as he returned to the swimming pool. The door bleeped again, giving Molly just enough time to pull her and Rocky through.

Inside, the space was aquatically blue. Molly and Rocky stepped nimbly into a dark-blue corner where they could hardly be seen.

"I wonder what's in there," Rocky whispered, nodding toward a dividing wall that hid the main part of the room. "I don't like this, Molly—it's weird here."

Molly was feeling uneasy too, especially as a low, muffled moan and a squelching noise were coming from the room beyond. "It smells of seaweed and salt, doesn't it?" Molly nodded.

Petula's nose picked up more. She could smell the young girl in the yellow dress. This girl's odor was very like that of the girl on the swing. She could smell a man too. An acrid stench of fear was coming from him. Both were behind the partition. Under the man's panic Petula caught a whiff of books and paper and ink and the plastic of computers, as well as cheese. The man liked cheese. Petula tried to stretch her mind out to see if she could sense more of the man's feelings, but all she got was fear. Intense fear.

"Wh-what *is* that noise?" Rocky stammered.

Petula hung back.

Molly gulped. Her blood was pumping through the veins in her temples at a galloping pace. She had a nasty feeling that the noise was Micky groaning. She stepped toward the screen and peered around it. Above her head, as if on hangers, hung the yellow dress and the high heels of the little girl. Beside them were a black all-in-one suit and a pair of brown rubber shoes. Then there was another partition.

Molly leaned forward and saw beyond it something giant and gelatinous and blue and watery. The thing squelched and quivered.

And then Molly caught a glimpse of the girl. She was dressed in a shiny turquoise sleeveless wet suit, with trousers that stopped above the knee. Molly couldn't see who was making the pained noise. Now convinced that it was her brother being tortured, Molly decided to step up to the screen and take a proper look.

As she did, an extraordinary and shocking thing happened. The moment Molly entered the zone between the partition walls, a current—some sort of force field—surrounded her body, causing the zipper of her white outfit to unzip. But not only that. Quicker than Molly could react, her feet were tilted forward and an invisible force removed her sneakers. Her clothes were effortlessly peeled off and, in a flash, her precious crystal necklace was sucked off her neck. Before she could reach up and grab it, it was over her head and hovering three meters above her, along with her clothes, sneakers, and rucksack. The plastic strip that was one half of the hospital band that had once been around Molly's twin brother's wrist, with its letters GAN TWIN written on it, floated down to the floor. For less than an instant Molly was left standing stark naked, and then something even odder happened. Blue lights shone at her body, and before she could blink, she too was wearing a shiny turquoise outfit made of the glowing electric-blue material. All this happened silently and took no more than five seconds flat.

Molly touched her new outfit and desperately looked up at her necklace, dangling far out of reach. She shot a scared look back at Rocky. He had his hand over his mouth in horror. Then, hearing another moan, Molly inched toward the lower wall. She crouched down and poked her head around it.

Now she could see the blue squelching thing in all its glistening glory. It looked like a massive jellyfish floating high in the air. Its strands and tentacles dropped down into deep, slimy, bubbling water.

Beyond it was a platform and on this a seat. A man also dressed in an electromagnetic wet suit sat gagged, with his body and arms apparently constrained by invisible forces. He was desperately trying to release his hands. A silver dome crowned his head. In front of him the girl stood like a DJ at a panel of switches and controls. Molly wondered whether to run forward and hypnotize her. She felt sure the girl was about to do something extremely bad. But before Molly was able to make her decision a heavy hand grasped her throat and another caught her arms in a full nelson.

# Seven

Molly gave a yelp and then began to struggle, but getting out of the grip of whatever Goliath was holding her was impossible. There was a scrabbling of claws on the floor as loyal Petula rushed forward to help her mistress. Immediately she was also given an electromagnetic dog-sized wet suit. Looking like a blue merdog and baring her teeth, she went for the legs of the man who held Molly, only to be kicked and hurled across the floor.

"Don't, Petula! Don't try!" shouted Molly. At the same time she heard Rocky struggling behind the screen. Molly wriggled and attempted to turn her head so that her hypnotic eyes could be beamed at her captor, but she couldn't. There was no choice but to just hang listlessly. In front of her she could see the princess and the blue jellyfish creature. The girl turned to see what the commotion was, put her hands on her hips in consternation, and then, calculating that the situation was under control, turned back to her complicated computer. To the right, Molly could see Petula recovering from her violent knock. How she wished Petula would use her doggy hypnotism now! That pug had hypnotic skills, Molly knew, because once, with a clear crystal in her mouth, she'd made the world stand still. It had saved Molly's life.

Petula barked weakly and staggered to her feet. If only the blue-suited man holding Molly was as easy to hypnotize as mice were. But she wasn't as in control of her hypnotism as Molly—Petula's hypnotism always felt like a fluke when it happened, and, anyway, right now she was in too much pain to even try.

"Rocky!" Molly cried.

"Yeahhuhhh—" came Rocky's reply as a hand clamped around his mouth.

This annoyed the little princess. "Be quiet, would you?" she snapped angrily, with a voice just like her older sister's. "Can't you see dat I'm working on my mind machine?" Giving a sharp trill of irritation, she resumed her work, jabbing at buttons and clasping dials to turn them. The blue jellyfish began to pulsate, then spark as tiny currents of electricity broke through it. It looked as if miniature lightning bolts were flashing inside its flesh. The princess donned a silver skullcap, very like the domed cap on the trapped man's head. Then, flinging her control disk onto the monitor desk, she stepped up onto the platform where her captive sat.

"Here we go!" she exclaimed, and she sat back in a long, black, comfortable chair as if ready to enjoy some show. The man looking petrified, the princess perfectly calm, the operation began. Green and blue sparks started to explode from the man's domed cap. His limbs twitched and jerked as though he was being electrocuted, and his body pulsed with light, showing its very bones. The jellyfish's insides lit up with a bright white fiery display, and then pictures of diagrams and numbers and letters, like complicated mathematical sums, sprang out of it to pose for a second above its gelatinous head before disappearing.

Turquoise sparks flew into the girl's headpiece, apparently causing her no discomfort. Shutting her eyes and smiling, she declared, "Ohhh, I seee!" and, "Ahhh, now dat makes sense." As the man's body twisted, spasming at every spark and flash, she cried gleefully, "Oh, of *course*!" And so the process went on. Molly watched helplessly from her captor's grip. Twice the girl recited a scientific equation as if reciting poetry.

"Pi equals *MC* squared plus the watio of two cubed minus fwee over four . . . hmm." And three times she clapped her hands in delight.

Petula lay on the floor, feeling bruised and scared. She too could see the strange performance around the jellyfish. She wondered where Rocky had gone. She sucked on the tag of plastic that she'd found on the floor. She knew it was Molly's and that gave her comfort.

Then finally the sparks stopped. With a sigh of pleasure the princess girl lifted the cap from her head. Her captive's silver domed cap levitated from him as if lifted by invisible strings. His body was released from the chair.

"Fank you *vewy* much," said the child with an insane politeness. "Dat was most intewesting."

The man stared ahead of him as though trying to focus properly. He attempted to get up, but his legs, as if boneless, gave way beneath him. He looked like someone who didn't know who he was, or where he was, as he was assisted to his feet by a servant and brought to the changing area, where his blue electromagnetic wet suit was magically stripped from him and instantaneously swapped with his original clothes.

The small girl strutted toward them. Without looking at Molly she stood in the changing area and was reclad in her yellow dress. As a gold bracelet was making its way to her hand she pressed a button on the wall and at once all of Molly's things thumped and clattered to the floor.

"Hmm, twenty-first-centuwy twainers and an 'owiginal' pug dog. Uuurgh." The princess nudged Molly's sneaker with the toe of her yellow shoe. Then her dark eyes lit up as they fell on Molly's string of special crystals. "But what are dees?"

"It's just . . . just a necklace," Molly stuttered, hoping that she didn't know as much about time travel as her sister had. "I wore it around my neck, here. Look . . ." Molly was desperate to get the child to look at her. *It shouldn't be too difficult to interest a six-year-old,* she thought. "Look at my neck. I've got a scar here," now Molly lied, "in the shape of a puppy."

But the royal child wasn't to be distracted. She picked up the gems. "It doesn't take a wocket scientist, although actually I am a wocket scientist—ha!—to guess that you, girl, are a time twaveler. I know these sorts of gems well. So it's obvious you're a hypnotist too. I wecognize the dwoning voice. Cover her eyes, Number Twelve."

"Please! You don't underst—" Molly began.

"And don't speak!" The girl slammed her hand over Molly's mouth. "Or I'll have your mouth taped up!"

As a black piece of material was tightened around Molly's eyes, her world went dark. Molly suddenly felt really frightened. This girl reminded her of the sort of children who pulled the legs off insects or who threw stones at frogs. Molly felt worried for Petula and Rocky. She wondered what the girl would do with them all. Where was the Redhorn man? And *where* was Rocky?

"So you're a time-twaveling hypnotist," the girl said, peering up at Molly. Molly could smell her breath. It smelled of bubble gum. "But, de question is, *what* has bwought you here? Not a good hairdwesser—I can see dat."

Molly felt scared and absurd both at once. She couldn't believe what a complete mess she'd got herself, Rocky, and Petula into. Then, as the peculiar child in front of her prodded her in the nose, Molly heard another voice from behind the screen.

"That's right," the voice was saying. "Look into my eyes." It was Micky Minus.

In an instant, Molly realized that he too was a hypnotist. And then she felt *really* stupid. It hadn't occurred to her that Micky might be a hypnotist! How had it not! Hypnotism obviously ran in the family.

Now Molly saw that, of course, this was the reason these people needed her brother. Molly could just imagine his green eyes working on Rocky. Though blindfolded, Molly pulled away to get to him.

"No!" she shouted. "Rocky, don't lis—" But this time a large hand clamped down on her mouth.

"Now . . ." Micky was saying, "now you are completely under my power. I seal this instruction in with the words . . ." His voice trailed off to a whisper. Molly knew what he was doing. He was locking his hypnotic instruction in with a password. In a few seconds she heard Rocky complying.

"I'll do—whatever—you say," he said in a dead voice.

Molly was mortified. This was an unbelievably dreadful situation. But then, as if to prove that things could get a lot worse, the princess child in front of her declared hatefully, "I fink we'll put *you*, Miss Whoever-you-are, on de mind machine!"

Molly's stomach tightened. "Wh-what? The machine over there?" She pointed, her blindfolded eyes darting in the direction of the giant jellyfish.

"Yes," the mad little girl replied. "Or I might put your dog on first!" She paused. "Only joking. It can't decipher animal foughts . . . yet."

Behind the wall Molly heard Micky questioning

Rocky. "So who are you and who is the girl?" he asked.

"I'm—Rocky Scar-let and she—is Molly—Moon," Rocky answered blandly.

"Minus, COME HERE!" screeched the little girl. "Come and see de worm I've caught!" Molly heard the now familiar hum of Micky's floating couch.

"Her name is Molly Moon," came her brother's weak voice.

"Is it now, my sick one? Moon! Hmm. Look at dees." Molly heard her necklace being rattled. "And have you ever seen anything as disgusting as *dees*? And as for her, I'm not sure I can stomach looking at *her* ugly face ever again. Her nose is almost as ugly as yours, Micky!"

"Those shoes are ancient," said Micky. "What period are they from?"

"Early in the twenty-first centuwy, I fink," said the little girl. She picked up Molly's rucksack and began to look through it. With her lip curling, she pulled out Molly and Rocky's jeans and dropped them on the floor. Then she inspected Petula's can of dog food.

"What is in dis obscene-looking parcel?" she asked, fingering Molly's cellophane-wrapped sandwich. The man holding Molly removed his hand from her mouth for a moment so that she could speak.

"That's a ketchup sandwich," Molly guessed nervously. "Delicious. Try it if you like."

The girl grimaced as though Molly had just invited her to eat a raw snail. She looked at the compass, the flashlight, and the camera, and then read the date on one of Molly's banknotes. "You are poorly equipped for a twip to your future," she commented drily. Then she addressed the boy. "But she's a danger to you, Minus."

"Why is she here?" he asked.

At this point Molly just had to speak. With the fury of an angry bulldog she bit her guard's hand. As it jerked away she shouted, "I'm your twin sister from the twenty-first century! Look at me—you'll see I'm your exact twin!"

"Shut your cakehole!" shouted the young princess. "Dat's porky-pies! Tape up her mouf!" There was the sound of running feet as something was fetched. Soon Molly's mouth was zipped shut with uncomfortable sticky tape.

"Don't listen to her, Micky," continued the little girl. "She's been sent here to destwoy you. Quickly, we must get her on de machine."

So as helplessly as a chicken being taken to the ax Molly was pushed toward the platform chair. She heard the squelching jellyfish and Petula's loyal feet as she trotted along beside her. She smelled the minerals in the air. Molly desperately rifled through her brain to try to find some way to escape this fate. She didn't want to end up like the man had. She felt the seat beneath her as she was pushed into it, and the invisible force as her arms, legs, and torso were held down. Struggle as she might, she simply couldn't escape. Then one of the egg-shaped silver-domed caps was lowered onto her head too.

"Mnnhummmmmhm!" Molly tried to shout. Petula began to bark relentlessly. Hands untied Molly's blindfold.

Molly quickly drank in the situation. No one was going to be foolish enough to look at her. Rocky stood beside Molly's twin brother in the blue light. He was totally hypnotized. Both wore blue electromagnetic suits and both looked calmly on. How Molly hated Micky now!

"MMMHHMMMMUURGH!" she yelled angrily at him through the tape. She wanted to shout, "You pathetic, stupid person. Can't you see I'm your sister? I came all this way for you, and you're just standing there waiting to watch me *fry*!"

Petula whined. She could feel Molly's fear and her anger. She knew her feelings were directed at the boy who smelled so strangely similar to Molly. Similar in the same way that puppies from the same litter always smelled alike. She began to bark at him. Molly turned her head. From the corner of her eye Molly could see the freakish six-year-old, now back in her shiny blue outfit, programming her machine, and she could just make out the words to a horrible nursery rhyme that she was quietly singing.

*"Fwee blind hypnotists,*
*Fwee blind hypnotists,*
*One dead, one tamed, one fwee,*
*One dead, one tamed, one fwee.*
*Dey all have minds of deir own, you see,*
*So keep dem down or dey'll eat you for tea.*
*Dis one's memowies will be my fee,*
*Fwee blind hypnotists."*

Molly didn't understand the rhyme. A fee was what a person paid someone else when they had done something for them. The princess hadn't done anything for Molly, so why did Molly owe her anything? And how would Molly's *memories* pay her fee? What did this machine do? Molly's hands began to sweat profusely. Her temples became moist as fear seared through her.

Then the sinister child said slowly, "Operation . . . suction . . . COMMENCE!"

Molly felt every hair on her head rise as an electric current passed through her. Her face tickled. And when she looked down at her hands she was filled with horror. Her skin pulsated so that every other second it became see-through and the bones there were visible. Her flesh tingled and then, as if the jellyfish was sending its tentacles into her thoughts, she felt her brain being rummaged through. She felt memories come alive in her mind and then she sensed that they were being snatched—they were being targeted by the electric sparks of the jellyfish machine and taken from her. Suddenly she found herself remembering reading and learning about hypnotizing. She saw pages flashing inside her head as though she was really reading them, but a hundred times faster, and then the memories disappeared. It was as if her thoughts were being vacuumed out of her skull. Then Molly remembered her early experiences of *using* hypnosis. The memories were stark and vivid. For instance, there was the time when she had practiced with a pendulum. She remembered how she'd hypnotized Petula for the first time. But as swiftly as she recalled the moment, the memory was snatched from her. Suddenly Molly couldn't think how she'd mesmerized Petula *at all*.

Molly winced and moaned with sadness as, time and time again, thoughts were taken from her. It was terrifying, as she had no control over the exodus. The riches of her mind were being stolen and she was being reduced—to what, Molly dared not imagine. Then, finally, the jellyfish stopped sending out its arcing sparks. Her brain had been robbed of every piece of knowledge about how to hypnotize. Molly could remember her life and what she had done using hypnotism, but she couldn't remember *how to do it*.

The flashing of the jellyfish quieted and Molly opened her eyes. She felt dazed. In front of her the huge blue blob quivered as it digested the information. Molly could see images of Petula and the words of the hypnotism book hovering above it before they were finally sucked in. Petula whined at her feet.

"Youf isn't evewyfing," said the strange six-year-old girl, switching the controls off. "*Knowledge* is power." She glanced at Molly. "Dis machine has just wemoved all your knowledge of how to hypnotize; derefore you are now no fret to us." She laughed gaily, then her face dropped to seriousness. "Sadly, technology is not yet developed enough to take *talent* fwom a person, only knowledge. *Talent*, in case you didn't know, is de natural ability of a person to do somefing. And flair, or talent, is a major ingwedient for hypnotism. So dis is fwustwating, to say de least. But I'm confident dat in a few years de technology will be dere, and den we will be able to extwact talent fwom people, and den I can put my cap on"—the girl mimed putting a cap on—"and absorb all dose lessons you've just given me *and* your talent, cos I'll have dat by den too. Why, my bwain will suck it up like a bee sipping nectar from a flower!" The little girl did a twirl, pirouetting on her toe. "We'll have to keep you for a few years, but we'll harvest de talent fwom you as soon as we can. And when we do—*ooh, là, là!* I'll be a hypnotist too. Fank you *sooooo* much."

The child turned to a servant. As she did her bracelet moved to reveal a star-shaped birthmark. It was exactly the same mark the six-year-old child in pink had possessed eleven and a half years before. So it wasn't a birthmark, Molly thought. It must be a tattoo, just like her big sister's.

"Take her to Miss Cwibbins's quarters," the princess instructed the guard. "De girl needs top secuwity." With that she clicked a switch on the flower of her dress. "Cwibbins! Got a bit of twouble here. She's called Milly Moon. Sorted now. Twelve is bringing her over. Keep her guarded. I'll explain."

With that, Molly found herself being firmly pushed and escorted to the blue dressing area. Here, her electric-blue magnetic suit vaporized to be replaced by her original white outfit. As her old sneakers were being slipped back on to her feet her brother Micky hobbled out of the shadows and stared at her. Rocky stood behind him—a shell of the real Rocky

Molly knew. Molly glared at Micky with smoldering, angry eyes. She wished she could have used them to hypnotize him. But that was impossible now. She had lost all memory of how to do it. Her mind felt full of holes, and at the blank look on Rocky's face she felt a giant hole *inside* her too. A hole that was the emptiness of lost friendship. Petula was all she had now. And as she stood there shocked, dazed, and sad, the small girl taunted:

*"Baby, baby, stick your head in gravy,*
*Wrap it up in bubble gum*
*And send it to the navy."*

Molly looked down at her pet, who blinked loyally up at her. As Molly was led away, Petula trotted after.

# Eight

Molly felt numb. Her head was whirring. And as a servant dressed in a woodcutter's outfit led her and Petula along a path she began to get the oddest sensation. Everything felt more *real* than it normally did. The sky seemed bluer, the red stripe on her sneaker was redder, and the grass was fluorescent, it was so green. An insect flying past buzzed extra noisily; the gel in Molly's hair smelled very, very fruity and the blood that she could taste in her mouth from biting her lip when she'd been on the mind machine tasted richer and supermetallic. It was as if all Molly's senses were on overdrive. And to heighten the surrealness of it all, she found that things she thought about suddenly appeared. First of all, as she walked, the rhyme "Sing a song of sixpence, a pocket full of rye,

Four and twenty blackbirds baked in a pie . . ." plucked its tune soundlessly in her head. This was odd anyway, as Molly had no reason to be remembering nursery rhymes. But even more curiously, as the refrain ended a mass of ten or twenty blackbirds flew up over the wall of the palace and away into the blue sky.

This coincidence felt bizarre enough, but to make things even weirder another crazy coincidence followed. The music in Molly's head now had a xylophone playing the jingle to the chocolate commercial she knew so well.

*Choc-o-late!*
*Choc-o-late!*
*Every day is a chocolate date!*

The words and the tune of the ad sang in her head. Then, through an open window, the same melody, recorded and played by a full orchestra, came drifting out.

The two events shook Molly. They made her feel raw and unstable and extrapeculiar after her ordeal on the mind machine. But before she had time to dwell on them she was taken to a bare room to meet Miss Cribbins.

As she was ushered in, the red-haired, beautiful

woman turned and opened some shutters to reveal a spectacular view of the valleys below. Her cat-spider let itself down from the ceiling on a silken thread, so that it dangled five paces in front of Molly. It narrowed its eyes and hissed at her. Petula growled. The woodcutter-costumed servant bowed and left.

"Interesting to see a twenty-first-century person," Miss Cribbins said, her voice sharp as broken glass. "You, Moon, will have dinner with us tonight." She scrutinized Molly as if she were a netted butterfly. "And," she said, stroking the beauty spot on her rouged cheekbone, "you will answer questions that Her Royal Highness and I have for you."

"And if I don't want to?" said Molly, wiping her mouth, which itched where the sticky tape had been ripped off.

"Why, you will go hungry."

Molly was still feeling dizzy from the mind machine and the peculiar coincidences on the path. And now, to make things worse, she began hallucinating. Strange little pictures floated above the Cribbins woman's head. Pictures of sausages and a jar of what looked like vitamins and a doctor's syringe. Molly felt really scared. Her hair felt all prickly, as though it was rising up from her scalp. Was her brain falling apart? She rubbed her eyes. She dreaded to think what damage the electric sparks had done to her mind.

"What are you going to do with me?"

"Supper is in an hour in the dining room. What will happen to you tomorrow I haven't a clue. But count yourself lucky—Her Highness wants to preserve you."

"I'm not a kipper to be put in a jar," said Molly.

"No, but you are a juicy specimen for us," Cribbins replied. "You are interesting. Her Highness wants to keep you, mostly in order to harvest your hypnotic talent. This won't be possible for a few years, so you are fortunate—you have some time."

"Time before what?"

"Time to appreciate your whole mind before it is lost to you. For after she has your hypnotic talent Her Highness will take the rest of your thoughts too and you will be left a hollow vessel. Until then I am in charge of your education." The woman stepped forward and her pet dropped silently onto her shoulder. She paused by the door. "Ah, and by the way, don't try to escape. The grounds are alarmed and monitored with cameras. You don't want to be darted."

"Darted?"

"Shot with a paralyzing dart."

Molly stared fixedly at the muddy, trailing lace of her sneaker until the woman had gone. Then she knelt on the ground and hugged Petula. "At least we're still together."

Petula licked Molly's face. As she did, the plastic tag with its letters GAN TWIN fell into Molly's lap.

"Oh, Petula, where did you get this?" Molly fingered the white strip and put it in her pocket. "I can't believe my brother turned out the way he did. Can you, Petula?" Petula whined. "I mean, what happened to him?"

Molly felt dreadful. Her situation was a living nightmare. She was stuck like a pigeon in a drainpipe. Her predicament was hopeless. Her best friend was hypnotized, all her time-travel gems had been taken, and to cap it all her hypnotic know-how was now completely gone too—as gone as a page of penciled instructions that had been erased. She was now an ordinary girl lodged in the wrong time. And in the meantime (and, Molly thought, it really would be a mean time if that horrid woman had anything to do with it), Miss Cribbins was to be her teacher. But why? What for? Molly couldn't see the point of lessons if it was all eventually going to be sucked away by the mind machine. She rubbed her forehead and tried to work out what to do.

It seemed clear the royal child would never give up Molly. She seemed convinced that the technology to "harvest" talent would arrive. And what about Micky, her brother? He seemed a dead loss. Micky was a weak, sick, bullied person with no will of his own. Molly wished she'd never come for him. If it wasn't for him, she and Petula and Rocky would be safe at Briersville Park with all those nice people who cared about them.

"I'm sorry, Petula. You didn't even ask to come," she said, staring into Petula's eyes. Petula stared back, wishing with all her heart that Molly could understand *her*.

As they looked at each other, Molly's mind played tricks on her again. Above Petula's head a sequence of pictures popped up. Molly saw a misty image of the daisy-dotted fields and the hills around Briersville and then a picture of a rabbit hopping across the grass, its tail bobbing. Molly screwed up her eyes and shook her head. But when she looked again the rabbit was nibbling a dandelion. Then the rabbit dissolved to become Petula's basket and then morphed to become Amrit, the pet elephant at Briersville. Finally Amrit vaporized. Molly's hair felt as though it had static electricity in it.

She thought of the pictures she'd seen above Miss Cribbins's head and then of the jellyfish and the thoughts that had floated above it too. And then a strange idea hit her.

"Is that what you're *really* thinking, Petula?"

Petula tilted her head. She'd felt Molly's fear and panic when she'd been caught on the chair with the lightning hitting her head, and she'd felt Molly's anger when Rocky had been hypnotized by the boy—the boy who smelled like Molly. But she couldn't decipher Molly's thoughts and she could only comprehend *some* of Molly's barks. Petula shut her eyes and nestled up to her mistress. As Molly ruffled her ears, she wished again that they were back home.

Molly tried to work out what she'd been doing when the pictures had materialized. She'd been apologizing to Petula, that was all. But since she'd known that Petula wouldn't understand the words of her apology, she'd also sent, she supposed, her feelings in a little mind message to her. She'd tried to communicate her apology by thinking it. Had some sort of invisible gate opened up so that Petula's thoughts were also visible to her? But, Molly considered, she'd often thought things to Petula and this had never happened before. She recalled the images of sausages and pills that had leaped up above Miss Cribbins's red hair. Then she remembered the way the world had felt super-real when she was on the path and she recollected the coincidences that had occurred. The nursery rhyme that had sung in her head and the blackbirds suddenly flying over her, the chocolate-ad jingle that had trilled through her mind and then been echoed by the same music somewhere in the palace. The logical conclusion was that Molly's mind had been altered by the machine. Or maybe she was light-headed from being on the mountaintop. Or perhaps the mind machine had scrambled her brain and she was simply going *mad*. Molly was alarmed by this idea. Quickly she decided to try asking Petula another question.

"What are you thinking, Petula?" Nothing happened—nothing at all. Molly squeezed her eyes tight and concentrated hard. Her scalp began to prickle. *What are you thinking, Petula?*

Lo and behold, this time when she looked a faint bubble filled with moving images bounced above Petula's head: the jellyfish, wobbling blue and full of sparks; Rocky, as seen from below, staring straight ahead like a soulless person; and Molly herself, looking scared, with a silver dome on, the skeleton of her face visible through her skin.

Molly's mouth fell open. The pictures had popped up before Molly had had time to conjure up a single thought. This meant only one thing—something quite incredible and completely spectacular. The fact was, unbelievable as it seemed, *Molly was seeing Petula's thoughts.* Molly was amazed.

"Oh, Petula, don't worry!" Molly hugged her little pug and marveled at the new power in her. How had it come about? The electricity from the mind machine must have triggered it. And why did her hair feel all floating and strange when it happened? Would it work on humans too? Could Micky mind read? What about the princess and Miss Cribbins? Molly doubted it. Maybe this new skill was special to Molly—maybe it had lain dormant inside her ever since she was little, woken by the jellyfish's sparks scissoring through her brain.

Molly shook her head, ran her hands through her hair, and took a deep breath to calm down. For now she was starting to feel, she had to admit, just a little bit excited. If she could mind read, then being here wasn't a hundred percent bad. If she could *see* something of what her horrible hosts were really thinking, perhaps, just perhaps, she might find a way to get her hypnotic skills back off the machine.

Molly spent the time before supper exploring her surroundings. She walked through the gardens near Miss Cribbins's schoolrooms and looked at the exotic plants growing there. They were unlike the plants from Molly's time. They were bigger and more colorful. And their perfume was ten times more powerful. There were orange roses that smelled of raspberries and purple lilies with the scent of black currants.

Huge, fluffy bees the size of mice buzzed under arches that were heavy with fragrant, rainbow-colored blossoms. A massive dragonfly zipped past Molly's ear. Her eye followed it to a balcony. She scanned the horizon and saw what looked like a flying cow. Screwing her eyes up, she approached the balcony to get a better look. But here Molly took in a breath of awe, at once forgetting the cow.

The view was incredible. On either side of her were craggy cliffs and the zigzagging profile of the mountain range. Below was a sheer drop. Thousands of feet of air hung between her and the valley below, and the view stretched for hundreds of miles. Molly stepped back, suddenly overcome by vertigo. The palace certainly was in a perfect position. It was comfortably cool with a breeze that was clean and dustless. But down below on the valley floor, beside the giant lake and the large fields, Molly saw that it was quite different. Away from fields and the oasis of green around the waterside igloo mansions, the land was brown and dusty. Molly grabbed a pair of binoculars lying on the table nearby. As she twiddled the knob, people tending and watering crops in the fields came into focus. Molly let the binoculars pass over them to the dusty part of the town. Here there were colored houses. They looked like cottages from a fairy-tale book. Their walls were crooked, their front doors and window shutters were brightly painted, and their roofs were thatched. There were thousands of them, all clustered together in streets that led past lots of big buildings to a fishing village on the shore of the lake.

Between this desert town and the beautiful silver igloo residences was a wide moatlike band of grass. It was as if there were two towns down there, Molly thought. There were the winter homes of the rich and powerful, and the poor town that was lived in all year round. Molly adjusted the dial on the powerful binoculars. What interested her was that the only barrier between the rich and the poor was a strip of grass. There must, she thought, be something that stopped the poor people coming into the rich territory. Maybe there were robot guards with poisonous darts at the ready. Or perhaps the moat of grass was electrified, or it was some sort of futuristic, man-eating grass. But the palace servants all seemed so calm and obliging, as though they accepted their lowly positions. Maybe everyone in the town felt like this about the unfairness. Molly thought of the servant who'd picked up the princess's shoes and carried them to her. He had done it automatically, as though he'd been brainwashed. Perhaps he'd had his will sucked out by the mind machine. Could all the people of the town have been put on the mind machine?

And then, like an answer in Twenty Questions, the truth of the situation appeared. One very good way to keep people under control was to hypnotize them. Hypnotize them to work without complaining, to live not caring where, to do exactly as they were told. The people in the valley must all be hypnotized. It all became suddenly very clear. *So that was why Micky was needed here!* He'd been stolen as a baby and brought here to work for the palace *to keep the masses hypnotized*, but why did he do it for them?

Molly heard a gong behind her. It was time for dinner. She licked her lips in anticipation. Maybe now that she was a mind reader she would be able to deduce exactly how this place worked and outwit the princess.

Molly smiled. She could now see a glimmer of hope.

# Nine

Molly followed her ears. The sound of the supper gong led her and Petula to a tunnel of flowers and a large open door at the end of the garden. She stepped through. As she walked, doubts niggled her like fishes nibbling at a piece of bread. The idea of being able to mind read now seemed so outlandish. Molly was already finding it difficult to believe that the pictures she'd seen above Petula's head had been real. Perhaps it had simply been Molly's imagination playing tricks on her. After all, knowing Petula so well, Molly could have easily made up Petula's thoughts.

A small servant dressed in bright clothes and wearing a frog mask walked past. He, Molly said to herself, was a complete stranger to her. Could she make up his thoughts too?

*What are you thinking?* she asked silently. Above his green froggy eyes a bubble popped up. It was filled with the images of a vacuum-cleaner-like object, an electric mop, and a silver spiked ball. Molly watched him walk away. Could she have made that up herself? She didn't even recognize the spiked thing. She had to admit that, crazy as it seemed, she did appear to have a new extra-special power. Molly shook her head and blew out a big sigh of amazement.

She and Petula came to a long, open-topped out-door hall with a broad pink staircase at its end and a fountain that sprayed a cloud of mist. To the left was a large window. Through it they could see the dining room and people gathered for supper. A gleaming white, rectangular table with a glowing pool set in its center stood in the middle of the room. Small violet lilies floated on the water. The table was laid for eleven, with large and small tulip-shaped glasses at each place.

The princess was sitting at the end on a high stool, her dark hair now piled up in a tall spiral on her head, with a scattering of shiny jewels set into it. Sparkling shoes dangled from her feet. She was reading from a small white box that shone light up into her face. An imprisoned turquoise grasshopper sat in a tiny golden cage on the table in front of her, chirruping loudly. At the other end of the table Miss Cribbins tapped her red clawlike nails on a glass. Her hair was now auburn and her lips had been painted with black lipstick so that her skin seemed extra white. Molly nervously stepped inside.

At once she saw Rocky. For a moment, she forgot he was hypnotized and her heart leaped. But then she saw his dead, hollow-eyed stare and she went cold. He sat obedient as a well-trained pet between two beautiful but very unfriendly-looking women wearing tailored suits. Behind them was a vast window through which was a wonderful view of the mountains.

Five children of varying ages and heights occupied the other seats around the table—a serious-looking Mongolian girl with her hair stuck up in a wiggly pony-tail sat beside a stern Asian boy with a Mohawk. A black boy sat next to them. He was consulting a palmtop computer and showing it to a freckled white boy in sunglasses. A blond girl with green-and-orange artichoke-shaped hair was shuffling a pack of cards. None was smiling. Who were they? Where were their parents? Whatever, they weren't having much fun. The atmosphere in the room was as controlled as a TV channel and the volume was most definitely on low. The children didn't seem hypnotized, for the Mongolian girl was talking freely to the Asian boy about trade regulations and tax in the Far East and the others were having similar hushed discussions, but Molly knew it was possible to be hypnotized and act completely normally, so she couldn't be sure.

Redhorn, the man with the quiff, who had kidnaped her brother, was nowhere in sight. Neither was Nurse Meekles, nor Micky. Molly took the last empty seat and Petula curled up at her feet. As Molly observed the people around the table none looked up, but when she turned away she could feel the heat of their eyes on her.

The meal began. Stony-eyed fancy-dressed servants filled their glasses with water. Then one in an Aladdin outfit of baggy silk trousers, bronze waistcoat, and turban brought in a bottle of purple wine. He poured a tiny amount into the princess's glass. She put her gadget down and took the goblet up in her small hand. Shutting her eyes, she sniffed at its contents. Then she took a sip and swirled the liquid about in her mouth. Swallowing, she nodded her head. This prompted the servant to fill her glass completely and to fill Miss Cribbins's and the suited ladies' as well as the other children's. Molly prepared to put her hand over her glass to stop the waiter, but she wasn't offered any wine. Neither was Rocky. They were given water. More servants, all looking like characters out of the Arabian Nights, now came around with dishes of food. Molly eyed the green squidgy stuff that the princess was piling on her plate.

"Lakeweed, Milly, full of essential vitamins," the

princess informed her, picking up some chopsticks. "A delicacy when pwepared like dis, with mussels. It's a starter."

"Don't suppose I could have my ketchup sandwiches back," Molly said hopefully, but her question was ignored.

"When you addwess me, you will call me Your Majesty or Pwincess Fang. My real name is wather long so Pwincess Fang will do . . . Fang is a lovely name—it means 'fwagwance'! And," she said, smiling and showing two small Dracula-like teeth that Molly hadn't noticed before, "it weally does suit me, don't you fink?"

Although her stomach was rumbling as if an underground train was driving around inside it, Molly shook her head when the lakeweed came to her. Raising her eyes sadly to Rocky, she saw he was eating it without objection.

She knew that deep down the real him would be screaming to get out. From its little cage on the table, the grasshopper chirped madly.

CHACK! CHACK! CHACK! CHACK! CHACK!

"He's stwidulating," the princess said. "In udder words, he's wubbing two bits of his body togeder—his legs, in fact. It's a bit like playing de violin. Lovely, isn't it?"

"Perhaps he's trying to tell you that he wants to get

out of there," Molly replied coldly.

"Oh poppycock and poo!" said the princess, tossing her head dismissively and turning away.

As she and the other children ate, Molly, who was itching to take her new powers out for a test drive, decided to take this opportunity to see what pictures might appear above their heads. So, staring at Princess Fang's forehead, she sent out a very simple message to her.

*What are you thinking?* Molly half expected the small girl to look up and answer, but instead, oblivious to Molly's probing, she continued munching on her lakeweed. Molly thought harder. This time she shut her eyes to focus, and the prickling sensation on her scalp began. *What are your thoughts?*

"Are you pwaying?" the six-year-old remarked. "It's no use, you know, and it's wude to sit wid your eyes shut at de table."

*What are your thoughts?* Molly beamed again. Her hair began to feel like it was rising off her scalp.

Slowly she opened her eyes. When she did, she saw that, like smoke from a fire, a hazy wisp had appeared above the girl's head and inside it were pictures. Molly swallowed hard. "WOW! I CAN'T BELIEVE IT!" she wanted to shout out loud. "IT EVEN WORKS ON YOU, YOU HORRID LITTLE BRAT!" but she had to behave as if nothing out of the ordinary was happening. Princess Fang was thinking a *lot*. Many moving pictures were appearing and then vaporizing above her—so fast that it was difficult to understand them all. Molly saw images of aircraft and foreign countries, of government buildings and official-looking people in smart, futuristic clothes. Images of particular faces kept appearing and disappearing: a Chinese man, an Indian woman. There was a scientist in a laboratory, green lakeweed, and then a ride down the huge spiral slide outside. Princess Fang was very perplexing. In some ways she was like a typical spoiled brat, with her huge playroom and toys, but her thoughts were so grown-up. She was completely unlike any child Molly had even heard of. It was grotesque. There she was, in her tutu dress, swinging her feet childishly but sipping wine and thinking the thoughts of a prime minister. Molly decided to strike up a conversation.

"I have never met a six-year-old as grown-up as you," she said. Fang looked up and laughed a shrill, superior laugh. Above her head were images of a Chinese woman of about sixty, who looked like she might be her grandmother. "If you don't mind me asking," Molly continued, "where are your parents?" Images of an aircraft crash shot quickly over Fang's head.

"Dead," she said. "Died twenty years ago." Molly

nodded, but silently she was doing calculations. Even though she wasn't very good at math, Molly could already see that this didn't add up. Fang was six, so her parents must have been alive not more than six years ago—unless they'd died years before and Fang had somehow been kept as a test-tube baby in a laboratory for fourteen years. Molly supposed this was possible. Anything seemed possible in this place.

"Erm, I'm sorry to hear that," she said, remembering her manners, "but you have a big sister, don't you?" She thought of the girl in pink who'd received Micky as a baby. "Your sister must be about seventeen by now." Around the table the other children began to titter and chuckle. Above the spiral of Fang's hair popped up an image of Molly's face—her curly hair; her potato-shaped nose; and her green, closely set eyes. A second later fumes and piles of muck surrounded Molly's features, and in the princess's thoughts a toy drum came down over Molly's head so that she couldn't be seen.

Molly was insulted. "Looks aren't everything," she said.

Princess Fang lowered her almond eyes as if she'd been caught doing something she shouldn't. "I have many acquaintances, Milly, but I have no sister," she said frostily.

Molly felt frustrated. There was something going on with Princess Fang, she knew, but finding out what was like solving an impossible riddle.

"By the way, my name is Molly, not Milly." The princess ignored her. Molly changed the subject. "Why do some of your servants wear masks?"

The princess wiped her mouth with her napkin. "Because," she explained with a sneer, "dose servants are far too ugly to look at. If I look at dem, dey make me feel sick. I hate ugly fings and *old* fings. So please do not make me fink of dem now—it will put me off my dinner."

As though the entertainment was over, the girl with towering artichoke-shaped hair began talking to the Asian boy about nuclear travel in space. Molly looked at Miss Cribbins and rolled her chopstick between her finger and thumb. She decided to read her mind next. Like an athlete warming up, she began to prepare herself. Her scalp started to prickle as she concentrated, and then her hair felt like it was lifting from her head. Molly knew she was ready.

*What are you thinking?* she silently asked. Slowly, as Cribbins unclipped a small silver box and took out four lozenges, a bubble of images materialized above her auburn bun. Images of the same Chinese sixty-year-old woman Princess Fang had been thinking of appeared. And then, as Cribbins swallowed her pills with a sip of wine, there were pictures of thick books and a whip.

"Where's Micky, Miss Cribbins?" Molly asked her out loud. Images of Micky lying on a couch eating celery and being given spoonfuls of medicine quivered above the woman's head.

"He's out of earshot of you," she said as a servant brought her a tray with a syringe on it. "We can't have you filling his mind with ridiculous nonsense, like the idea that you are his twin sister." Then, as calmly as if she was checking her watch, she rolled up her sleeve and gave herself an injection.

"But I *am* his sister," Molly said, trying to ignore the sharp needle piercing the pale flesh. Around the table conversations stopped. Molly began to lie. "Now that I know he is safe and sound, and well looked after, I am happy." She suddenly thought of a cowboy film she'd watched, where a very fine Indian chief proclaimed, "Go in peace." Addressing both the princess and Miss Cribbins she pleaded, "Can't you just let me go in peace? If you give me my gems back and my knowledge of how to hypnotize and time travel, and Rocky too, we'll just travel away to our time and never bother you again."

The princess smiled broadly, her fangs exposing

themselves as her mouth spread. The Aladdin waiter bent down to her with a dish of sausages and another green spongy vegetable.

"But I need all your information on how to hypnotize and how to time twavel *in de mind machine*," she said petulantly. "I told you. When I have learned to extwact talent as well as knowledge, den I will have de ultimate guide on how to become a master hypnotist." The little girl rubbed her small manicured hands together and clicked her fingers. A servant brought her a knife. "Dere is a mountain of knowledge stored in my machine!" She sliced her sausage with the precision of a surgeon and then picked up her chopsticks. "All sorts of people have given me deir minds. I don't see why you shouldn't give me yours too." Children around the table murmured approvingly.

"But why do you want to put all the information on the machine?" Molly asked, watching the air above Princess Fang. The little girl was thinking of herself in a skullcap next to the giant blue jellyfish.

"Youf isn't evewyfing, Milly. It's nice, yes," the child said patronizingly.

"You*th*, you mean? And it's *Molly*."

The princess ignored Molly's corrections and went on with her self-important speech.

"Oh, we all love de fountain of youf! It's wonderful

to have agile limbs and bones dat don't cweak! You have no idea what old age is like!"

"And you do?" said Molly, a bit sick of this six-year-old's clever-clogs ways.

"Yes. I've seen it." The picture of the sixty-year-old woman flashed again above her head. "But de point I want to make," continued the small girl, "is dat youf is wonderful, but actually *knowledge is far supewior.* My pawents were quite bwilliant inventors, you know—the best this countwy has ever had—and dis beautiful mind machine dey made, well, it *collects knowledge.*"

Molly was offered sausages. She took one and some of the green spongy stuff as well. Her next question she thought to the princess. *Collect it for what?*

Again images of Fang in a skullcap appeared. Molly assumed that the princess could in some way put the knowledge from the machine into her own brain in this way. That must be how this weird six-year-old had become so knowledgeable and wise beyond her years.

"I see," Molly said, as though none of this impressed her. "So you absorb all the knowledge from your machine into your head. Suck it up like drinking water."

"Not as silly as you look, are you?" said the six-year-old rudely. Then, taking a balloon from a drawer in the table, she blew it up. As it grew, Molly saw that it was a replica of a globe, with all the countries and oceans of the world printed on it. Most of the land masses were colored in pale pink, and the seas were blue. "De light pink bits indicate which countwies we plan to take over," the little girl explained proudly. "De *dark* pink shows the countwies we alweady contwol. All dat part is called Yang Yongia—after my middle names. It means 'beautiful' and 'fowever bwave.' De mind machine has been ever so useful. We invite udder countwies' officials over and dwain deir bwains, you see. Den we can learn deir national secwets and den deir governments are easier to manipulate and destwoy."

"And I expect you use Micky Minus to hypnotize them. I bet he makes sure that the people you've brain drained go back to their countries secretly working for you." Molly paused. "And he hypnotizes them not to tell anyone about what you're up to."

"Hmm. Yum, yum, bubble gum!" the child replied irritatingly, and she let go of the balloon so that it shot up into the air and around the room, making a raspberry noise. As the last bit of air escaped from it, it hit the ceiling and then plopped onto the floor.

"Where are my gems?" asked Molly suddenly.

"None of your beeswax." The children around the table laughed. To them, the conversation was like some delightful Ping-Pong match. Molly watched as moving pictures of her gems being deposited into a safe in a wall spun and disappeared above the princess's head.

"What program should a person set the mind machine in order to get back their thoughts?" she asked.

"Nosy parker!" screeched the girl. But as she sipped her wine, numbers and buttons flashed above her. They flipped up and away too fast for Molly to understand or remember. Molly picked up her chopsticks and, giving up the idea of using them properly, stabbed one into the sausage on her plate, holding it up to eat as though it was on a barbecue stick.

"How long have you kept all those people who live in the dust bowl down there hypnotized?" she asked bluntly, chewing the sausage.

> *"Silence in de courtyard,*
> *Silence in de stweet,*
> *De biggest fool in de world,*
> *Is just about to speak!"*

The princess looked delighted with herself. Then she crossed her arms and stuck her tongue out.

"We're not in the playground, you know," Molly replied. She looked with interest at the pictures above the small girl's head. There was a bearded man and then Redhorn and then Micky Minus, as if Fang was casting her mind back to all the hypnotists who had helped enslave the people. It had obviously been going on for ages.

"She's not as dumb as she looks," said the Mongolian girl, taking a cube-shaped puzzle out of her pocket and beginning to fiddle with it.

"I agree," said Miss Cribbins, observing Molly as though she was a performing seal. "But whether she'll absorb a lot of information in her lessons is another question." Above her head were pictures of Molly sitting at a desk with piles of books about her.

Molly interrupted them. Her mouth was full as she spoke, and she was glad. "I hate to disappoint you, but I've always been a terrible student."

Miss Cribbins looked at the mashed food in Molly's mouth and frowned. "I have ways of making you work." A tight smile crossed her lips.

Molly felt a shiver of fear, but she didn't show it. "Where is Redhorn?" she asked.

"Dead as a doornail," said Fang. A coffin floated above her right ear.

They continued eating in silence. Molly mused on all that she'd learned and ate her supper, scooping up the spongy vegetable mash using both her chopsticks at once as though they were a flat spade. The sausage tasted of cod and the vegetable tasted like a mixture of apples and buttered toast. Under the table, Petula heard a *splat* by her back leg. Molly had dropped some sausage for her. She ate it up gratefully. Then, she noticed an acrid smell. It was the unmistakable whiff of the cat-spider, Taramasalata. Petula sat up, alert.

*Only just noticed me, have you?* came the nasty drawl of the creature as her thoughts wormed their way into Petula's mind. Petula looked about, trying to see where the animal was. She was amazed it could speak dog so well.

*Up here.* The cat-spider was hidden, hanging upside down from the underside of the table. Now it let its thread drop and landed on its eight pink furry feet. Petula jumped.

*Ha!* The thing laughed. *Tricked ya!* "Miaaaowwww!"

Petula's skin prickled as she recovered from the little shock. She didn't like this animal at all. Then she suddenly thought how marvelous it would be if she could hypnotize it. So far she had been useless to Molly—she needed to practice hypnotism. Taramasalata would be the perfect subject. Petula ignored the creature's purring and instead tried to focus on her own breathing. She wanted to become calm enough to tune into the cat-spider's vibrations and for her eyes to throb hypnotically. In Los Angeles she'd once charmed a director so thoroughly that she was sure she'd actually hypnotized him. As her forehead bristled and her ears tickled she felt she was ready. And so, slowly, she looked up.

Her huge brown eyes bored into the creature's unblinking yellow ones. Petula gritted her teeth and sent out what she thought was a hypnotic blast. But nothing happened.

*Dogs always stare,* said the cat-spider. *So rude. No manners.*

Petula gave up. It wasn't working. *I'm sorry*, she apologized.

*Don't try and get smarmy with me,* came the cat-spider's frosty reply. *I want nothing to do with a ball of fur and guts like you. Just came to inspect you, that's all. You are quite as repulsive as I suspected. Horrid popping-out eyes and a face like a bottom!* With that, she wound herself back up to her cavelike hiding place under the table. Petula frowned and snarled. At least now she knew exactly where she and this Taramasalata stood.

Above, waiters were bringing the diners coffee, salted plums, and ginger slices. Then Princess Fang was brought a selection of cigarettes. She chose a green one and lit it. Three of the other children began smoking too. Molly was amazed. To see children smoking was as peculiar as seeing a horse dressed in clothes.

"So, Monsieur Povolay is awiving tomowow,"

Princess Fang said, leaning back against an invisible rest on her stool and puffing smoke into the air, "but I shan't look at him; he is far too wepulsive!" She winced. "He should be put down." An ugly, whiskered man in a suit hovered above her forehead.

*Another poor victim,* Molly thought.

Across the table the young boy of six or seven with sunglasses on consulted a glowing pad.

"Yeah, M'sieur Povolay is tomorrow. I fink we h've ve Chinese biologists arriving in ve afternoon as well."

"And," whined the princess, "dere must be a show. Cwibbins, you *pwomised* us all a pantomime dis week. And a magic act. We're bored. And I want to play dat game where if de servants get it wong dey have to chop up onions blindfolded. It's so funny when dey cut demselves!"

Around the room the children all nodded in agreement.

"Smoking gives you cancer," Molly said.

"Ha! Oh, silly Milly! You are so out of date!" sniped the princess. "Cancer was cured two hundwed years ago. It's a disease of de past. Why don't you have a cigawette? I always have one at de end of a meal."

"It still makes your breath smell something rotten," Molly said icily. "And by the way, it's Molly, not Milly." But it was as if Molly hadn't spoken, for the princess did not reply. Her attention was all on a big bowl that was being brought to her.

"Oh, it's my favowite fing!" she cried. "I do so love it when we have fortune cookies! Quick, quick. Me first, me first!" Obediently the waiter tilted the bowl so that she could choose a cookie. The little girl greedily dived her hand to the bottom and fished out a red parcel. Ripping its wrapper off, she found the slip of paper. Throwing her glowing cigarette over her shoulder, she took a bite of the biscuit and, munching, read her fortune.

"Oh, dey're always so stoopid!" she exclaimed. "It says, 'Never play leapfwog wid a unicorn.' Ha. Ha, h-ha! Dat's actually quite funny!" Everyone else at the table had also now chosen a cookie. "Tell us yours, Milly." Molly uncurled her white slip of paper.

"'The robbed one who smiles steals something from the thief,'" she read.

"Silly, see? Now dis is much better. Listen to dis poem I know:

*"Ooo-errr, ooo-errr, ooo-errr*
*Milly fell down de sewer,*
*She pulled de chain*
*And up she came*
*In a chocolate aiwoplane."*

All around the table the other children laughed. Then, as though suddenly bored, the small girl clapped her hands. A servant appeared with the air moped. Gathering her tutu dress and snatching the grasshopper's cage from the table, Princess Fang hopped aboard her scooter and shot out of the room.

Molly felt strangely satisfied. Although she was still stuck without her powers of hypnotism, she was feeling excited about her amazing new skill. She thought of her fortune, "The robbed one who smiles steals something from the thief," and Molly smiled inside.

She looked across the table at Rocky, who sat waiting to be told what to do.

"I'll help you," Molly found herself silently promising him. "I got you into this mess; I'll get you out of it."

Miss Cribbins dabbed her black-lipsticked mouth with a napkin and then pushed her stool back. "We will start your lessons this evening, Molly," she said sharply. "No time to waste." Molly was taken by surprise. Outside the window the golden sun was setting. It was time to wind down, not wind up, she thought.

"But I'm a bit tired for lessons now," she said.

"My lessons will wake you up." Miss Cribbins retorted unsympathetically. As she stood up, her cat-spider scuttled up her leg and perched on her shoulder. It eyed Petula.

"Miaaaaaoww SSSSSS!" it hissed. Then Miss Cribbins snapped her fingers by Rocky's ear, and like some tamed animal he got up. "You, Moon, will meet me in the classroom by the weeping willow in an hour."

# Ten

The air in the palace gardens was thick with scent as evening jasmine flowers opened. Molly was outside the nursery. She pushed the pad on the wall and the door slid open. She'd decided to pay Nurse Meekles a visit.

Inside, three beautiful women dressed in long white robes like maidens out of a fairy tale sat holding babies. One held a tiny infant a few weeks old. The other babies, both very pretty, were bigger and were holding their heads up and squawking like parrots. Four young children ran about, chasing one another on the flowered lawn of the nursery garden. Then Nurse Meekles, dressed in a blue-and-white-striped pinafore over a pale yellow dress, came out of the building. She was holding a bowl of peaches.

"Five more minutes, my little prawn dumplings, and it will be ion time," she announced. The children halted for a moment as they grumbled. Then they continued romping around. Nurse Meekles watched them fondly, then her eyes caught sight of Petula and Molly. A flash of recognition crossed her face as she matched Micky's looks with Molly's, and for a second the bowl nearly slipped from her hands.

"Can I . . . help you?" she asked uneasily as Molly approached.

"I just wanted to say hello," said Molly.

"Princess Fang's quarters are back through there." Her voice trembled slightly as she glanced toward the door. Her face was tanned, round, and flat and smile lines creased the skin beside her blue, slanted eyes. Her black hair was arranged in a cottage-loaf style. She reminded Molly of the kind lady, Mrs. Trinklebury, who'd looked after her when she'd been little. Molly suddenly felt homesick and full of tears.

"Can't I stay for just a few minutes? It's so nice here." Molly watched the kids beside her kick a ball. "I've got no one to talk to." Nurse Meekles furtively checked that the camera trained on her garden was looking away. Then she put her hand up and touched Molly's cheek.

"Had a bit of trouble with your hair, haven't you,

my petal?" she said with a smile. "You're the split image of him. Micky told me that a girl had arrived, a girl called Molly Moon, who claimed to be his twin sister. He said it was a trick. But I remember the day he arrived here with Redhorn. I know about this time-traveling malarkey." She shook her head and sighed. "I hear you've been on the machine." Molly could feel a dry lump rising in her throat. She didn't want to cry—not now, with this woman she barely knew. She glanced about for the children, who were now digging about in the sandpit.

"Who are these children? Where are their parents?"

Nurse Meekles rearranged the peaches in her basket. "I c-can't tell you," she stammered and shook her head. Above it swam pictures of mothers in long dresses sitting outside what looked like gingerbread houses. Then, as if talking to the peaches, she said, "I know what goes on here. I'm ashamed to be part of it, but someone has to do the job. I love my children. I love Micky. I hardly get to see him these days." She looked beseechingly into Molly's eyes and whispered, "I'm lucky to have my mind, Molly. I fear that machine, you see. Anyone with their right mind would. I'm sorry about what they did to you. I can't say any more." A small boy tugged at her pinafore and pushed a muddy rubber toy squid against her hip.

"Can I get squid's dirt off in the ionic cleaner?" She nodded to him.

"I'd better be going," she said hurriedly. "You must too." The old woman stroked Molly's arm. "Good luck, dumpling." Molly watched as she rounded the children up, like a goose with her goslings. And they went inside. The three women got up to follow. The one with the tiniest baby took slightly longer. Her eyes were empty, except when she looked at her child, when they shone.

Molly and Petula left the nursery area, and the green door slipped shut behind them. They took a left turn and came to a balcony. This one overlooked another mountaintop residence and below, in a walled garden, Molly could see a group of children sitting at a garden table. A servant poured them drinks. These children were behaving oddly, just like the children in Princess Fang's palace. One was reading from a screen, two were immersed in serious conversation, and the fourth was smoking a cigar. Molly supposed they had all been on the mind machine and so were now super-intelligent. At least, Molly thought, the princess wasn't too mean to let her friends have a go on her jellyfish toy. The curling cigar smoke wafted up to Molly's nose. She waited a while to see what the children's parents looked like, but no one came.

Molly leaned her elbows on the balcony wall and watched as small flycopters buzzed about the cliff lower down. She scanned the horizon to see whether she could spot another cow with wings, but instead, against the ember-orange sky, she saw the silhouette of a flying *person*. Molly rubbed her eyes. It must be the dusky light and her tiredness playing tricks on her. She picked up Petula and gave her a hug.

"How many of these weird people live up here, Petula? Two hundred? Three hundred? And how many hypnotized people are down there? *Fifty thousand?* This is a terrible country, Petula. It's got a creepy royal family that has everything, and people working for them all dressed like characters from nursery rhymes and fairy tales, who have nothing—not even their own minds. Oh, what are we going to do, Petula? We can't get back to our own time. I don't think we can escape this place either. And even if we did, where would we go?"

Petula licked Molly's cheek. It tasted salty. Molly's hair, now hanging from her head like a limp wind sock, stank of gel. *Oh Molly, what are we doing here?* Petula whined. Then a metallic bell chimed. Molly groaned.

"That's the seven o'clock bell, Petula. Come on. It's time for 'Fun with Cribbins.'"

# Eleven

Miss Cribbins was waiting expectantly in the classroom, clicking her spiky heels on the floor. Her hair was now black. Molly wasn't sure whether she was wearing a wig or whether her hair actually changed its color. The dark hair made the woman's powdered face look even paler.

"You're late. Five minutes late," she said, pointing to a strip of numbers on the wall that looked more like a section of a measuring tape than a clock. The door bleeped shut. Molly and Petula cast their eyes about the room. It was bare except for a table in the center of it that was piled with books. Old-fashioned books, as far as this time was concerned. Molly eyed their spines. There was *The Oxford Companion to Philosophy* and another called *War and Peace*. There was an instruction manual entitled *Nuclear Fusion Power Explained* and a thick tome called *The Dictionary of Theology*. Molly felt tired just reading the titles. She dreaded to think how the *insides* of the books would make her feel. Beside the table was a metal, shoebox-sized machine with a screen displaying a graphlike picture. And on the table lay two brown rubbery things the size of hazelnuts.

"Sit!" Miss Cribbins instructed, pointing to the chair by the table. Her cat-spider suddenly appeared and crept up the front of her suit to settle on her shoulder. "These are what you'll be working on. Open the first book."

Molly didn't like being ordered around in this way, but she did as she was told. She opened *Nuclear Fusion Power Explained* and scanned the first page.

"Umm, Miss Cribbins," Molly said, "I'm not really interested in learning about nuclear stuff. And to tell you the truth"—Molly threw a cursory glance at the other books—"I don't really fancy reading those books either. Haven't you got anything that I might find more interesting?" Molly felt she was being more than reasonable. Half of her was yelling, *Molly, you don't have to do any lessons at all! This isn't school, you know!*

Miss Cribbins stroked the bridge of her perfectly straight nose. "Later you will have the pleasure of absorbing some eighteenth-century poetry. But at this moment these subjects are your task."

"But these books are for adults," Molly objected. "I wouldn't understand the stuff that's in them, let alone learn it."

"You can just learn it off by heart. Then it doesn't matter whether you understand it or not."

Molly gawped. "You must be joking! Anyway, what's the point? If you're going to put me on that mind machine again in a few years to extract my hypnotizing *talent*, and suck all my thoughts out, then why should I bother learning anything at all?" Molly closed the book. "This book isn't of any use to me!"

Miss Cribbins's beauty spot twitched on the side of her cheek. "Who said it had to be of *use* to *you*?" she said, pulling a thick, silver traylike contraption out from the wall behind her and locking it onto the table. All at once Molly understood why she was having lessons. The information in these books was intended for Princess Fang and her machine. Molly would learn about philosophy or whatever it was Fang wanted stored on her machine, and then eventually they would put that electric cap on her and suck out all the information from it. They wanted to use Molly's brain to learn and remember, and then they would rob it.

"I'm not a hard drive for a computer," Molly said angrily.

"Put your hands in this," Miss Cribbins directed, ignoring Molly's comment.

Molly now looked at what was on the table. The silver block in front of her was indented with the shape of two hands. Molly's hands were now starting to feel a little sweaty in apprehension. She lay them down so that they were cradled in the silver molds.

"Other way. Palms up!" Miss Cribbins tutted impatiently.

Molly followed her instructions and then regretted it. At once her hands were stuck. Molly wished she'd refused. Miss Cribbins now attached the two rubbery things to Molly's temples. Then she switched on the screen. A red dot pulsed there on its graph, sinister and threatening. Briskly Miss Cribbins took the book about nuclear fusion and held it in front of Molly's eyes.

"Is this the correct level for you to read?"

"Yes . . ." said Molly uncertainly.

Miss Cribbins pressed a button on the desk, and a blue ray of light shot upward until it surrounded the book. When she released it, the book now floated magically in the air.

"To turn the page you will say, 'Now,'" said Miss Cribbins. "You will work for three hours, then a servant will come and lead you to your sleeping quarters."

Molly scowled. "I'm not going to do this," she said. "You can keep your books." She tried to pull her hands out of the silver hand molds.

"Up to you," said Miss Cribbins. She extracted an old-fashioned wooden ruler from a drawer. This she placed above Molly's hands and pressed another button so that it was suspended by green lights. "This device"—she pointed to the screen—"will judge whether you are absorbing enough information. If it considers that you are not working hard enough, it sends a message to this machine." She pointed to the box under the monitor. "The ruler will then punish you. An old-fashioned method. Charming—don't you think?" Miss Cribbins smiled, flashing a perfect row of pearly teeth. Her cat-spider hissed as if laughing in agreement, and without another word the nasty woman left the room.

Molly was left with her hands stuck fast and the ruler hovering above them. The book floated in front of her face and the expectant monitor, attached to her head via its rubber-ended cables, blipped. She wondered how much the ruler hitting her hands would hurt. And so she didn't even look at the book. A flat red line began to be traced on the screen.

"Are you all right down there?" Molly asked Petula, nudging her gently with her foot. Then she noticed the monitor was making a quicker bleeping noise. The flat red line was now quite long. And the bleeping was becoming more insistent. And then it happened. The ruler came down on her right hand with smart THWACK.

"Owww!" Molly winced from the stinging pain, only to see the ruler slicing through the air to hit her other hand too. "Owww!" Petula put her front paws upon Molly's knee to check if she was all right. The monitor was now starting on a *new* red line. Molly eyed it nervously. Already it was half a centimeter long. Three minutes later the ruler came down twice more.

Molly had received this punishment before at school when she was younger, from a vicious teacher called Miss Toadley. But she'd never had more then five pairs of thwacks.

Five smacks from the ruler had hurt a lot when she'd been seven. Perhaps she'd bear the pain better now that she was eleven. The ruler came down for the third time. The palms of Molly's hands were now branded with pink ruler-shaped marks, and they were feeling sore. After the fourth lash the marks had turned a raspberry pink and her hands were going blotchy. Only twelve minutes had passed. This was torture—torture that Molly could definitely not endure for three hours. Her hands would be raw in half an hour.

Molly couldn't bear it. There was nothing for it but to do what Miss Cribbins wanted and learn about nuclear fusion. Molly began to read.

> *Nuclear* fusion *power stations must not be confused with nuclear* fission *power stations. Nuclear* fission *power stations split particles of uranium to produce energy. There are dangerous waste products. Nuclear* fusion *power stations make clean, safe energy.*

"I'll get you for this, Miss Cribbins," Molly said under her breath.

To start with she was so angry that she couldn't concentrate. But after a few more whacks from the ruler Molly focused on the book. She soon worked out how much concentrating she had to do to stop the red line on the screen growing. Whenever she read something and made her brain remember the information, a nice green line grew on the screen, reaching up like an electronic beanstalk. Three nuggets of learned information kept the ruler at bay. So Molly read on.

> *In nuclear fusion power stations, hydrogen is compressed with hydrogen, and miraculously helium is made. While this*

*is happening, vast amounts of energy are also produced. This energy can be turned into electricity.*

It was tricky stuff to remember and very tiring. The minute hand on the flat clock on the wall seemed to crawl slower than a slug. After an hour Molly's eyes were heavy. After two, she kept nearly falling asleep. Each time her eyelids dropped the ruler gave her a sharp shock to wake her up. Eventually three hours were up and the torture stopped. The monitor gave a little whistle and, with huge relief, Molly pulled her hands free. Her arms and back were stiff from being in the same position for so long. She had pins and needles in her bottom. She lay her head on the desk.

"That was horrible, Petula. Horrible! I can't do that again."

Then a servant came and escorted Molly to her sleeping quarters. Molly lay down exhausted in her cell-like room. Petula jumped up and snuggled next to her. Molly switched off the light. Pajamas lay on the chair in the semidarkness, but before Molly had even pulled off her shoes she was asleep. The night drifted by. Molly slept deeply. Then she had nightmares about being trapped down in a dark pit, with a ruler chasing her. The ruler had Princess Fang's face and the cat-spider's legs.

Just before dawn, when the sky was pale indigo, Molly woke to find someone in her room. She sat up quickly, expecting to be knocked on the head or handcuffed at any second. But instead a familiar, soft voice whispered, "Come with me now. There's no time to waste. Chop-chop! And be ever, *ever* so quiet!"

# Twelve

As soon as Molly's eyes adjusted to the light, she recognized the plump form of Nurse Meekles. She was in a pink fluffy dressing gown with her hair up in a net. Molly slipped out of bed, and she and Petula followed. Three courtyards later, after a tunnel of vines, the nurse stopped at one of the cloisters, where there was a stone seat.

"Wait here with your dog," she said nervously. "The cameras won't catch you because that pillar blocks their views. In a while I will be back with Micky. I will walk through that door with him."

Molly recognized the silver entrance at once. "That leads to the jellyfish room."

"Yes. When you see us, don't show yourself. Give me two minutes to get us into the main machine room, then come inside and get your electromagnetic suits on too. But, remember, keep yourself hidden from us at all times."

"What are you going to do?"

"Molly, I can help you a bit, dumpling," Nurse Meekles whispered, "and I am going to help Micky too. Once we are in the mind-machine room I want you to assist me, and we're going to have to work fast. Remember, whatever you do, don't look into Micky's eyes." With that she took off.

Molly waited in the darkness and breathed in the sweet smell of night flowers. She wondered what Nurse Meekles was planning. Ten minutes later Petula's nose pricked up. Micky, swathed in a light blue dressing gown, followed the nurse, leaning heavily on her as he limped along. At the silver door he picked out the combination of numbers on its lock, and Nurse Meekles beckoned him through. She left the door slightly ajar.

Molly counted slowly to one hundred and twenty. Then she and Petula went in too.

Inside, the familiar blue glow of the giant jellyfish greeted them. Molly could hear Micky's voice in the main chamber.

"But why did you wake me up to tell me that?" he was saying. "If I don't get my sleep, I'll get more sick.

Why didn't you wake *her* up and tell her about these faces?" Molly realized that the faces must be something to do with a story Nurse Meekles had fabricated to get him to follow her.

"I wanted *you* to see them first, dumpling," Nurse Meekles said.

Molly and Petula stepped into the changing zone. Silently Molly's jumpsuit was hoisted up on an invisible hanger above to join Micky and Nurse Meekles's nightclothes. And Molly and Petula found themselves clad in the blue electromagnetic outfits.

"I can't see them," Micky was saying in the machine room.

"There's one," said Nurse Meekles. And then there was the distinct sound of sticking tape being peeled off its reel.

"What are you do—" Micky's sentence was cut short.

"You can come in now, Molly," Nurse Meekles called softly. Molly walked in, to see Micky struggling with his hands held behind his back and his mouth taped. Nurse Meekles looked extraordinary in her electromagnetic suit—rather like a shiny blue bouncy ball with arms and legs and a head stuck on.

"We have to move it, Molly. I've muffled the microphones and turned the cameras away from us, but they can't be like that for long. Hopefully the guards in the monitor room will be too dozy at this time of night to notice anything suspicious. Help me take him to the chair. Come on."

Molly faltered.

"Molly, I *had* to gag him," the woman whispered gently. "Micky maybe can't run very well, but he certainly can shout. Help me put him on the chair. Once he's there we can sort him out."

"Sort him out?" Molly still held back. She wasn't sure she wanted to be part of this. "What are you going to do to him?" She watched the nurse pull Micky toward the chair as easily as if he was a tightly rolled-up duvet.

"The same as they did to you."

"What? Take away all his knowledge of how to hypnotize?"

"Exactly that. The machine is on the same settings. Typical! Her Highness never tidies up after herself—lets servants do it all. Lucky for us, she was too lazy to put this machine back into neutral too. All I have to do is press this one." She pointed to a large green button with GO printed on it. Micky was now pinned into the chair, his hands held down, his body and legs firmly trapped. Nurse Meekles lowered the silver dome down over his head. "I'm sorry to have to do this to you, Micky," she said, speaking to his feet and avoiding his hypnotic eyes, "but you wouldn't listen. This is for your own good, my darling. You need to get your feet back on the ground. Your sister here will help you."

Micky tried to wriggle out of the imprisoning chair, but it was impossible.

Molly knew how he felt. She was extremely confused. "Why are you doing this?" she asked.

The stout woman walked toward the control panel of the machine. "He needs to see something of the real world," she said quietly. "He has no idea what he's done. He needs to know. They've nearly changed him forever, Molly. He used to be such a nice little boy. It breaks my heart to see how my little plum cracker's changed. But I know him, Molly. He's still good underneath; I'm sure he is. I can see he's your brother. Get to know him. Try to forgive his bad habits and help him. He has to lose his hypnotic skills because only then can he escape with you."

*"Escape?"*

"Yes. I know a way." She put her finger on the green button. "This is difficult for me to do, but I know it's for the best." She closed her eyes and pressed. The machine was activated. Sparks shot through the blue gelatinous gloop of the jellyfish, and the domed cap on Micky's head flashed. Micky tried to kick and shout, but his efforts were futile. Molly knew how furious he was and she really felt for him. Soon Micky stopped thrashing. His anger subsided as he accepted that all his hypnotic knowledge was being drained from him.

"I think you can look at him now," Nurse Meekles said.

Molly's eyes met her brother's. They were molten.

"Do you know how to put the memories back in?" Molly asked hopefully.

The woman shook her head. "There's no time for regrets now. Keep looking back at yesterday and you'll trip over tomorrow! Now come on, quick, let's get out of these ridiculous outfits."

Nurse Meekles fixed the cameras and microphones in the room so that everything was back to normal. Then Molly helped her pull Micky, his hands now taped together in front of him, toward the changing zone and their clothes were sluiced back on to them. Keeping to the shadows, they hurried through the courtyards, half dragging Micky, to a blue door, beyond which was a corridor. At the end of this was a waist-high oblong opening. Nurse Meekles pressed a button beside it.

"This is the chute that goes to the laundry rooms," she said, bending to give Petula a stroke. "There are no cameras there." Hearing a noise behind them, she suddenly grew very panicky. "Yes, so . . . oh my goodness, where was I? So there's the entrance to the secret mountain passageway in there. Go through it. Like I said, ride the pincers. Princess Fang won't know where you are." She reached into her pocket and passed Molly a matchbox-sized object. "A flashlight, Molly. But that is all I can do for you."

She turned to Micky. "I did this for you, honey puff. Might get my whole mind washed away if they find out, but I had to take the risk. I had to do it for you, dumpling." She bent to kiss him, but Micky blazed with anger and ducked away. He tried to shout something from behind the tape on his mouth, but all that he could produce was a hoarse grunt of complaint.

The nurse kissed Molly softly on the forehead. "Good luck," she said. "Now hurry, hurry, hurry, and thank you for coming to rescue him." She picked Micky up in her strong arms and posted him through the hatch. "He'll have to manage without his hover chair," she said. "It'll be good for him."

Molly touched Nurse Meekles's shoulder. A new courage had blossomed inside her.

"What do you mean, 'ride the pincers'?" she said. But before she had time to hear the answer, she and Petula had slipped down the hatch and they too were shooting away into the darkness.

# Thirteen

The laundry chute was a large metal tube angled steeply so that the ride down it was dark and very fast. Molly, with Petula in her lap, landed in a sofa-sized basket of dirty linen, just missing Micky, who had rolled over to the side and was floundering about, trying to get up. With his tied hands he wiped a sock from his head and grimaced at Molly accusingly.

"Don't you *dare* look at me like that!" Molly said reproachfully. "You're not the only one who's been put on that machine. Imagine what it's like for me. I only came here to check that you were okay. Now look at me! My best friend has been hypnotized *by you*; I've lost my powers; and Rocky, Petula, and I are stuck in a time that isn't even our own."

While Micky stubbornly sat on the floor, determined to make her life as difficult as possible, and Petula sniffed about, Molly began searching for a way out. The laundry room was fairly big, with large white machines along the length of it. Each had a dashboard of buttons with Chinese writing on them. One was switched on, and through its square window Molly saw one of the princess's frilly dresses. Instead of being tossed in water, the dress was being stretched and cleaned by green light. At the far end of the room was a door. This was locked. Above their heads, long mechanical arms, which Molly assumed sorted the clothes, hung dormant. Molly ran her hands along the surface of the wall. It was completely smooth. There didn't seem to be a seam line of a door at all. Desperately she pushed trolleys of laundry aside to search. Micky began to laugh. It was a mean laugh and muffled behind the tape on his mouth. Molly ignored him.

The next second there was a thud. Molly jumped as the engines of the room cranked into action. Micky had found the buttons that operated the laundry machines.

The cranelike arms of the sorters began swinging into action. The first made a swoop for Molly. Thinking her a large, unwashed piece of clothing, it dived, claws open, to pick her up. Molly turned, horrified, and ducked for cover. The second went for Petula, who wasn't so lucky. Rubber clamps embraced her body and lifted her up. She let out a howl of fear, but the machine ignored her. Swiftly it lifted her, making its calculations about which machine to put her into.

"You moron!" Molly shouted at Micky. "Switch it off!" Micky shook his head and shrugged his shoulders. Molly watched aghast as Petula was lifted higher and higher, right up to the beams of the ceiling. Pushing wheeled baskets of laundry out of her way, Molly ran to be directly below Petula in case she was suddenly dropped.

Up above Molly, Petula went stone still with fear. She hated heights. Seeing a beam close by to the right, she forgot her fear of falling and began to struggle. If she could just wriggle out of the sorting claw's metal and rubber grip and get onto the beam, things would be better. Below, Molly was craning her neck and holding her arms out.

The mechanical arm was now losing its hold on Petula. She could feel herself slipping. If she fell, it would hurt. It would be far worse than the time she fell off the garden wall when she was a puppy. There was nothing for it. The next time the machine moved toward the white beam, Petula made an immense twisting effort. She pulled her body out of the mechanical grip and pushed away toward the beam. Suddenly she was flying through the air like a plump black squirrel, and for a split second she thought she wouldn't make it. Then her front paws caught the beam and, kicking with her back legs, she was up.

"Oh, Petula, be *careful*," she heard Molly saying from below. The mechanical arm moved away, confused but resigned that it had lost its load, ready to pick up another piece.

Petula looked down from her perch. Her world swayed. Determined not to fall off the beam, she stared ahead, but her furry knees quivered as she realized she was stuck. She tried to pull herself together and willed herself not to feel dizzy. If she walked to the end of the beam, she thought, she'd reach a ledge that was wider. She'd be far safer there. So, plucking up courage, Petula pretended she was walking along a thin path on the ground. She ignored the scraping of her claws on the metal beam. She ignored all thoughts of plummeting to the ground. Soon she was by the wall, and so relieved was she that she flung herself at it. When she did, a very unexpected thing happened. The wall gave way.

From below, through the metal of the laundry-machine arms and the sheets that were being lifted and sorted, Molly saw the opening. She marched over to Micky and pulled him up.

"Thanks," she said, tugging him toward the center of the room so that they were prime targets for the laundry sorters. "You've actually just shown us the way out. We have to do what Nurse Meekles said—'ride the pincers.'" Micky looked wide-eyed at the beams high above. As he did, one of the mechanical claws spied what it thought was a tablecloth and swung down to grab it. Molly jumped onto its articulated arm. The machine swung Micky up high and hovered near the beam for a moment as it tried to decipher whether he was linen or cotton. Molly caught the beam with her legs and gripped it tight between her knees. Once she was balanced, she tugged at her brother. He tumbled onto her, and the machine, confused again, went down for more laundry. Micky's hands were still tied. He was obviously petrified that he might fall.

"Just keep still," Molly said, trying to be reassuring. Micky was as rigid as a wooden broom. "I'll pull you over here and you'll be fine." She inched backward toward the ledge, dragging him with her. When they got there she kissed and hugged Petula. "Good girl, clever girl!"

Petula was very impressed with Molly's brave ascent, although she wondered why she had brought the boy up. And she didn't know how they were all going to get down again. She'd already sniffed at the tunnel beyond. It smelled of damp and old burned-out fire. It wasn't the sort of tunnel any dog, or person, would want to venture into. So it was with great surprise that Petula found herself being pushed into its blackness.

Molly checked the laundry room for any telltale signs that they'd been there and then carefully she shoved Micky and posted herself through the secret trapdoor. Its hatch snapped satisfactorily shut.

# Fourteen

For a few moments Molly sat perfectly still. The tunnel was dark and smelled of old burned cabbage, but she didn't care. Relief washed through her—they had made it out. The princess and her entourage behind the secret door would be sleeping and so, for a little while at least, they were safe. She thought of Miss Cribbins's slapping ruler and hoped with all her heart that she would never see it—or feel it—again. Micky's muffled grunting brought her to her senses. She couldn't see him, but she could feel him. His back was in front of her legs.

"Mrrmmhmmm!" He was trying to shout behind his gag. Molly knew how horrible it was to be gagged. On top of this, Micky had his hands tied. With the cobwebby darkness engulfing him, he must be feeling claustrophobic and scared. She reached for the flashlight Nurse Meekles had given her and switched it on.

Micky turned, his eyes wide and watery. He brought his hands up and waved them in front of the light. "Mrwrrwwhhhmm!" he demanded.

"I *will* free your hands," Molly whispered, "but not until we are away from this door. I don't want you taking off your gag and shouting." Micky turned away. Molly softened. "I'm sorry," she said. "It wasn't actually my fault you were put on the mind machine. Nurse Meekles thought it was the best thing for you." Micky grunted angrily. "Okay," Molly said. "Well, you tell me later. For now let's get going. You first. Lead the way." She gave her brother a little nudge with her knees, and he began to edge down the tunnel.

At first the slope was gentle. Petula went first, using her nose and the light from Molly's flashlight. She moved forward very reluctantly. To her sensitive canine nose the tunnel smelled of a mixture of dogs and snakes, as though creatures of both types used this place as a playground. She smelled their thick scent in the air. It was fresh. Her hair prickled up on her back as she examined it. Petula had come across a viper in the grass at Briersville Park once. The smell from these snakes was fifty times as powerful. She had a horrid feeling that these snakes were probably fifty times as big. Couldn't Molly smell them too? And as for the dogs, they would be furious to find another dog on their territory. She twisted toward Molly and whined quietly, *This is dangerous Molly—let's go back.*

Edging down the tunnel was like moving through the stone vein of some great rock beast. The walls were clammy and cold, and the ground beneath them, rough rubble. Molly supposed that the tunnels had been cut away by ancient underground mountain streams, when in times past the snows had melted each year. Yet *someone* used, or had used, the tunnel too, for someone had built the secret door to the palace laundry room. *Who?* Molly wondered. *And how did Nurse Meekles know about it?* She imagined the vast, heavy mass of the mountain all about them. It felt oppressive—as though it might suddenly squeeze them to death. This tunnel might go on for miles, Molly thought. Already her legs were aching and she was thirsty.

Then the rocky channel took a sharp, earthbound turn that they skidded down, landing in heaps at the bottom. Molly leaned toward Micky with the flashlight in her teeth and undid the knots around his wrists.

"I wouldn't try anything if I were you," she said. Her voice sounded extrafierce in the dark, stuffy air. "I'm not in the mood to be tackled. You know I'm stronger than you, plus Petula would bite you if she had to." Molly didn't like to be mean but knew she had to make Micky scared of her or he might attempt to fight. Micky rubbed his wrists and peeled the tape off his mouth.

"You idiot," he snarled. "Nobody asked you to come. You should've stayed where you came from. We're in deep trouble here. I mean, who built this rat run? Have you thought about that?"

"As far as I'm concerned," Molly growled back, eyeing the royal crest embroidered on his dressing gown, "*those* people, those vicious *friends* of yours back there, are the rats. Whoever built this tunnel must be better than them!"

"You're so stupid. You don't know what this place and this time are like." Micky practically spat his next words. "How *could* a prehistoric person like you know?"

"I may not be a person from this time," said Molly through gritted teeth, "but in my time people were a thousand times nicer than they are here. Those people—*your* people—are sick in the head. The only one who was anything like a proper human being was Nurse Meekles. And *you're* sick too, by the way."

"I know I am. *You're* sick, to make fun of my illness!"

"I wasn't talking about your body," said Molly. "You are sick to have hypnotized all the people who live around the lake."

"If I could hypnotize you, I would make you think you are a pile of muck," said Micky, "a rotting pile of cow-flapper muck!"

"Very nice," said Molly icily, "but you're not a hypnotist now, are you, Micky? Now you're just an ordinary eleven-year-old boy, so you'd better get used to it." Molly shone her flashlight to inspect their surroundings. They had landed in a passageway that went to the left and to the right.

"You're like a mole lost in a hole," said Micky drily. "And I'll tell you what—there are creepy things out there that hunt moles."

Molly ignored him. She took a deep breath. Her words sounded braver than she was feeling. "Which way, Petula?"

Petula cocked her ears and sniffed the air. Both routes were unattractive. Both tunnels were dank and smelled of snake dung and dogs. She chose the mossiest-smelling one and poked her nose toward it.

"You trust your *dog* to show you the way?" asked Micky derisively.

"Animals," Molly replied coolly, "have far better senses than us. Petula has got her head screwed on. She's helped me in lots of dangerous situations." Molly suddenly remembered her new mind-reading powers. They were so new to her that in the panic of their escape she had forgotten about them. Would they work in the dark? If she could read Micky's thoughts, she might at least see if he was planning anything nasty. So she sent out a question to him. *What are you thinking?*

Immediately a pale blue bubble rose above Micky's head with a bedroom in it, then a glass of water, then a picture of Molly with ropes tied tight around her, making her look like an Egyptian mummy.

"I certainly trust Petula," Molly concluded, "more than I trust you. I expect you are having horrid thoughts about tying me up till I can't breathe." She shone the flashlight in her brother's face and saw his amazed reaction. "Am I right?" she asked.

"Wr-wrong . . . weirdo," Micky stammered.

"Let's move."

They shuffled down the slope in silence.

"This passage is freezing. What if it goes nowhere?" Micky taunted. "It might lead to a dead end. Then what? We'll get hypothermia."

"Then we go back and try the other tunnel."

"What if I can't?"

"Then I'll pull you back." Molly answered flippantly, as if pulling Micky would be as easy as pulling a helium balloon. The truth was, she was tired and she didn't like the very real prospect of hitting a dead end. She was worried that farther on the tunnel might have caved in. The air in it was so stale Molly already felt buried alive.

The passageway twisted and dipped on and on. Molly even began to doze off as she shuffled. And then, as if the mountain itself was whispering to them, Molly heard noises. Was she asleep and dreaming? She snapped awake. She could definitely hear a swishing noise and she was sure that was a growl too. She, Petula, and Micky froze, and Molly switched off the flashlight.

Petula's tongue tasted bitter as fear shot through her. The dogs and snakes she'd smelled before were now horribly clear, as a current of underground air brought their stench to her nose. She doubted that they had picked up her scent yet, for a breeze in the other direction was needed for that. Nevertheless, the dogs and snakes were approaching. She heard the swishing noise too and another growl. Ignoring Molly's wishes, she turned. Pushing past Micky and Molly, she ran up the tunnel they had just come down, her claws skittering on the damp rocks.

"Seems like either your dog's head has come unscrewed or she knows something you don't," Micky said sourly. Then he stiffened as he too heard the strange growl coming from the dark ahead.

"I think we'd better follow her," Molly said, her hands starting to sweat. She gave Micky a tug. "Come on—I'll help you." Frantically Molly scrabbled back up the sloped tunnel. Micky was far heavier than she'd expected him to be, and her feet, slipping on the rubble, sent stones rolling. A shower of mud and flint kicked up behind them.

Petula paused to try to sense the feeling coming from the creatures behind. How she wished Molly and the boy would hurry up. Didn't they sense any danger at all? Didn't they see that they might be breakfast to whatever was back down the tunnel?

*Come on!* Petula whined, and as soon as she'd uttered this, wished she hadn't, for, as if in reply, a howl came up the tunnel.

*WHO'S IN OUR TUNNEL?*

*Something's in the run!* another dog snarled. Petula yelped.

"Crumbs. Sounds like they've discovered us!" Molly exclaimed. And with a useless, desperate pull, she lurched herself and Micky another foot up the pitch-black passageway.

The swishing noise was now really loud, as though a giant broom was sweeping its way toward them. And the growling had given way to a host of enthusiastic barks.

"We're dead!" Micky gasped, crippled with fear.

"Don't stop here," Molly begged. "If you stop, we're

definitely done for. For goodness sake, Micky, just try to move." She was terrified too. They were really close now. In the dark their harsh panting and slobbering sounded as though they were just around the bend. "Oh, Petula!" Molly cried out, fear stricken. "You just run, Petula. Let them get us. You escape."

And then it was too late. Molly felt them all around her. She felt smooth, scaly skin, soft, with strong muscle beneath it, running under her hands, past her neck, under her back. It was as if huge tentacles had swooped under her. In fact it was as if she lay on a bed of snakes. And the smell of dogs and their growling echoed down the hollow tunnel. Molly could feel two dogs panting only inches away from her face to the left and the right of her body. Their breath smelled of old meat.

"Aaargh!" Micky cried as he was scooped up and carried off.

*We're sorry,* Petula barked to the two dogs that she could smell in the darkness near her. *We didn't mean to trespass. We were lost! We meant no harm!*

But the big dog in front of her growled, *Keep your mouth shut, you palace Peking. Or I'll shut my mouth on YOU.*

Petula found herself being lifted by the thick, sinuous bodies of two snakes. The dry scent of them was overpowering. They clasped her around her front and back legs. Then they carried her down the passageway. Seeing that a struggle would be futile, she shut her eyes and let the journey unfold.

Ahead, exactly the same thing was happening to Molly and Micky. A multitude of dogs growled and barked and snarled.

"We've been caught by a pack of mountain wolves!" Molly screamed. Ahead of her, Micky was yelling too.

"Aaarghh! SNAKES! Stop! *Stop!* I'm allergic to reptiles!"

Now Molly wished that Princess Fang *could* hear them. Life at the palace was at least life. Here she was going to end up as a pile of bones with every last bit of life chewed off her.

Down and down the dark spiral slide tunnel they were carried. It was like being on some sort of crazy fairground ride, with the snakes beneath Molly and Micky rippling, carrying them forward and downward with the utmost ease. Molly didn't dare turn her flashlight on for fear that this would anger the creatures. She tried mind reading their thoughts, but the bubbles were moving about so much as they sped along that she couldn't see the pictures. And so, like Petula, she shut her eyes and let the nightmare unfurl.

Finally the slope of the mountain leveled out and the beasts sped along the ground. And then they stopped. The next thing Molly knew, something had opened a trapdoor above their heads.

Dim light and a strong smell flooded in. It reminded Molly of home—of Amrit the elephant. Strands of straw floated down, catching in her hair. Then Molly's surprise was swamped by astonishment. As her eyes adjusted to the light she began to make out the shapes of the creatures. They weren't dogs and they weren't snakes; they were a *mixture of the two*. They were giant snakes with Labrador heads. Some black, some rust colored, some sandy. They all had yellow teeth. As Molly was lifted into the dusty space above, she realized she had been riding on a sort of snake chariot.

Behind her she heard Micky yelp. Then, with a swift movement, they were all carried up through the hatch.

They were now in what seemed like a giant hutch. The wooden boxlike structure around them had heavy crisscrossed wire spanning the far end of it and a water feeder, like a giant version of the type stuck onto the sides of hamster cages, was fixed to one wall. The floor was covered in straw. Molly felt the scaly creature beneath her squirm and wondered whether they were about to be dumped and devoured.

Petula worriedly sniffed at the air. An odor of rabbit and elephant was coming from under a large blanket at the other end of the hutch. There were either an awful lot of rabbits there or the rabbits were peculiarly big. The blanket moved. Micky finally found his voice.

"I think this . . . is the Yang Yongian Institute of Zoology," he said in a terrified tone, "and that big thing under that blanket there is an elethumper. I don't—" The blanket slid off the massive animal, silencing him.

Molly now saw what looked like an elephant crossed with a rabbit. The creature had dry gray leathery skin and was as big as an elephant, but instead of a short whiplike tail it had a massive round fluffy one. Its legs were like a rabbit's, except not furry—leathery. Its ears were like a rabbit's. Its eyes were large and yellow, but it had no whiskers. Instead of a button nose it had a trunk. This it now waved suspiciously in the direction of the new arrivals, raising its massive body from the ground.

The dognake closest to Molly barked at it, while another, using its muzzle, busily covered the trapdoor with straw. The elethumper lifted a giant back foot and began thumping the ground. The hutch shook.

"Elethumpers are very, very d-dangerous," stammered Micky, his face now ashen with fear. But before the elethumper could do anything dangerous he, Molly, and Petula were once more scooped up by the dognakes and carried through a big dog flap in a gray metal door.

Outside it was the start of a bright, sunny day. Temperatures were already beginning to soar. Wide paths leading to the left, the right, and straight in front of them were lined with buildings that housed strange-looking animals. A zebra-striped giraffe poked its head out of one rooftop and blinked at the sky. Beside the door of a nearby pen was a sign:

**BEARUNKEY**

This breed produced by the Qingling Team in 2425
at the Yang Yongian Institute of Zoology.
**Eats shoots and leaves and anything warm-blooded.**
**Extremely ferocious.**

But Molly scarcely had time to read it, for in the next moment they were off again, heading for a giant, low, spreading tree with a complex of huts and walkways built into its many gnarled branches.

They passed another pen with a sign:

**SABRERAT**

This breed produced by the Qingling Team in 2420
at the Yang Yongian Institute of Zoology.
**Eats anything.**
**Extremely aggressive.**

Desperately Molly looked around for anyone who might help them, but the zoo appeared empty of people. No one was about. At the foot of the tree's broad trunk one of the dognakes began to bark. Moments later, twenty feet up, a wooden door opened.

Someone appeared. From where Molly was he looked like a tiny old man with brown skin that was rough and thick and barklike. He wore a dirty loincloth, tied loosely around his waist. His black, shoulder-length dreadlocks were filthy, and his mouth seemed set in a permanent snarl. But the scariest thing about him was his eyes. They were an extraordinary bright green color and were mad and staring. His half-tree half-human looks made him seem like he might also be the result of an experiment done by the Qingling Team wherever they were.

Micky, who up until then had been quiet and seemingly exhausted, suddenly lurched forward and shouted up at him.

"HELP! Do you know who I am? I'm the boy from Yang Yongia Palace. She has abducted me!" He pointed frantically at Molly. "Tell these animals to release me and take me to safety. Then report this to the high authorities. I command you with the Yang Yongian power that is vested in me and in the name of Princess Fang!"

# Fifteen

Molly's stomach turned and she felt sick.

"Please . . ." she begged the little person up the tree. "Please don't! Please hide me. I can't go back—they'll kill me. I'll do anything. Please hide me."

"GO!" Micky now shouted furiously. "In the name of Princess Fang!"

But the small leathery man didn't move an inch. Instead, he clapped his hands together and two of the oddest-looking people Molly had ever seen appeared from behind the base of the tree.

The first person was a tall, thin, birdlike man. Instead of hair, he had a cockatoo's crest of white feathers. His pale orange nose was hard and sharp like a beak, and below his small, mean hawk eyes were brown feathered cheeks and a feathered chin. His back was humped and cloaked in brown silk, and he wore a rust-colored waistcoat and orange leggings. His clawed feet were like those of a bird of prey, with talons.

The man beside him was just as strange. He was ancient—he looked at least a hundred and fifty years old. His scalp, face, and neck were grayish green and scaly, his huge eyes looked out from above creased bags of skin, and his nose was wide and flat. His gray hair hung curtainlike down to his chest, while the top of his head was wrinkled and as bald as a nut. He wore a long, flowing olive-green robe with green, pointed cloth shoes. His neck was stooped so that his hunched shoulders were at the same level as his ears, and covering the whole of his back was a giant shiny tortoise shell.

"Mu-mutants!" stammered Micky with a gulp, so softly that only Molly heard him. Then he shouted, "Did you hear what I said? In the name of all that is Yang Yongian, call the palace guards!"

But the strange animal people did nothing. Molly's instincts told her they were hypnotized but not in the way that Micky obviously expected them to be. Then the wrinkled midget man up the tree spoke—although he seemed to be talking to himself more than to anyone else. His voice was high and childlike.

"So that's what she was yabbering on about. And

old Fake Face. Saw them both on the screen. *'Bring them back, hypnos, and it'll be cake for tea.'* So that's what she's lost." He leaned over the wooden balcony. "Where did you get them, Schnapps?" The dognake carrying Molly barked. The little person rubbed his hands together and his wild eyes flashed like a tiger's. "Aha!"

"Please, *please* don't hand us in," Molly blurted out. "We're running away from the palace—we don't want to go back there. My brother here has been so scared by your dognakes that he's talking gibberish. He doesn't really want to go back."

"I DO!" Micky bellowed. "In the name of Princess Fang, tie this girl up at once and call the Lakeside guards."

"He's frightened out of his wits!" Molly continued.

"I'm NOT!" Micky screamed. "Don't believe her!"

All this squabbling was far too much for the midget man up the tree. In a high pitch he screeched, "BE QUIET! Or I'll feed you to the dognakes." At once both Micky and Molly were silent. "So," he asked threateningly, pointing a tiny dirty finger at Molly, "who are you and why are you on the run?"

Molly took a deep breath.

"Well, it's a long story really, but in nutshell it's this: I'm called Molly . . . er . . . Molly Moon. And, you may not believe this, but I come from five hundred years ago. I came here to find my brother. You see, he was taken from the hospital when we were born—we are twins, you see. Well, I traveled here but it's all gone wrong. The princess up there put me on her mind machine and she took all my hypnotic powers away so now I can't—"

"*You* are a *hypnotist*?"

"Er . . . yes, but NO." Molly gulped. "I was, but I'm not now."

"Bad," said the midget man darkly.

Molly panicked. "But I come from a different time," she explained. "This place and all the hypnotism here has got nothing to do with me. Nothing. I've come from a time of . . . of smelly car engines and oil, a time before hydrogen engines, before all the weather changed. In my time Mont Blanc was still covered in snow and this place was called Switzerland and people used to come here to ski. Look at my old-fashioned sneakers," she gabbled desperately.

But the midget man up the tree wasn't listening. He was pacing up and down his rickety balcony.

"Tasty," he was saying. "Well, keep them under lock and key. Have to pack them away before the hypnos start coming in. Snarlers' pit? Too dangerous. Bearunkeys' cage? Don't be stupid. We want to save them for me. Sabrerats? No. No, no. Ah, now there's an idea. Worm pit. WORM PIT." Now he leaned down and called out, "Job for you, Wildgust and Tortillus. Take them to the worm pit."

"Yes—Professor—Selkeem," the hawk-man, Wildgust, said. Picking Molly up, he tucked her under his arm. Then he reached out for Micky too.

"You can't do this!" Micky objected, the cord of his now-dirty blue dressing gown dragging on the ground. "I'll c-catch something. I'm fragile. Princess Fang will . . ." But his words were ignored. And up in his tree, the midget professor was talking to himself again.

"Nearly opening time. No, I can't put them in the cooking pot here. She'll sink her fangs into them if I do." He glanced up at the mountaintop. "Fank you, Pwincess Fang. I'll sink *my* fangs into them instead. Take them *now*, Wildgust! To the worm pit!"

With that, the small mad professor stepped back into his tree house and shut the door. As he did, the dognakes slithered up the tree trunk into its branches. A plume of nasty green smoke wound its way out of a chimney up into the leaves above and the sky beyond.

The last dognake let go of Petula and she found herself on the ground again. Shaking herself, she saw with horror that Molly and the palace boy were being carried away. At once she set off after them.

Up at the mountaintop palace, Princess Fang was in her nightclothes—a floaty, white chiffon nightie with pink rabbit fur along its hem and mother-of-pearl buttons up the front. She was pacing back and forth in front of a picture window, sucking on a yellow-and-white stick of rock candy. Outside, the shark's-tooth-shaped mountains quivered in the morning light, and miles and miles below the great lake shimmered. The sky was a cornflower blue.

The six-year-old princess flung her sweet on the floor and stamped on it as though killing a scorpion. Her grasshopper chirped madly from its cage. Miss Cribbins sat silently on a half-invisible purple stool in the corner, dressed in a gray night robe. She stroked her pet cat-spider.

"HOW DID SHE DO DAT?" the princess shouted furiously. She pointed a pudgy finger at Miss Cribbins. "Dat Milly Moon girl turned de camewas off! Minus must have shown her." She narrowed her eyes accusingly. "He was too weak, Cwibbins. He was easy meat for her! She obviously got de better of him." She picked up a long-legged doll by its ankles and, venting her fury, beat the ground with it. Then she said darkly, "Dat was a foolish oversight of yours, Cwibbins, not to twain him to be tougher. Foolish! Foolish!" And she began to chant:

*"Build a bonfire,*
*Build a bonfire,*
*Put de teachers on de top,*
*Put de schoolbooks in de middle,*
*And den just BURN DE LOT!"*

"There was never a threat," said Cribbins frostily. "There was no threat until Moon came along."

Princess Fang snorted. "You do wealize dat if we lose Micky Minus, Cwibbins, all our plans fall down. Dere will be no big empire. We won't be able to contwol other countwies because we will have lost our little hypnotist."

Cribbins's grip on her cat-spider tightened. "Of course I realize that. It's obvious," she hissed.

The princess now screamed. "SO WHERE DID DEY GO? Vanished! How? Moon can't time twavel anymore and Minus can't either, because he doesn't even know about time twavel. Anyway, you keep his cwystals. You *do have* his cwystals?"

Miss Cribbins nodded, pulling two chains with red, green, and clear gems from her pocket.

"Old dead Redhorn's are here too," she explained. "And you have the Moon ones locked up. There's no way Minus can time travel or stop time—even if someone could teach him, he's not got the tools."

Princess Fang snatched the crystals and hung both strings around her neck.

"So," she said crossly, taking two chocolate truffles from a black velvet box and stuffing them both in her mouth at once. "So, dat means dey could still be here in de building. Hiding under some toys, or under de trampoline or somefing. I like a game of hide-and-seek. I'll just get all the servants to look for me." She chewed her chocolates thoughtfully, wiping her messy mouth on her chiffon sleeve. "Or," she said, throwing a cursory glance in the direction of the valley bottom, "or dey have somehow hitched an elevator down dere to Lakeside in one of de food planes or somefing." She picked up a green cigarette and lit it. It smelled of limes.

"They won't last long," said Miss Cribbins with a bitter smile, "I assure you. You've put out your message on the street screens with Minus's picture. The hypnotized plebs will do as they're told. They'll hound Moon and Minus out. Just say the word, and the whole place can be turned upside down."

"Mmm. But," said Fang, blowing a smoke ring and

lassoing her finger with it, "when we do catch him, what den? That ugly Milly girl—uurgh, she's so unattwactive it makes me sick—she will have worked on Minus. He may fink diffwently. He may not be under our influence anymore."

Miss Cribbins sneered. "If we net them quickly, she won't have had time to change the way he thinks. He will still be like us. He will still understand that our way is the only way."

Taramasalata miaowed.

"Huh! And if he doesn't?"

"Then he'll have to be destroyed. Just as Moon will have to be destroyed."

"Destwoy her, yes, but not Minus. In a few years de machine will be able to extwact talent. When it can, we'll extwact de talent for hypnotism and time twavel fwom *Micky Minus*, not fwom her. And once it's ours, why, den we can dispose of him as well. Imagine it, Cwibbins! No more dependency. We'll be able to hypnotize de people ourselves."

"I look forward to it."

"So let's concentwate now. Dat Milly's started a game of tag. She wants a game, does she? Well, lovely! I *love* tag, and I'm *vewy* good at it. So let's see who wins!"

# Sixteen

As they were bundled along, Molly's eyes swiveled around, taking in the details of this strange new place. The Institute of Zoology was enormous. From one large stone building as big as an airplane hangar came bouncing, thudding noises. A sign to the side of its giant stable door read:

**KANGARAFFE**

This breed produced by the Qingling Team in 2418
at the Yang Yongian Institute of Zoology.

**Vegetarian.**

**Extremely excitable.**

Molly wondered who these brilliant scientists, the Qingling Team, had been. Every creature in the place seemed to have been developed by them. And the zoo was enormous, so they must have invented hundreds of new animals. As far as the eye could see there were leafy enclosures, stretching all the way down to the lake.

The path meandered past a copse of trees until they came to a massive gray shed. While the tortoise-man, Tortillus, unlocked its metal door Molly read the sign nearby:

WORMUS MAXIMUS

This breed produced by the Qingling Team in 2419
at the Yang Yongian Institute of Zoology.

**Eats rotting matter.**

**Mostly harmless.**

The hawk-man, Wildgust, deposited Molly and Micky on the ground and in halting, hypnotized phrases he warned, "Sit—on ledge—don't go on soil—or you drown—or get squashed—by worms." He roughly nudged Molly toward some steps that led down into a dark pit.

Micky limped forward and peered inside. "It's pitch-black down there," he said with a look of revulsion and fear on his face.

"Window later," the tortoise-man said. "Tinted—Worms don't—like strong—daylight."

Petula sniffed at the pong of manure in the air. She wasn't sure about this place either. It smelled of wet soil and fat, slippery worms. Petula had never been a great digger, never the sort of dog that shot down rabbit holes or buried bones.

"Come on, Petula," Molly coaxed. "I'm going, so you'd better come too. Come on." Molly put her finger through Petula's collar and gave a gentle tug. And the three of them entered the gloomy dungeon.

Once inside, they found themselves standing on a thin metal ledge. Behind them, the door closed. Molly waited for her eyes to adjust to the darkness. She thought she could sense something very large close to them. There was a squelching sound and a crumbling, splattering noise as clods of soil parted and moved.

"Look where you got us now!" Micky hissed with repulsion into the darkness. "Captured by *mutants*!"

"We might not be in here if you hadn't thrown that lunatic fit out there," Molly replied irritatedly. She felt the slimy wall behind them and tried to work out where it would be best to sit. "There's no point in yelling for help like that. Now that you've lost your hypnotic power, you are no use to Little Miss Fang."

"You really are thick, aren't you?" Micky replied. "I mean, you're very, very stupid. The princess can easily fix me."

"Not after Nurse Meekles breaks the machine," Molly lied. "When the machine is broken, then what? Unless there's some other way you could learn how to hypnotize people again." Molly was suddenly struck by the possibility that a hypnotism book might still exist. If one did, she might be able to get hold of it herself. She must find out, but she didn't want Micky guessing what she was after. So she casually said, "Look, this is silly. Why don't we make friends? We've got so much catching up to do. For instance, how did you learn to hypnotize anyway? Was it from a book?"

"No, Redhorn taught me," Micky said sourly. "There were never any books involved. But I *will* get my skills back. They'll catch that stupid woman before she gets back into the mind-machine room." He folded his arms and turned away.

"Don't count on it." Molly began to lower herself and Petula down to sit on the metal ledge. "And you should realize something, Micky. Without your powers, you really are of no use to Pain-in-the-neck Fang and Ghost-face Cribbins. They don't care about you unless you are a hypnotist. And what do you think of the mind machine, now that it's been used on you? Don't you think its sick to drain people of their thoughts like that?" Micky said nothing, but she could hear his quiet huffing breath as he silently cursed her.

"Anyway," Molly continued, "Fang will think you're contaminated by me now. She won't trust you anymore."

"That's rubbish," Micky retorted. "I'll get my knowledge back and everything will be as it was."

Molly coughed a large lump of phlegm into her mouth, making as revolting a sound as she could, and spat it into the mud in front of her. "You need your head examined if you think that would be a good thing."

In the darkness, Micky screwed his eyes up with hatred. "You are a complete stupid," he hissed, slowly sitting down. "You know the palace will find us very easily. You've signed your death warrant."

"I can't believe I risked everything for you," Molly replied angrily. "It's obvious that you wouldn't have ever risked *anything* for me."

The two of them stared silently ahead of them, dangling their legs over the ledge as though on a giant swing. Suddenly a worm moved under them, nudging their feet upward.

"Whaaah! Disgusting! Oh cat-spider turds!" yelled Micky, pressing himself back against the clammy wall. Molly squinted into the darkness. Twenty feet away she could just make out the frame of the window that the tortoise-man had spoken of. As if on cue there was a juddering, creaking sound as two mechanical metal shutters ground apart. Dim light poured through the brown glass. Now Molly saw the expanse of soil in front of them. It was like an earthy swimming pool filled with seething monsters. Their pink backs glistened slightly in the wet soil.

"Oh noodle puke!" Micky said, revolted. "Uuuurgh!"

Just then some people approached the window. They were dressed like peasants from a fairy-tale book, in patched trousers, tattered skirts, jerkins, and straw hats and were consulting books. They came up close to the thick glass and cupped their hands to their eyes, trying to block out the sunlight and see the worms. Micky immediately jumped up.

"Farmers! Help!" he yelled. "In the name of all that is powerful in Yang Yongia, help! Help me! I'm in here!"

"They can't hear you," said Molly calmly. "That midget Professor Selkeem guy wouldn't have put us in here if it wasn't soundproofed."

"HEEEEEEELP!" Micky screamed, waving his arms about and ignoring her.

"They can't *see* you either. I should think all they can see is the first few meters of the pit by the window." Molly looked at the stew of worms in front of her. "And that bit is too dangerous for you to get to."

It was then that she was completely caught by surprise. For Micky—limping, pathetic Micky—did something crazy. He threw himself, just like a rock star throws himself off the stage and into the crowd, into the mass of heaving worms. He landed on a hump of one of the worms. And then, like some mad stuntman in a fancy flowing dressing gown, he began hopping across the stepping-stone-like humps of various worms, toward the window.

"Micky, come back!" Molly shouted. "It's dangerous! Don't you remember what the hawk-man said?"

But it was too late. Micky had already misjudged the distance to the next worm and his legs had slipped into the soil. Now he was scrabbling to mount the worm, but it was diving under the mud and disappearing.

"You idiot," Molly said under her breath and then, with Petula barking madly at her, she too leaped into the pit.

The first worm she landed on was unsuspecting, as was the second. Therefore, stepping on the fleshy pink islands, Molly was able to get halfway across the room. But in the middle of the chamber things got difficult. The worm she had jumped on didn't like the sensation at all and shrank into the mud, taking what was going to be the next landing place down too. Molly's feet sank into the soil until mud was up to her knees. Ahead,

Micky was in an even worse predicament. He was already up to his waist in wet mulch. His eyes were wide with desperation. Petula howled from the metal ledge.

"I'm—I'm s-sinking!" Micky yelped. "The worm's s-sucking me down."

Molly was desperately trying to fathom how to stay up herself. If only she could see where the worms were under the mud! Then a bright idea struck her. If she thought a question to the worms, perhaps bubbles would show her where their heads were. And so she probed with her mind: *What are you thinking?*

Hazy gray thought bubbles suddenly hovered all around her. She could hardly tell what the worms were thinking—their thoughts were bendy and mostly pictures of soil. But Molly didn't care if she couldn't read the images; they showed her where the heads of the worms were. Some of the bubbles were half visible, their worms being deep in the earth; other bubbles were higher up. *These* worms were near the surface. There was one like this beside Molly and another close to Micky. She pulled her right wrist out of the sludge and, with a hefty effort, jumped. Sure enough, there was a worm just under the surface. Before it had time to shrink again Molly was on to the next one. From this balancing point she was able to grab Micky's arm. With a tremendous heave she dragged him toward her. Of course, the worm she was on was now fast sinking, but behind she saw that another was close to the surface. Molly tugged Micky toward this one and from there on to a wet concrete ledge away from the window at the side of the pit. They slumped down with relief.

"Don't try that crazy stuff again," said Molly, gasping as she caught her breath. "Next time you might drown." Micky gritted his teeth and said nothing, but Molly could tell that he'd been impressed by her rescue performance. He wouldn't have guessed *how* she'd judged where the worms were, and she was glad, for she wanted to keep her mind-reading skills a secret.

They were both now shivering from the wet. Micky was filthy and very shaken up. He slumped down in a shocked heap. Then, out of the corner of her eye, Molly saw him take a tiny rag out of his pocket. He sat rubbing it between his fingers as though it was a huge source of comfort.

A medieval-looking farming family approached the window. The mother was dressed like a milkmaid, and the father and son were in leather knee-length trousers and floppy white shirts. The boy peered in. He had a vacant look. It was the same mindless stare of his parents.

"It's so sad," Molly said. "In my time families going

to the zoo have fun. That boy should be jumping about going, 'Wow! Look at that giant worm! Urgh! Yuck!' Here people have had their feelings ripped out. They're like zombies. I'm amazed they're at the zoo at all."

"They're studying the worms because there is a plan to use them on the farms," said Micky, replacing his rag in his pocket. "The plebs are given enough freedom of thought for the greater good of the empire."

"I see," said Molly. "I know Princess Fang's plans, Micky. By stealing people's minds with her weird machine and by using hypnotism she wants to take over the world. I expect she's promised that you will be a *prince* of this empire if you help her. She's probably promised you whole countries for yourself! But, Micky, who, by the way, is going to do the hypnotizing now that *you* are not around?" Micky picked mud from his nails. "Because there are no other hypnotists in Ying Yongia, or whatever it's called, are there? That old Redhorn man who took you as a baby, he's dead, isn't he? You hypnotized everyone, didn't you?"

"Not *all* of them," Micky snarled back. "Redhorn had done lots before I started."

"But still," said Molly harshly, "because of you, lots of the lake people are hypnotized. That boy there can't think straight—all because of *you*. Didn't you ever think you might be ruining people's lives?"

"It's for the good of all," said Micky automatically.

"Sounds like Cribbins has brainwashed you too," said Molly curtly. "For the good of *all*? You are nearly a complete nutter, Micky. For the good of that snobby lot living up there, you mean!"

"The people are violent and unruly if they are not hypnotized," said Micky mechanically, as if reciting a boring poem. "They are dangerous and murderous. It is for everyone's safety that they must be on hypnotic leashes."

Molly couldn't help laughing. "Ha! The dangerous people around here are those lunatics up there! They're power mad and so spoiled and selfish that I shouldn't think they've *ever* done something nice for anyone else, not *ever*. Fang is wicked; so is Cribbins. They should both be put in loony bins." Molly pointed up at the boy, who was now being offered a stick of something woody to eat by his mother. "Think about him, Micky. He'll never know what it's like to have fun." Molly looked at her brother's downturned mouth. Micky probably hadn't ever had real fun either. She put her head in her hands. "I can't believe you did that, Micky. You've taken away his freedom to think for himself and you've killed his fun in life. That's the worst thing you can do to someone! That boy's not really living." Molly looked at her sulking brother and felt just a bit sorry for him. He had no idea what people were really like because he'd been told so many lies about them. "How did you hypnotize them?" she asked.

"Through a screen, that's how," said Micky tetchily. "They put blue makeup on my face and my eyes were decorated to look extra large. Then my face was filmed. There are big screens all around Lakeside. People would just look up at me and my eyes did the rest."

"And what was the password you used?"

Micky laughed cruelly. "You must be mad if you think I'll tell you that." But as the words came out of his mouth a thought bubble, cunningly summoned by Molly, appeared above his head. In it was a picture of a white meringue pudding on a dish. Molly digested the image.

"I know why you want the password," Micky continued, sneering. "You think you'll be able to dehypnotize your friend."

"Have *you* got any friends, Micky?" Molly said, her voice full of contempt. "No. If you did, you would understand how I feel. Rocky was ready to be your friend. You might have liked him." Molly, furious with frustration, now shouted as loudly as she could. "I CAN'T BELIEVE YOU ARE MY BROTHER!"

"I am not your brother," Micky replied uninterestedly.

Molly scrunched up her face with fury and then turned back to him. "How come we look so similar then, Potato Nose?" She glared at him in the dim light.

"We don't," he mumbled, turning away from her.

"How come Nurse Meekles believed I was your sister then? Believed it enough to help me escape, and you too?"

"She's gone mad."

Molly shook her head. "Have it your way, Micky. You'll see the truth in the end."

They sat staring away from each other for a little while, then Molly broke the silence.

"By the way, what is this place?"

Micky tutted disgustedly. "Are you a moron or something? I *told* you before. It's a zoological institute." He paused and sighed. "All the world's most amazing cross-breeds were developed here. Princess Fang's grandparents the Qinglings were very brilliant scientists, and they advanced the technology of genetic engineering. The institute still does scientific work. Mutations and stuff."

"Who does? That midget, Professor Selkeem?"

"I have no idea about him," Micky answered. "He looked like an evil little mutant boy to me. I've only visited this place a few times, when I was small. Meekles brought me."

"You know," Molly said, "I don't think Selkeem is hypnotized. But Wildgust and Tortussus—"

"Tort*illus*," Micky corrected her.

"Yes, him, well, it's obvious he and Wildgust *are*, and they did exactly what *Selkeem* asked them to do." Then she added mischievously, "Seems like Fang kept secrets from you, Micky." She said nothing more. Instead, welcoming Petula, who came to sit beside her, she thought and thought and thought. About the scary Professor Selkeem in the tree, about the cooking pot he'd spoken of, about the salivating dognakes and what they might eat for supper, and about Fang and her spied-upon kingdom.

Time ticked by. After a while Molly said, "You have to admit, it was quite nice of me to save you from drowning."

Micky snorted. "You were only trying to stop those people from seeing me. You weren't interested in saving me."

"Micky, you were much too far away for them to see you. In the next few seconds you would have gone under."

"A worm would have come up under me like it did you."

"I doubt you would have lifted a finger for me," Molly continued, ignoring him. "In fact, I have a nasty feeling that, if you could, you would definitely have pushed me in." Molly turned and sent a silent question to him. *Am I right?* At once, she saw the answer—horrible pictures of her disappearing in the mud hovered over Micky's head.

"Such a pity." Molly got up. "Right, I'm going back now." She felt the wall and prepared to walk along the thin ledge to the broader balcony part near the exit.

"D-don't leave me here. I'm ill. I might faint any second."

"I can't believe you!" Molly said. "On one hand you want me to drown, and on the other you want me here to help you in case you faint. Well, come with me now if you want."

And so the day slowly passed. Molly spent most of it stroking and hugging Petula.

At lunchtime two bottles of water were thrown in to them, along with a bag full of circular doughy sandwiches. These had a fish filling. Micky refused to touch even one. By the end of the day Molly's bottom was cold and numb from sitting on the metal ledge.

When Wildgust finally opened the door and smiled nastily down at them, Molly was almost glad to see him. Until he opened his mouth and reminded her of the professor's cooking pot.

"Dinnertime."

# Seventeen

Molly and Micky stepped out into the late afternoon sun and squinted and blinked as their eyes adjusted to the light. They were both completely filthy, caked in dried mud. Molly put Petula down. The heat of the day shimmered from the ground under their feet.

"You . . . disobeyed," Wildgust commented crossly, eyeing them. A scruffy black bird was perched on the hunch of his back. It had large yellow legs and claws that it dug into the brown silk of his cloak, and an intensely orange beak. It turned its bright blue eyes toward the children and their dog.

"Micky fell in. I had to help him out," said Molly.

At once the bird began to squawk. "Chaaarp, chaaaarp! Lay-er! Lay-er!"

Wildgust studied Molly suspiciously. Then he said, "Zoo—shut. You—animals'—food. No running. I—on to you like eagle on—mouse. This—private access—area. —No cameras here."

Molly nodded. Inside she was a storm of nerves. Did the hawk-man mean that she and Micky were tonight's food? Surely they wouldn't feed the zoo animals human meat? She summoned up a thought bubble to see what was passing through the hawk-man's mind. He was thinking of an eagle swooping down on a mouse with the face of a little girl, then of a bowl of food and a huge bearlike animal. Molly gave Micky a panicky sideways glance. He stared back stubbornly as though he couldn't care less what happened to them.

"Follow," the hawk-man said, giving a fierce hoot that made Molly jump.

So, being as good as gold but also trying to work out how to make a run for it, Molly stepped up to his side. She gripped her brother's wrist and yanked him with her. He limped lamely along. Petula followed. The black bird hopped onto Wildgust's head and curved its beak downward to stare at Micky.

"Does your bird talk a lot?" Molly asked. If she could charm the hawk-man, she thought, perhaps he would be kind to them. He turned and scowled. Molly looked down at the path and decided to keep quiet.

Micky on the other hand seemed to be on a suicide mission, for he suddenly sullenly said, "I hate birds."

Wildgust didn't reply, but the bird on his shoulder cocked its head and whistled.

"Chiiiirp, chaaaarp! Lay-er! Lay-er!"

"Especially ones that shout like that," Micky elaborated. "They're dirty and disease ridden and carry the flu. It was probably a bird like yours that spread that flu virus four hundred years ago that killed everyone."

Molly felt like hitting him. Why didn't he just shut up? If he carried on hurling abuse like this they'd probably get pushed into somewhere like the bearunkeys' cage. She scowled at him and clenched his arm even tighter.

Wildgust spat on the ground so that the gob landed directly under Micky's foot and Micky trod in it. "This mynah bird—genetically engineered—not carry disease.—Uses bird toilet.—Flushes away.—Eats everything.—WILL EAT YOU—WHEN I TELL IT TO."

The hawk-man strode ahead down a slope toward a large green shed.

Molly hung back to chide Micky. "What are you doing? If you carry on, we'll get chopped up into little pieces."

"I'm dead anyway," Micky replied bitterly, stopping to pause for breath. He wasn't used to walking around so much. "Animals carry infections. Everyone knows that! My immune system is so bad that if I catch anything I'll get much more ill than normal people. My temperature will go so high I'll have a fit and then die. Probably caught something nasty in that worm pit. Wouldn't be surprised if I had a fever tomorrow. The day after tomorrow I'll probably be dead, *all because of you*."

"You were the one who 'fell' in the pit," Molly quietly reminded him. "Anyhow, it's good for you to get ill sometimes. It can make your body stronger." Saying this, Molly reminded herself of the nasty orphanage mistress, Miss Adderstone, who had made her early life so miserable. Molly hadn't meant to be that harsh. Underneath, what Micky had said worried her. Could he really die from a cold?

"Move," the hawk-man called back to them impatiently.

They stood in front of a big red door. The label beside it, half covered by a plastic board, read:

**COW FL**

This breed produced by the
at the Yang Yongian Insti
**Eats s**
**Extremely**

Molly was sure that some terrible beast was beyond it. Above Wildgust's head she saw pictures of strange brown creatures. As he pressed a few digits on a control pad beside the entrance she wondered whether she ought to make a run for it now. And then the door swished open. A strong smell of cow manure and straw filled Molly's nostrils, and Wildgust tugged her and Micky into a cool, air-conditioned barn. Petula sniffed the air. Then she entered too.

They found themselves in a large central walkway with caged pens on either side. The floor was green concrete, and the ground in the pens was sloped toward steel bars and drains near the central aisle. Every so often, jets of water shot out of the ground, sluicing muck away down into them. And behind the bars was a sight so extraordinary that Molly, full of astonishment, forgot her fears.

"Cow flappers," Micky murmured.

The creatures were cows in every way, brown ones with patches of white on them, but these animals had huge tawny angel-like wings on their backs. The hunched hawk-man unlocked a cupboard at the end of the shed and dumped three big buckets into a bin of cow food. He handed one to Molly and one to Micky. Petula sniffed at the hay-smelling nuggets.

"Put—in troughs."

Molly eyed the winged cows in wonder and saw that each cow had large plastic clips holding its wings in place. "Do you let them out to fly?" she couldn't help asking. She remembered the creature she'd seen flying when she was on Fang's palace balcony, and how she'd thought it was just a trick of the light. Wildgust ignored her and walked to the end of the barn to distribute feed.

"There are wild ones," Micky said, holding his nose. "Princess Fang hates them. Hates anything ugly. It's one of her sports to get out her supergun and take potshots at them. She killed one last year."

"When did cow flappers first . . . um . . . happen?" asked Molly. She sprinkled some of the nuggets from her bucket into a trough. Micky gave her a look as if she was the stupidest person he'd ever met.

"You don't know anything, do you? Hundreds of years ago. That was when animal design really took off."

Molly looked at Wildgust, at his cockatoo-feathered head and his hawkish nose. *He must be genetically designed too,* she thought. Then she tipped some more food out for the cow flappers. The huge one closest to her suddenly made a very loud trumpeting noise from its rear end and the ground beneath it was covered with cowpats. Immediately the water squirters began cleaning the floor.

"Uuuuurgh!" Micky complained, stepping backward.

"Crumbs!" Molly said. "They say *bird* poo is supposed to be *good* luck if it hits you, but I don't think you could say the same about a flying cowpat." And as she said this, a very odd thing happened. It happened in a second and was gone in another. But Molly was certain that she'd seen it—a flicker of a smile had crossed Micky's face. "I mean," she continued, pretending that she hadn't spotted Micky's amusement, "I mean, if one of those landed on your head, you'd be—"

"You'd be chocolated," Micky said quietly, in a deadpan voice.

Then, seeing that Wildgust had turned and was coming toward them, Molly got on with quickly doling out the cow feed from Micky's bucket.

And so they fed the cow flappers. Molly patted a few on their dappled heads while Micky kept away, convinced that he would catch something nasty if he touched them.

Petula sat patiently by, sucking the stone that she'd picked up the day before. She was very relieved to be out of the worm pit. She glanced about the shed at the strange beasts, comforted by their farm smell. It was then that she noticed the scruffy black bird hopping toward her.

*That's brave of it,* Petula thought. She tilted her head and sent out a good-natured doggy greeting. To her surprise a "hello" came back and the bird winked at her.

*Had a bad day, haven't you?* it said. *Caught by those nasty dog-nakes and then dumped in the mud!*

For a moment Petula paused. She'd never met a bird that spoke dog before. But then she remembered her manners.

*I'm quite surprised that you think dog so fluently. Are all birds here like you?*

The bird hopped from one leg to the other. *No,* it thought back, whistling. *My breed is special.*

Petula was impressed. *Very special,* she thought.

The bird nodded. *So where are you from?* it asked.

Petula sighed, then dropped the stone she had been sucking onto the ground and lay down with her head in her paws. The bird seemed nice enough; she didn't see any harm in talking to it. In fact, she was pleased to have someone to confide in.

*We've come from a long time ago, I think,* she thought. *We came to find this boy here. He's a right pain in the rump. My mistress was put on a big machine up in the palace that made her skeleton show. She seems to have forgotten how to hypnotize people.*

*Hypnotize. Is she a hypnotist?*

*She was.*

*You seem to have some sort of power yourself,* the bird thought back. *I can feel it.*

*Maybe,* thought Petula. *I have done some hypnosis. But I don't know whether I'll ever be able to do it again. If I could, we wouldn't be in this mess. Can you do it?*

*I am a very fine mimic,* said the bird, giving a little whistle, *but only for tunes and people words.*

*Strange place this,* Petula observed, *with all the hypnotized people about.*

*Not good,* the bird thought back.

*And that hawk-man is a fierce one,* Petula added. *Smells of greasy feathers.*

*You have to watch him. That's for sure,* the black bird agreed. *By the way, what's your name?*

Petula gave a small bark and the bird mimicked it exactly. But before Petula had a chance to ask the bird its name, Micky was there with his hand around her collar.

"No, bad dog," he said.

*I think he likes you,* Petula thought to the black bird.

The bird whistled again and squawked to Micky, "Chaaaarp! Cheeeerp! Dawg good! Dawg good. Okay, leet-le chuppy!" And with a sudden flutter, he flew up to sit on Micky's shoulder.

"Urggh! Get off me!" Micky shouted, and brushing the bird off him he lurched off down the central aisle.

*That boy isn't quite sure who he is,* the bird thought to Petula. *My name's Silver. Pleased to meet you.*

*Nice to meet you too,* replied Petula.

Petula and Silver sat side by side and waited for Wildgust to shut the nugget trough. Then Silver hopped back on to his hump and off they set.

Wildgust led Molly and Micky along pathways to a white, water-filled enclosure where tubs of fish were waiting for them. Here happy red-and-pink penguins lay about in the still scorching sunlight. There was a sign on the fence.

**PINGINS**

This breed produced by the Qingling Team in 2420
at the Yang Yongian Institute of Zoology.

**Eats anything.**

**Extremely fierce.**

Wildgust handed Molly and Micky a bucket of fish each and then went to get one for himself.

"Are they at all like Antarctic penguins?" Molly asked Micky quietly, as she threw the birds their fish.

Wiping his hands on his pajama bottoms and then lodging them firmly in his dressing-gown pockets,

Micky shook his head. As though he was extremely bored by her question, he answered, "They've been genetically modified so they can take the heat. They bite. Bet we catch something from them. You wait till you're writhing around later like a caterpillar with stomachache. It's not a joke, you know. That's why I'm not frightened of that hawk-man—because I know I've caught something and I'm dead already."

Molly ignored him. "So what other animals have they got?"

Micky sighed peevishly and talked as though he was teaching a kindergarten child its lessons:

1. Clamels—camels with four humps, and claws, not hoofs.
2. Kangaraffes—obvious.
3. Piggybears—ditto.
4. Quogs—dogs mixed with ducks—webbed feet and beaks but otherwise dog.
5. Deer geese.
6. Sabrerats—giant, oversized rats.
7. Eagle hoppers—grasshoppers mixed with eagles.

"Could go on to fifty, but I'm not going to. There's tons of weird animals here. Lesson over."

Molly looked down at Micky's thin legs. His bony

knees showed through his muddy silk pajamas. He wouldn't make much of a meal for a hungry animal. She glanced up at Wildgust, who was emptying the last of his fish into the pingin pit. Was he taunting them by showing them all these hungry zoo animals? Or were they destined for the filthy tree midget's cooking pot? Molly's imagination whirred so that when Wildgust came up behind her and spoke, she jumped.

"Now—before night falls—feed hippishes," he declared.

"Hippishes?" Molly asked, worried, looking up at the darkening sky.

"Fish crossed with hippos," Micky whispered to her as Wildgust beckoned them on.

"What do they eat?" Molly asked nervously.

"Eleven-year-old girls," Micky replied.

# Eighteen

Contrary to what Micky had said, the hippishes didn't eat eleven-year-old girls. They were fed fish. After watching the creatures splash around for a bit, Wildgust led Molly and Micky, with Petula following, away from their pools, along a lake-side path lined with low cherry bushes.

"No cameras—here," he said simply. "Private access area.—Princess Fang—doesn't want to watch us.—We're too—ugly."

The sky was turning really dark now. Night was quickly drawing in.

Molly began to feel very worried again. She thought of the tiny professor's threats about cooking pots and his talk about supper, and she wondered whether they were being taken to some ghoulish chef. Without talking,

Wildgust led them toward a large circular building with a thatched roof. Micky leaned on Molly as he limped along, wincing from the pain in his legs.

Drumming was coming from the big hut. It stopped as soon as they entered.

Inside it was hot and humid. At a metal table sat two skinny, bright pink people with flamingo-thin legs and flamingo feet. The female wore a full black skirt and a red corsetlike waistcoat over a floppy white shirt, and the male wore black britches and a baggy green shirt. Their faces, crowned with locks of fair hair, were human, but were covered in pink feathers with huge, curved noses like flamingo beaks. They were drinking a yellow frothy liquid from tall glasses. On the next table sat a flamingo-boy and flamingo-girl, dressed like their parents. Their faces were feathered too and their small hands were leathery. And on the last table sat a tortoise-shelled woman, like the man they met earlier. Each table was laid with dull pewter cutlery and candles that stood in earthenware holders.

In the corner a doglike woman, with the droopy black ears and the wet nose of a spaniel but the face and hands of a human, held a drum. As Molly and Micky were led in, everyone turned to stare, as if they were the out-of-the-ordinary ones. Molly's hands began to sweat. She was reminded of a time at school once when, in front of everyone, she'd been given ten strokes of the cane across the back of her knees. She hoped she wasn't about to be punished now.

The drummer woman broke the silence.

"OOIIHH!" she shouted, to start the music up again, and then she picked up a rhythm on her drum.

An aroma of onions wafted toward Molly's nose. Micky looked petrified. Molly's heart skipped a beat as it struck her that they might be about to join the onions in their pan. Were she and Micky on tonight's menu?

Then Wildgust pushed them to the back of the room to where the tortoise-man, Tortillus, sat in the shadows.

"Sit!" he ordered in a dry voice, pointing a bony finger at the floor. Molly sank to the dirt ground, pulling Micky with her. Now faced with this low-lit room and the hungry animal-people, he had lost all his bravado of before.

"Do you think they'll eat us raw—sushi style?" he whispered as he shuffled his legs under him.

Molly shook her head and began to concentrate on mind reading Tortillus. This wasn't easy though. For when she tried to summon the tingling sensation on her scalp, a wave of nerves washed the electric feeling away. Finally she managed to make her hair feel static, as though it was standing up on end, and on cue a bubble popped up over the old man.

Inside the bubble were misty pictures of Micky with blue and green and purple lines shooting through his body and yellow and orange circles rotating around his head.

Tortillus's mind was throbbing with color like a disco light. It looked as if he was thinking of ways to cut Micky up. There was a long silence and then he declared, "You—ill."

"Yes," Micky quickly agreed. "Stomach problems. I've got rotten insides. My kidneys don't work properly, and my legs are weak . . . some sort of arthritis. I'm not a healthy specimen. I've got things you can catch. It wouldn't be sensible to eat me."

The tortoise-man squinted at Micky's head. Then he clicked his gnarled fingers. The tortoise-woman brought him a cotton apron and some white paper.

Molly was very alarmed. "You can't eat him," she blurted out.

But Tortillus ignored her and stepped toward Micky, pulling out of the pocket of the apron some sheets of white paper, a comb, and a pot of paste. A ripple of excitement passed around the room. Molly was bewildered. Was this a slaughter ceremony? Gripping Petula, she tried to think clearly and logically. *What would Rocky do?* she thought.

"Remove your dressing gown and your pajama top," the strange old man said.

Trembling, Micky did as he was told. His pale, thin chest showed all his ribs—bare flesh waiting to be cut. But Tortillus didn't come for him with a knife. Instead he began methodically combing Micky's curly hair up, away from his face, the comb catching in the clods of dried mud. Then the tortoise-man started to daub paste along the edges of one of the pieces of paper. Once it was wet with paste, he stuck it on Micky's forehead and wound the paper around his head. He continued dabbing and sticking until Micky had a crown of paper glued to his head. Then Tortillus wrapped a bandana around the crown.

Behind him the tortoise-woman was heating oil in a large pottery jar. Tortillus took it from her.

"You can't put that on my head!" Micky exclaimed, pulling away. "You'll burn me!"

Molly got ready to attack the old man if he brought the hot oil anywhere near Micky. But when he stuck his finger in the oil and left it there, she saw that it could only be warm.

As the drumbeats became more regular and solid, the light in the hut was dimmed, and slowly Tortillus began tipping the warm oil into the well of the paper crown on Micky's head.

"Ancient herb recipe. Oil soaks into skull. Close eyes."

Molly was horrified. It sounded like Tortillus was preparing Micky with some sort of marinade. Quickly she glanced about the room to see how difficult it would be to escape. Wildgust stood in the corner, like a perched hawk waiting to swoop. Tortillus meanwhile dropped onto his knees and pulled his head inside his shell, so that he looked like some strange headless creature. The powerful drumbeats made the hut claustrophobic and cramped.

"Ahhhh . . . !" Tortillus muttered from within his shell. He dropped his hands beside him and flapped them a bit before bringing them up to Micky's shoulders. Petula whimpered. "Hmmmm," the headless tortoise-man hummed. Now it was as if his hands were feeling for some invisible thing in the air around Micky's body. He knelt on the floor and touched Micky's foot. He put his thumb on Micky's knee and tapped it. He got up and cupped his hands over Micky's head as though he was concentrating on extracting something from him. He prodded Micky's shoulder blades and spine. Molly felt sure that in the next second he was going to start to strangle him. And then she jumped as his head popped out of his shell.

To her complete surprise he said, "You poor boy."

The drums stopped. As they did, Molly realized two things at once, and both hit her like great swinging clubs.

The first was that Tortillus meant Micky no harm. The second was that he was *not hypnotized*.

"Please lean slowly forward toward this bowl," Tortillus was saying to Micky in a gentle voice. Micky did as he was asked, and oil from the crownlike bucket on his head tipped into it. The old man removed the crown and wiped the oil from Micky's forehead.

"You may put on your clothes," he said and then to Molly, "The others aren't hypnotized either." Molly nodded amazedly at him. "I am Tortillus," he went on, taking Molly's hand in his own and shaking it firmly. Molly nodded. "And you are?"

"Me, um, my name's Molly—Molly Moon, and this is my dog, Petula. And this is my brother, Micky, who we came here to find. And, um, Mr. Tortillus, why and how are you not hypnotized?"

No one said a word. The animal-people in the giant hut all looked on expectantly, as if they wanted Molly to talk. So she did. But as the sentences flowed from her mouth Molly saw that her story sounded like a pack of lies.

"I'm a time traveler and a hypnotist, you see," she explained. "At least I *was*, but Princess Fang put me on this machine and stole all my hypnotic knowledge and my special crystals, so now I'm not a time traveler either. She took my friend Rocky too and had him hypnotized—"

"By whom?" Tortillus asked.

"By . . ." Molly paused. Instinct told her that it was best not to tell Tortillus that Micky was partly responsible for all the hypnotized people who lived around the lake under the sweltering sun.

"By Redhorn or by Axel?" Tortillus asked.

Molly faltered. Tortillus seemed well-informed about Fang's inner circle. She had never heard of a hypnotist called Axel, and Micky had said that Redhorn was dead.

"Who's Axel?"

"He's a hypnotist I knew once. You didn't meet him?"

"No. All the hypnotists are dead." Molly made a mental note to find out more about this Axel person.

"Then who hypnotized your friend?" The old man's eyes bored into Molly.

"I don't know," she lied. "Look, all I want to do is go back with Rocky and Petula to my own time." Molly suddenly realized she had omitted Micky from this return trip. The fact was, she didn't like him enough to want to take him home. To the tortoise-man she went on, "And Micky can come too—if he wants. And . . .

and I don't really expect you to believe all this because it sounds crazy, but actually it's not crazy. Believe it or not, it's all true."

"Hmmm," Tortillus turned his attention back to Micky. "And what about you, boy? If what your sister is saying is true, do you want to go back in time with her?" He scrutinized Micky's face. "What do you say, boy?"

Micky pursed his mouth, hesitating. Then he stammered, "I'm—I'm ill. Don't think I would live long there, five hundred years ago. I'd die. I'm safer here. All the illnesses they have in those times . . ." His eyes darted timidly up to meet the old tortoise-man's.

"Hmmm."

Micky sat down beside Molly and put his hand in his dressing-gown pocket. Molly could see that he was fingering his comfort rag. With his other hand he gave Petula a stroke. Molly was very surprised. She doubted Micky had ever touched a dog before.

Then Tortillus took a deep breath. "I have news for you, Micky." Micky looked up. "Although you are frail and weak, and your legs hurt because your muscles have wasted away, you are not actually *remotely* ill. You are not sick at all."

Micky gave him a patronizing look. "I am sorry to disappoint you," he objected rather pompously, "but you really don't know what you're talking about. I've had the best doctors in the world visit me. Experts. Real professionals. Are you trying to say they were all wrong? Don't be ridiculous!"

The tortoise-man smiled. "What I am saying is true. Believe me, I am a healer, an energy man. And I tell you, young Micky, your energy is good. But it has been trampled on. Somewhere along the line bad energy has influenced you. Your spirit feels flattened, as though something has been sitting on it, holding it down. This something wants you to feel small, worthless, ill, weak, useless, powerless. Why is that? What is this thing that has been suffocating your life force?"

Thousands of feet up, at the top of Mont Blanc, Princess Fang stood in a purple organza dress in her crescent-shaped drawing room. Above her was a massive skylight, and on one side of the room was a long, high picture window, so that the overall effect was of being outside. The dark evening sky with its froth of silver stars hung above and the mountain's crags and its splendid moonlit views dropped away below.

The princess sipped at a pink cocktail. Reaching for a glass bowl, she ate a few honey-coated almonds. Then she stared down at Lakeside. The valley below was dark except for lots of tiny twinkling lights that came from the fishermen's boats on the lake. Taking a yo-yo from her pocket, the princess wound it up and let it spin away from her finger. And there she stood in silence, the only sound being her luminous yo-yo shooting up and down, like a trapped animal on the end of a string. Then the princess began singing.

*"Milly had a little lamb,*
*It used to leap so high.*
*It leaped into a butcher's shop*
*And now it's mutton pie."*

She wound her yo-yo up tightly and put it in her pocket.

"I will get you, Miss Milly and young Micky," she said confidently. "In fact, I am going to lure you in. Just like dose fishermen entice de fish with de bwight lights on deir boats, I will lure you. What we need is some bait. Somefing to get you up to de palace again. For dat's what you want, isn't it? You want your mind back, Milly Moon. And Micky, you want your medicine. Just like a couple of dumb fish you'll come. You wait and see."

# Nineteen

In the hot communal hut Molly and Micky tucked into plates of lakeweed bake. It was surprisingly good, as the lakeweed actually tasted a bit like broccoli and was mixed with crispy potatoes. What was more, Molly was very pleased to find that the sauce served alongside it tasted very like tomato ketchup. Petula was gobbling up chicken giblets. When she had finished she curled up beside Molly's feet and fell asleep.

Tortillus came and sat down opposite Molly and Micky and took out his pipe. "So," he said, pinching a fingerful of tobacco out from a pouch, "I expect you've got *lots* of questions to ask me."

"You bet," Molly replied with her mouth full. "Like why aren't you hypnotized and who is the tree man?"

"I'll tell you everything, and he's a boy, you know,"

Tortillus replied, "but first I have a few last questions for you. How did you escape from the palace?"

"Through a secret door in the laundry rooms," Molly replied, buttering some bread and dolloping some of the tomato sauce onto it. "There's a nice lady up there called Nurse Meekles—she's the only nice person there—well, she told us about the secret door. It leads to some tunnels inside the mountain. Then the dognakes found us and carried us down to a hidden hatch in the elethumper's cage." She took a gulp from her glass of water and tilted her head questioningly. "Did you know about the laundry room door?"

"It's news to us," Tortillus replied. "We knew about the dognakes' tunnels—those have been there for thousands of years; they were made by meltwater rushing through the mountain. But I never knew they led to the palace. Hmm. I wonder who built that door." He watched Micky picking at his food. "And it's interesting Nurse Meekles helped you. She was Axel Meekles's wife, you know."

"Really?" Molly exclaimed. "The other hypnotist?"

"Yes. He was a good man too. Like his wife. And I have a feeling he must still be alive. Otherwise, who else would have hypnotized your friend Rocky?"

Molly felt her stomach twist, for her feelings and her logic were tugging at each other inside her. Part of her, the warm friendly part, wanted to tell Tortillus the truth about Micky, but the other part, the suspicious, calculating part, refused to let that happen, in case it led to trouble. So she changed the subject.

"How come you aren't hypnotized?" she asked again. And deciding to check that Tortillus's thoughts and words matched, she summoned a bubble to appear above his head.

"It's a long story," Tortillus began, "that begins like this. We animal-people weren't born like this, living like the animals you have seen in the zoo. We used to live up at the palace." He paused. "We are the true royal family of Mont Blancia. I am King Klaucus, and this"—he gestured to the tortoise-woman—"is my wife, Belsha, the queen. Wildgust"—he pointed to the hawk-man, who loitered in the shadows by the door—"is my brother, and these people"—he indicated the flamingo family and the dog-woman on the drum—"are our cousins." In the bubble above Tortillus's head a family picture appeared. All the members looked human. Tortillus continued. "Twelve years ago we were overthrown. You mentioned the hypnotist Redhorn."

Molly nodded. "Yes, he's the man who stole Micky from the hospital when he was a baby." Micky frowned as though this wasn't true, but Tortillus didn't register his look.

"Yes, well, at that time, twelve years ago, there was a very brilliant scientist up at the palace. She worked for us. She was the only daughter of the Qinglings. They, I am sure you have gathered by reading the signs around the zoological institute, were the team responsible for all the absolutely genius discoveries here to do with animal genetic design." Molly nodded. "Well," continued Tortillus, "the Qinglings were good people and brilliant scientists, but unfortunately they had a bad daughter. Her name was Fen Fang Feng Qingling. And she was the mother of Princess Fang." Tortillus sucked on his pipe. "To cut a long story short, Fen Fang Feng teamed up with Redhorn. Under her orders he hypnotized the people of our kingdom. She had the army hypnotized too. My family and I were locked up in the palace prisons and she pronounced herself *Queen* Qingling. But having us in the dungeons wasn't enough to satisfy her.

"Queen Qingling had all her parents' scientific knowledge at her fingertips. Unfortunately she used it for evil purposes. She took some of the mutagens that had been discovered by her parents and injected all my family with them. We were changed into what you see now. She even made up our names for us, as if we were her toys. 'Tortillus,' as you see, suits me down to the ground. These names have stuck and we have been using them ourselves for years now. We were banished to Lakeside, to live here at the zoological institute. For Queen Qingling, like Princess Fang, her daughter and heir, loathed anything ugly and so wanted us out of sight."

Molly didn't like the pictures she was seeing in the thought bubbles above his head. She now believed Tortillus was telling the truth, so she just listened to the deposed king's story.

"She had us hypnotized by Redhorn too," he continued, "but as you can see, his hypnotism didn't work. We can't be hypnotized. It's a side effect of the mutagen injections. This is our one strength. For Queen Qingling never knew we weren't hypnotized, because we *acted* hypnotized and have done so ever since.

"Princess Fang is even more dangerous. We run the institute and we watch. We watch our people live in this ridiculous theaterlike land, where fairy-tale costumes and nursery rhymes rule. Princess Fang forces everyone to behave as though they are her playthings. I think that's part of the reason she keeps them hypnotized, so that they are like her toys—and she calls us mutants!" Tortillus wiped his eyes and sighed. "For twelve years we have waited for a time when we might take our revenge and get our kingdom back and our people dehypnotized. I know of her insane plans to take over the entire world. Princess Fang must be stopped."

Belsha put a bowl of orange bananas on the table. "Help yourself," she said.

Molly smiled at her. "Have you never tried to fight back?" she asked.

Tortillus shook his head sadly. "There is no point. There are too few of us. Once we made the mistake of sending someone up to the palace, in a food plane. He was darted and killed. We cannot risk that again. For if Princess Fang discovers we are not hypnotized, she will have us all executed."

Molly gulped. So Princess Fang was capable of executing people. This bloodthirsty streak made her a thousand times more frightening. And Molly saw that King Klaucus and his family were in a worse predicament than her. She might have lost her freedom, but at least she still had her own body.

"Who is the tree boy?" Molly asked.

"His name is Professor Selkeem," said the tortoise-man. "He is related to Princess Fang. She didn't want him at the palace but because he is her relation she can't just get rid of him. Four years ago he arrived with all his test tubes and chemicals, and she instructed us to do his bidding. She gave him free run of the zoological institute and ordered us 'zooeys,' as he calls us, to do his work. She loathes him because of how he looks. *Why* he looks like he does isn't clear—perhaps she gave him a drug too, or perhaps he gave it to himself. He may have, for he is mad. He is only young, but like the princess he has knowledge beyond his years. It's as if his brain has been stuffed with so much knowledge that it's made him go crazy." Tortillus puffed pensively on his pipe and a cloud of smoke rose into the air. "Like Princess Fang, he is a scientist. His tree house is his laboratory—a dangerous place with all sorts of dubious experiments. He is working on more mutating drugs for Princess Fang, we are sure. She will use the drugs for some foul purpose. He is very peculiar in the head and not to be trusted. Today he may hide you and your brother, but *tomorrow* he may give you up to her. So beware of him."

"Does Princess Fang ever talk to him?"

"Sometimes. He has a direct link to the palace via a communication system, which he shouts into, when he's not talking to himself. And since he first came here, he has been summoned back to the palace twice. Perhaps Fang must put him on that mind machine you talked about, for each time he comes back his brain seems even more scrambled and his conversation even more of a riddle." Tortillus reached a long bony finger up to his neck and scratched the skin just inside his shell. "He once tried to get me to drink one of his foul brews.

Heaven knows what that might have turned me into. I threw it over the balcony when he wasn't looking."

Just then Silver flapped over and landed on the table. Micky put down his fork when he saw the black bird. But when Silver whistled, "Chaaaarp! Chaarp! Eat ap! Eat ap!" he relaxed and, Molly was shocked to see, he even gave the bird a morsel of bread.

Molly took a banana and began to peel it. Its inside was bright orange and it tasted like pineapple. She considered whether to tell everyone about her mind-reading skills but decided to keep it her secret for now.

Tortillus continued. "So, as I said, Molly, we have been waiting for years for an opportunity to overpower the palace. Now we meet you, a once-brilliant hypnotist. Perhaps"—he smiled and looked around the room—"you have come to set us free."

"I wish I could." Molly sighed. "With all my heart I do. But Princess Fang stole all my skills. The mind machine took all my hypnotic knowledge from me."

"Tell me about the machine."

"Well . . ." Molly described everything she had seen. "And as soon as the technology is there, Princess Fang will suck the *talent* out of me and then she'll have my hypnotic knowledge *and* the talent to use it. And then, once she's a time-traveling hypnotist, well, there will be nothing to stop her from taking over the world."

Tortillus nodded gravely as he digested what Molly had said. Micky, Molly noticed, was listening carefully too.

Tortillus tutted. "So simple and yet so impossible! If only we knew how to put the knowledge back into your brain. We'll just have to find a way to get you wearing that skullcap again."

"I know," Molly agreed. "But *how*, Tortillus? Princess Fang and her scientists are probably the only ones who know how it works."

"Have you seen the scientists?"

"Not exactly, although there seem to be some very scientific-looking children up there. And some women in smart suits."

Tortillus suddenly leaned forward and seized Molly's hand. "I believe there is a chance now, Molly. You must too."

Molly tried to smile. Tortillus made everything sound so simple, but what he was suggesting was impossible. And yet his hope was infectious. Molly couldn't help feeling excitement and she noticed a wonderful sense of something else was bubbling up inside her too: optimism.

Later that night Wildgust, giving every indication that it was a thoroughly unwelcome chore, took Molly and Micky to a hut by the starlit lake. Inside it had a dry, hard earth floor and two very basic beds with pillows and sheets. There was no need for blankets as the night was warm.

"Sleep," Wildgust said gruffly, but he patted Petula gently on the head.

From his shoulder Silver imitated him. "Slaap!" he squawked, adding, "Swet drems."

"Good night," Molly replied, and quickly she summoned a thought bubble to appear above Wildgust's head. Strange pictures were painted there. The hawkman was thinking about dark birds flying around the moon and then a view of the lakeside town from above. Next there was an image of Tortillus asleep on a pile of wood.

He left, locking the door behind him.

"He's creepy, isn't he?" Molly said to Micky. "Like he's angry or something." But Micky wasn't listening.

"Don't suppose there's an ionic cleaner here," he complained, inspecting the hut's bathroom.

"What's an ionic cleaner?" Molly asked.

Micky looked at Molly as though she had just asked what water was. "Oh, I forgot you're from the Stone Age. It's a machine that you step into and it cleans you with laser light and positive ions."

"What, instead of a shower or a bath?"

"Yes. But as I suspected, all they've got here is water."

"What's wrong with that?" Molly asked.

"Full of germs. I'm not going to risk it." Micky sank down on the bed, the mud on his dirty dressing gown cracking and falling in flakes on to the ground. "Ow, my legs. They're so sore." Molly watched him rolling up his pajamas and rubbing his leg. "What are you looking at?"

"What do you think of what Tortillus said about you not really being ill?" Molly asked.

Her brother shrugged. "He's wrong," he said.

"But—but it could be true," Molly mused. "I mean, if you think about it, all your life Cribbins has been telling you how sick you are, hasn't she? *Why would she do that?* I tell you why—because if you were healthy and strong you would be too powerful for her to control."

Micky continued to massage his leg, as if completely uninterested in what Molly was saying.

"Look Micky, with all her other hypnotists dead, you are, or rather were, the *only* hypnotist Fang had. Princess Fang needed you to keep hypnotizing all the people, didn't she? Without you she wouldn't have the people under control and she would lose her power. So of course this is the *last* thing in the world that she ever wanted you to know. She was probably even frightened that you might hypnotize *her* or take power yourself. So her and Cribbins had to make you think you were sick—so sick that you needed them. I know you won't believe this, but I heard Cribbins talking to herself once about you. 'Keep him down,' she said. 'Don't destroy him, but keep him down.' I didn't get it at the time, but now it's obvious. They wanted you to think you were nothing, Micky. Think about it. Even your name! Micky *Minus*. Minus is less than nothing. Cribbins gave you that name to make you feel like a nobody!"

Micky stared sullenly at the floor, grinding his teeth. Molly expected him to suddenly shout at her to tell her that he *was* ill, that Tortillus was an idiot and didn't know what he was talking about. But instead a very strange thing happened. Micky looked up and the agitation on his face melted. His mouth dropped open as he finally saw the truth.

"It's—it's true," he stammered. For a moment the two of them stared at each other, both stunned by the horrible truth of Micky's situation.

"So Nurse Meekles was right to get you out of there, Micky," Molly went on more kindly. "She's the only sane one up there, and she cares about you, Micky. You're better off here."

Micky frowned as he thought it all through. "This is freaking me out," he said quietly. He ran his hand through his oily, curly hair and turned to look out at the lake. "But I'm not your brother," he added. He pulled his comfort rag out of his pocket and began to rub it between his fingers. "Just give me some space, would you?" Petula jumped onto the bed and sat beside him as though in sympathy.

Molly left Micky to his thoughts. She knew that it must be very scary to see that you had been used like a slave all your life. She got up, went to the bathroom, and ran the tap. Out came very normal-looking water. She scratched her head. Her scalp was itchy from the dried gel.

It was a relief to get all the mountain-tunnel dirt and the worm-pit mud off her and to get the gel out of her hair. She liked the slimy weed soap, and the earthy, warm water was comforting. For a moment, as a stream of it tipped over her head and down her face, she could imagine she was back in Briersville Park on a hot summer's night. Lucy and Ojas might be downstairs, cooking supper. Primo and Rocky might be playing poker in the sitting room, with their hippie friend, Forest, tied up in some yoga knot on the floor. She wished with all her heart that she was back there. She felt powerless without her hypnotic skills. To Molly, the idea of time traveling was now as impossible as it might feel to any ordinary person. As she stood in the shower Molly ransacked her brain. Surely there must be some scrap of hypnotic knowledge still there, some snippet of information that the jellyfish machine had missed. But there wasn't.

Was she destined to stay here *forever* in this time—five hundred years away from her family and friends? If she and the animal-people couldn't get her hypnotic knowledge back, would she have to live hidden at the institute forever? And what about Micky? She couldn't trust that he wouldn't *eventually* give her away. Molly wished she'd never come. And she couldn't bear that she'd lost Rocky. Poor Rocky. Somewhere, deep down inside that hypnotized shell, the real Rocky was longing to get out. Molly could hardly stand to think of it. And her tears mixed with the Lakeside water and ran down the drain.

As Molly dried herself she looked in the mirror. Her face looked gaunt and her eyes had gray shadows under them.

"Come on. Pull yourself together," she whispered, tapping her face in the mirror with her finger. She made a large thought bubble appear above her head and forced it to fill with positive images. She imagined Rocky and her escaping in a helicopter with Micky and Petula. She thought of them all being back home, cooking together in the kitchen and then swimming in the Briersville Park pool with Amrit the elephant. "You can do it, Molly," she said to herself. "You've gotten out of other piles of mess. There must be a way out of this. You must think positively."

Getting back onto the jellyfish machine was her only chance. But who would know how to work it? She thought about Micky. Would he help her? He knew the combination code to the machine room door, but he'd said he didn't know how the machine actually worked. She must check whether he was lying. She didn't feel he was entirely on her side yet. Though he should be, after all the trouble she'd gone to just to meet him, he might need some more persuading. Maybe tomorrow he would start facing up to the truth. Molly put on a pair of lightweight cotton pajamas that hung on a peg on the wall and padded out to the bedroom.

Micky lay on his bed with his back to her. He was looking through the window at the lake. It was illuminated by what looked like thousands of twinkling fairy lights.

"What are they?" Molly asked, picking up Petula to give her a cuddle.

"Fishermen. The lights attract the fish. It's an old-fashioned way of fishing."

"It looks very pretty," said Molly. Micky didn't reply.

And so they went to bed in silence. Micky was asleep as soon as his head hit the pillow, but Molly couldn't drop off. Her mind was as busy as a city station. She went over to the window to look out at the lake. It was then that she noticed Micky's dressing gown, lying on the floor. She bent down and, a little guiltily put her hand in the pocket. She was interested to see his comfort rag. But instead of material, Molly's fingers curled around a piece of plastic. She held it up to the moonlight and gasped. The small strip of plastic was practically identical to the strip that she had been carrying around. The only difference was that instead of having the letters GAN TWIN printed on it, Micky's strip had the words ST. MICHAEL'S HOSPITAL and then MALE LO.

Molly was stunned. She crept over to her jumpsuit and retrieved her half of the plastic baby bracelet. Now she put the two together.

● St. Michael's Hospital MALE LOGAN TWIN ○○○○○

The identity band was complete. Silently Molly replaced Micky's half in his dressing gown and put hers down the side of her sneaker for safekeeping. That was why he was called Micky, she thought. It was an abbreviation of Michael. And the fact that he treasured the scrap of plastic Nurse Meekles had given him showed that Micky really did care about finding his real family, no matter what he might pretend. Staring up at the moon, Molly decided that she would find the perfect moment and show him how the pieces fitted together. Once he saw that he'd have to believe he was her brother!

Then something caught Molly's attention. A dark shape flew in front of the moon. Like a cloaked vampire the monstrous creature seemed to be part man, part bird. Molly quickly shut the window and jumped into bed. Snuggling Petula, she was soon asleep too.

# Twenty

In the early hours of the morning, when it was still dark outside, Molly was woken by Petula stirring and by a knock at the door of the hut. The key turned and Wildgust entered with a candle. The light from it flickered up over his brown, feathered cheeks. Micky rolled over and pulled his sheet up over his shoulders. Silver hopped onto the edge of his bed and sidestepped up to his face.

"Chierrrp! Cheeep! Out bed, lazzee bons," he whistled in Micky's ear, pecking at his earlobe. Since Micky was still half dreaming, this made him laugh. "Made laf, made laf, cheeeerp!" the bird trilled, fluttering up to perch on Wildgust's shoulder.

"The professor wants to see you both," Wildgust said. "So you'd better get out of bed fastish."

"Why?" Molly asked worriedly, bending to reach for her dirty jumpsuit.

"I don't know," Wildgust answered, shrugging his humped shoulders.

Soon Micky, wearing his grubby dressing gown and pajamas, and Molly were walking through the cool morning air, with Petula trotting close by, toward the giant tree in the center of the zoo. As they approached, Molly studied the podlike huts and rope ladders within its high branches. She tried to work out how wobbly it would be to walk on the swinging wooden balconies up there. Lower down were the bigger pods, and in the center was a round, yurtlike chamber with chimneys, out of which poured grayish-green smoke. Professor Selkeem's faithful dognakes lay asleep about the yurt, their bodies wrapped around the branches like bracelets.

"You don't think Princess Fang is in there, do you?" Molly asked as they stumbled along.

"No," Wildgust replied briskly. "Would have seen her flycopter arrive. Don't talk any more now. I'm supposed to be hypnotized. Remember?" From the thought bubbles above his head Molly saw that he was telling the truth, for there were pictures of Princess Fang in her bed, as Wildgust imagined it, up at the palace.

They came to the bottom of the tree, to a low door that was carved into the trunk there.

"In—you—go," said Wildgust in his "hypnotized" voice. He pushed the tree entrance open and ushered Molly, holding Petula, and Micky through. Nudging them toward some steps, he shut the door.

Darkness engulfed them. Then, as their eyes grew accustomed to the light, they noticed a faint glow coming from above and, holding on to a wooden banister, both began to climb the massive tree's internal spiral stairs.

"So you've never heard of Professor Selkeem before?" Molly asked Micky in the darkness.

"No, never," he replied tetchily. He sounded very irritated, as though annoyed by Fang's secrecy. Molly felt she'd won a point over the princess.

"He's a filthy little mite, isn't he?" Micky went on, changing the subject. "Bet he's got lice. *Pediculus.* That's the Latin word for *louse*."

"Just hope he doesn't want to roast us alive," Molly said.

At the top a door swung open to reveal a big, wooden space with a curved wall. It smelled sulfurous, like bad eggs.

Then, like a scene from a horror film, a giant seed-pod, which hung from the ceiling in front of them, opened like a clam, and the leathery-skinned professor popped out with his favorite dognake. Petula shrank into Molly's arms.

"Welcome to my humble abode," he said with a sinister smile, holding his loincloth as though it were a ballet dress and doing a strange little curtsy. "I'm fuddled and muddled but I won't be puddled. Sharp teeth I've got. See?" He smiled and showed them a row of yellowing teeth. "Haven't brushed them for years." Then he eyed Micky in his filthy pajamas. "You're a dirty bit of vermin, aren't you?"

Micky stood mute, rooted to the spot in panic. But Molly, remembering that in bad situations good manners were always a sensible idea, spoke.

"Pleased to see you too," she lied. "Really nice." The disheveled, wrinkled boy stepped toward her. He reached up and put a small, creased, lizardlike finger on her throat. Molly gulped. "Nice place you've got here," she said. "We'd love to have a look about." She looked in the boy's Chinese eyes. There was a glint of madness there. He was only six or seven, but the expressions on his face as he stared at her suggested that he was older. Molly knew that he'd probably been on the mind machine and wondered what worlds of knowledge his child's mind held. Too much had been stuffed into his young head. His hands were filthy, and his nails looked as though he'd been scraping up black paint with them. His face was dirty too. Molly wondered what had happened to his parents.

She decided to probe his mind. In an instant her scalp was tingling and her hair felt as though it was standing on end. A hazy thought bubble, with streaks of gray and brown in it, rose above the boy's head.

He was thinking of Molly beside Micky, and how they looked exactly the same. Then two giant peas in a pod filled the bubble, but were quickly replaced by two identical fleas, then two identical knees, and then two matching keys. He'd obviously got that they were twins. Then glancing out of the window at a sky golden with the rising sun, he suddenly said, "New day, the last day for some. I suppose you haven't eaten breakfast?" And the picture in the bubble above his head morphed into one of Molly and Micky on a giant slice of toast. Molly felt incredibly nervous and her stomach leaped as though genetically modified, extrafluttery butterflies were flapping around in it. Did the professor plan to eat them? As he bent down and patted his pet dognake on the nose—"Good boy, Schnapps!"—she gave Micky a worried glance.

Shakily Molly and Micky followed the tree boy into the main part of the oval-shaped hut. It looked like a real science laboratory built for six-year-olds. Revoltingsmelling liquids bubbled away in test tubes and glass vials. To one side was a very strange experiment. A large, glass spherical vat was being heated from underneath by a blue flame. In it were cracked rocks that were smoldering hot. And the green fumes that curled from the rocks went up a glass tube in the lid of the vat, into a transparent, doughnutlike container, where they were sucked through a spongy substance and emerged as a clear liquid. This liquid flowed down a pipe where it collected until a big drip of it was ready to plop out. When the drop fell, it passed through a very strong light and splashed into a jar. On the wall behind the falling drip, the light that had passed through it hit a screen, where it showed its colors—a wonky rainbow, murky and mud tinted. More green fumes from the sponge above spiraled up a glass chimney out of the roof of the laboratory hut. The innocent-looking clear substance in the jar looked like water, but, Molly suspected, was probably something badly toxic. Maybe it was even the dangerous mutating drug that Tortillus had said the professor was working on for Princess Fang so that she could turn other people into new forms of mutants.

Along the wall was a shelf filled with jars containing pickled animal bodies. Small mice and voles, a two-headed squirrel, and a cat with nine tails were a few of the dead creatures on display.

And at the far end of the room were glass boxes with squeaking animals inside. Then to Molly's horror, as they were led around the workbench, the sight of a dead meerkat-type animal, lying pinned out on a chopping board, greeted them. Here too, hanging from a beam, were strings with shriveled animal hearts, livers, and kidneys threaded onto them. Molly felt nauseous.

The boy opened a drawer. It was full of dried-up flat things. Some of them were covered in green mold.

"Toast?" he inquired nastily, pulling a withered slice out. "Here's a nice one from last week."

"I'm not hungry," both Micky and Molly said at once. "But, er, thank you very much," Molly hastily added.

"Really? Well I hope you don't mind if I do." The boy picked out the moldiest, greenest toast that he could find and took a bite. "Marvelous," he declared, crunching it between his small jaws. "So good for one's skin." Then he reached for a glass of something red and sticky and gulped it down. Molly was sure it was blood.

To stop herself from being sick she looked away, up at the walls of the building. There were fist-sized holes everywhere, as if someone made it their habit to hack away at the wooden walls.

"What are all the holes for?" she asked, hugging

Petula as closely as she could.

"Spies," the boy answered. "They're all over the place. Want my secrets. My inventions." He turned to a fridge marked SAMPLES, and opened it, revealing rows of jars containing red glistening things and plates piled with very unappetizing mounds of brown worms. As he poured himself some more of his evil brew, he muttered to himself. "They know about the laundry room door. So what are you going to do?"

As if in answer, another voice, but a higher voice that also came out of his mouth, replied, "Are they rats? That's the question. If they're rats, get the rat catcher around. The zooeys could do it. They're hypnotized. Just get Wildgust on to do it. He's got a nasty streak in him. Peck, peck and it's done."

The boy's two voices spoke in turns.

"Maybe you can trade with them. Fang wants them badly."

"Why?"

"For her maniac plans. Keep them safe for now though. Don't use the chips yet. Lock them up."

Just then there was a hissing noise outside the laboratory window. The professor ran over to look out. On the far wall of the zoo, Molly saw over his shoulder, was a giant screen. Princess Fang's spoiled face appeared on it.

"Good morning and hickowy, dickowy, dock!" she proclaimed with a laugh.

"Oh, blow your fat head up!" the boy shouted at her. "Put scabs in your mouth and suck out the gunk."

But of course Princess Fang up at the palace was completely oblivious to his mad ranting. "Oh, have I got news for you," she said. Her hair was perfectly coiffed into a hexagonal construction. "We have a special summit meeting tomowow. Some vewy important, intelligent people will be flying in from all over de world. So we must entertain dem. We'll need performance number firty-one, from the Yang Yongian Entertainment Catalog, wid all de twimmings. So get your costumes bwushed up and put dem on! Warm up your singing voices! Put on your dance shoes, evewyone! Because tomowow evening it's showtime at de palace!" The screen fizzed and she was gone.

"Ridiculous, sick-in-the-head plastic doll!" the young professor exclaimed venomously.

"But look," his other voice piped up with a shrill squeak. "What are those guards doing in my zoo?"

"She can't have them," the first voice whispered back. "They're *mine*." Then he turned to Molly and Micky. "They've come to get you, but they shan't have you. *I'm* having you." He put his hands on the windowsill. "EEEEEEEK!" he shrieked. At the same time three burly guards, hypnotized and dressed like toy soldiers, came charging along the path toward the tree house. The professor leaned out.

"Who goes there, in your underwear?" he shouted rudely.

The hypnotized guard beneath him, unable to be either angry or amused, declared, "Her—Royal Highness—has instructed us to—search your premises."

"Poppycock and weasels in a test tube!" the boy replied. "I'll eat my rotten legs if you find them here. So come up—it'll be a squeeze though because it's a small door and a tight staircase, pink face."

Below, Molly heard the guards mumbling to one another as they squeezed through the tiny door. She found herself instinctively reaching for her clear crystal, to stop time, but of course it wasn't around her neck. Even if it had been, she had no time-stopping powers now anyway.

"Where shall we hide?" she cried in desperation, hoping that the professor had some sort of plan. Just then, a door to the side of them opened. Wildgust was standing there.

"Hide them," the boy said, and Wildgust nodded. He pulled Molly, with Petula and Micky, out on to the tree-house balcony and shut the door behind them.

"We must leave the zoo immediately. They will search everywhere," he said impatiently. "I have permission to leave the zoo to get fish. I got you these costumes. You will dress as animals, like in the Musicians of Bremen." Frowning, he thrust piles of fabric into their hands. Molly had a cat costume and Micky a dog outfit. "My flamingo cousins will accompany us to town. Safety in numbers." With that he did something completely unexpected. He took off his cloak, revealing two huge brown folded wings, which quivered slightly and then opened like giant feathered fans. Wildgust shook them out. Then, roughly scooping Molly, holding Petula, under his left arm and Micky under his right, he dived off the tree-house balcony and swooped through a gap between the leaves and branches to land on the ground behind the elethumper hutch.

"You can fly!" Molly said, stunned. Micky looked equally amazed.

Wildgust just bent his hawkish beak nose toward them and said crossly, "Don't stare. Change. I'll put your old clothes in my sack."

As Molly wriggled into her furry cat suit she noticed her brother slipping his plastic hospital tag, or at least the half of it that he had, into the pocket of his dog suit. Above his head rose a thought bubble. Princess

Fang and Miss Cribbins were shouting at him. He obviously feared getting caught. This was a good sign, Molly thought, and she felt that she'd scored another point over Fang. At least Micky would want to stick with Molly, not run back to the palace. Now he was thinking about his motorized divan.

"By the way," Molly said, "you can always lean on me if you need to, Micky. I know you're probably missing your floating chair."

Micky gave her an odd, sideways glance. "Okay," he said.

Petula looked up at Molly and wondered why she had chosen to look like a cat wearing a peaked cap. At least she didn't smell like one.

Molly and Micky followed Wildgust to the gates of the zoological institute. Wildgust had covered his wings with his cloak again so that, as before, his back simply looked like it was badly hunched. At the gate, they met the flamingo children, who were dressed as a donkey and a cockerel, carrying a drum and a flute. The spaniel-woman from the night before was there too. She handed Micky a violin and Molly a flute. Then she took Petula.

"Now you look the part," she said. "And don't worry—I understand dogs." She nodded to Petula. "I'll look after her." And so while the guards ransacked

Professor Selkeem's tree-house laboratory they all set out for the town.

"I reckon those guards will be there for a good few hours," the flamingo boy said as they negotiated the slope outside the zoo.

"Won't they find Petula?" Molly asked, worried.

"No, Lola will make sure she's safe and hidden." Then Wildgust went on gruffly, "Don't behave stupidly. Remember, there are many more cameras out here than in the institute. You must all seem just like the hypnos."

"The hypnos?" Molly asked.

"The hypnotized people," the flamingo girl explained.

Molly fingered the whiskers on her mask. "Where are we going?"

"The harbor," Wildgust replied.

The sun was getting hot now. Molly started to feel warm inside her furry suit. She looked up at Mont Blanc and wondered what Princess Fang and Miss Cribbins were doing. Had they discovered that Nurse Meekles had been the one who helped them? As they passed their first hypno, Molly's stomach jittered.

Silver sat back to front on Wildgust's shoulder, cocking his head and eyeing Micky. It was, Molly thought, as if he suspected that the boy was the weakest link on this trip.

The road they trod was unkempt and stony. Micky hobbled along beside Molly, occasionally stumbling on the uneven surface.

"Try to walk a *bit* better," Molly pleaded, "unless you want the cameras to relay pictures of you limping up to Princess Fang."

On either side were gingerbread-style thatched cottages with timber frames and lopsided windows. A few hypnos, looking like they'd walked straight out of a pantomime, were awake and already numbly conducting their morning routines. One sat beside a spinning wheel; another walked by, carrying pails of water. Wildgust led them past a big billboard-sized screen. On it were the words SING THIS TODAY, and then, the words of a song.

*Hey, yiddley yiddley, everyone feeling just diddley,*
*Hey, yoddley yoddley, like peesalies in a poddley!*

"That's another one of Princess Fang's screens," the flamingo boy murmured between clenched lips. "When she wants to play with the hypnos as if they were her toys, or whenever she wants something done, she puts her ugly little face on that screen and shouts her commands out. That's where she's been advertising the fact that you two are missing. Those words are lines to a stupid song she wants people to sing for the big show. And those boxes on the right are more cameras for her to spy on everyone. And those over there"—he glanced furtively toward some silver igloolike buildings that Molly recognized at once—"those are the grand houses where Fang and her people live when it's winter and too cold on the mountain."

"Chaaarrp! She naw good," sang Silver. Wildgust reached up and cupped his hand around the bird's beak.

Pebbles crunched under their feet. They walked down a narrow street that could have been a picture in a fairy-tale book come to life. The houses were narrow and medieval looking, with wattle-and-daub walls and rickety doors and windows. A man dressed as a page, in a green jacket, short, puffy britches and white tights, and a plump cap with a feather in it walked past. His head hung down and he sang sadly:

*"Hey, yiddley yiddley, everyone feeling just diddley,*
*Hey, yoddley, yoddley, like peesalies in a poddley.*

Molly looked at the flamingo children in their stuffy outfits. She thought how difficult it must be always to have to pretend to be hypnotized.

"When do Lakeside children get hypnotized?" Molly asked the girl.

"As soon as they can talk," she whispered back. "But Fang thinks that us zooeys *can't* be hypnotized until we're seven years old. My parents made them think that because my brother and I couldn't have *acted* hypnotized when we were little. Once a month an instruction comes for the hypnos to take any of their new talkers to the Hypnosis Hut. The children go in, and when they come out . . ." She sighed. "It's awful. The poor little things come out like *little* zombies."

Molly looked back at Micky and wondered—had *he* been responsible for hypnotizing the toddlers or had Fang used a recording of Redhorn's hypnotic eyes?

Soon they were at the fishing harbor of the lake. Its small buildings were painted yellow, with mermaid-shaped flags flying above them. This should have been a rowdy place, with seamen shouting to one another and fishwives noisily selling their wares. But instead it was quiet as a graveyard. Women with rich brown skin, wearing dresses, white aprons, and bonnets, stood with trays of the night's catch before them. The fresh fish shimmered like jewels, scaly and shiny. Quietly the hypnotized shoppers stated their needs. Quietly the hypnotized sellers wrapped the fish but took no money. Small waves from the lake rippled on to the shore. Farther up, fishermen who'd been up all night heaved their simple boats in. Others mended their nets or rolled them up for safekeeping.

Molly shivered. It was creepy. The hypnos were like ghosts haunting a strange, quiet town. She watched Micky's thought bubbles. He was thinking about Miss Cribbins. She was holding out her bony hand. In it was a mound of pills. Micky's mind then turned to the lake and its deep water. He thought about dolphins playing there, chasing one another in circles.

Silver hopped onto his shoulder. "Chaaarrrp!" he whistled quietly. "Swim with dollll-phins!"

Molly was stunned. Could the bird read thoughts too? She wished she could see Micky's face behind his dog mask. She bet that had surprised him. She marveled at the brilliant bird. Did Wildgust know its talents? Or maybe that outburst had been a coincidence. While Molly mulled this over, Wildgust swung a sack of fish over his shoulder and they set off up the stony path again.

A flycopter's engines purred in the sky above. The day's heat was now really picking up. It seared down on the dusty road and the dry thatched roofs of the nursery-rhyme cottages. Molly began to sweat inside her cat outfit. She was boiling. In fact she felt like she was wrapped in an electric blanket, and the noisy flycopter's engines made the hot air seem even more intense. Then

Molly noticed that it was moving toward them. She began to feel worried. Had Professor Selkeem reported her and Micky after all? Was the flycopter coming for them? Her heart began to race. She tried to relax. To divert her thoughts she looked ahead. A very beautiful woman caught Molly's attention. She was sitting in a rocking chair under a yellow awning outside a timber house, with a very pretty baby in her lap. The baby was sucking its hand and practicing making noises.

"Mmmbaar, mmmbar, mmmbar," it went, looking as happy as any baby could be.

Then, its gurgling was drowned out by the approaching engine noise. Molly had to force herself not to look up. Instead, like the hypnos about her, she did nothing. She let her eyes dart over to check on Micky. Molly's heart thumped in her chest. If she or Micky gave the game away, they would both be caught immediately.

*"Don't react,"* said the flamingo girl from under her cockerel mask. "Remember, there are cameras everywhere. Keep walking."

The flycopter landed on a patch of scrubby land near the cottage of the mother and baby. Two hypnotized palace servants dressed in red silk tunics, white tights, and pointed red shoes got out. With the blades of their machine still whirring, they marched toward the small house.

"Cottage three twenty-six?" the first servant asked the woman. She nodded. What Molly saw next was horrifying. The palace servant reached toward the woman's rosy baby and said, "The time has come."

The woman's eyes were glazed and totally obedient. In the next moment she handed over her child. Without showing any emotion, the palace servant received the bundle. The baby shrieked and cried out for its mother, but its pitiful screams fell on deaf ears. It was carried back to the flycopter and taken inside.

Then, with a sudden leap from the aircraft, the second palace worker charged over to Molly and her companions. Reaching the two flamingo children in their donkey and cockerel costumes, he ripped their masks off. Molly found herself frozen to the spot. She watched a flash of disgust cross the man's face and he let the masks fall. Molly got ready to sprint.

"These—two," said Wildgust, talking in hypnotized monotone and indicating Molly and Micky, "are—tortoise-children. Beware—they bite."

This all seemed too much for the palace worker. He turned back to his flycopter, and moments later the aircraft took off. The woman beside the cottage stretched her hands up to it, toward her baby. Tears were streaming down her face, but because she was hypnotized, she was rooted to the ground.

Molly made herself stare ahead as though watching an invisible TV. And then, with Micky trying his best not to limp, they all walked, pretending nothing at all had happened. When they came to a quiet shady place under trees near the water, Wildgust stopped.

"There are no cameras here," he said. "You can take your masks off now and cool down a bit." Silver flew up onto a branch above as if establishing a lookout perch.

"What *was* that?" said Molly immediately, really upset. "That woman had her baby *stolen*!"

Wildgust nodded and stared stonily out at the water. Micky frowned. The two flamingo children came and sat down beside Molly.

"When a child down here takes the fancy of the palace," the flamingo boy explained, "it is taken. Fang always takes the beautiful ones."

"But why? And what for?" Molly pictured Miss Cribbins with lots of young children in a classroom. She imagined them sitting in a row beside lots of learning machines, with their little hands stuck to silver blocks under whipping rulers.

"The palace people," the flamingo girl said, "bring up the babies as their own."

Molly remembered the nursery where she had visited Nurse Meekles. There had been three babies there and other smaller children. Had they *all* been stolen? And did Nurse Meekles have something to do with this?

She turned to Micky, and for a moment couldn't care less what the zooeys knew about him. "How could you let this happen? Why didn't you stop them?"

"I—I didn't know that they did *this*," Micky stammered. "I was told that the Lakeside children and babies at the palace were orphans."

"Nurse Meekles seems so nice. How could she do it?"

"Maybe she was told they were orphans too, or maybe she thought that *someone* had to look after them so *she* might as well. She likes children."

But Molly was too furious to be reasonable. She was sick of trying to be patient and understanding. Something cracked in her, and all her fury and anger came tumbling out. "Are you blind, Micky? Can't you see? That baby is just like you were! That's *just* what they did to you, Micky. They stole you. And your mother, *our* mother, was too deeply hypnotized to do anything about it. THEY STOLE YOU JUST LIKE THAT! Do you believe it now, Micky? Do you see what kind of people they really are up there? Don't you see how wicked what they did to you was? They took away your real life and made it so that you grew up to serve *them*."

Then Molly was quiet.

"I'm *not* your brother," Micky said doggedly.

"What's this then?" Molly said. Without looking at

him, she tossed her half of the hospital identity bracelet into his lap. He picked it up and fingered it. Eventually he pulled his own tag of plastic from his pocket.

"Redhorn dropped it," Molly said. "He tore it off your wrist when he took you. Half the bracelet stayed on your wrist—that's the bit Nurse Meekles must have found. The other half fell on the ground outside the hospital. I found it when I started looking for you."

Micky put the two strips together and slowly read them aloud, "'St. Michael's, MALE LOGAN TWIN.'"

Molly nodded. "Mine probably said 'St. Michael's FEMALE LOGAN TWIN.'" For a moment she was silent and her temper simmered down. "You know, Redhorn nearly took me," Molly finally said. "I might have been the one that grew up here. Instead, something different happened to me. I never grew up with our parents either. I was taken too, but by someone else. I grew up in a nasty, cold orphanage."

Micky sat very still. Then he looked Molly in the eye. "I'm sorry," he said. "Thank you for coming to get me, Molly."

Molly sighed. At last, she thought, I've won a game from Fang.

On the way back to the zoo they passed the old-fashioned town clock, where one of the princess's screens sparked into life.

MIDMORNING MEALTIME, it proclaimed in purple lettering, and a recorded Miss Cribbins wagged her red-varnished fingernail at anyone watching.

"Eat nutritiously, not greedily," she said. "Keep Lakeside tidy." Then she disappeared and pictures of fruit floated across the screen—an orange banana, a pineapple with a skin like a strawberry, and some rainbow-colored berries.

"The hypnotized population is very healthy," the flamingo girl pointed out. "The hypnos are told exactly what and how much to eat. Not too much salt, not too much fat, lots of vegetables—that sort of thing. Everyone drinks lots of water. Princess Fang's work-force is hardly ever off sick."

Molly looked at the screen. It reminded her of the billboards and commercials from her own time. "Buy this, do this, be this," those commercials used to say to promote their shampoos or holidays, their fast cars or sweets.

*Qube if you're cute . . . Qube if you're rude . . .*
*Everyone loves you, cos you're so Qube.*

The jingle from the fizzy-drink commercial sang in Molly's head and she thought of Rocky. They'd always laughed so much when they imitated the commercials.

She could imagine him impersonating Cribbins now. "Eat nutritiously, not greedily. Actually, hypnos, you will stop eating! Yes, you will *stop* eating!" His voice practically echoed in Molly's head. And she saw how much she missed him. She clenched her fists inside the furry paws of her cat costume and shut her eyes to make a promise. Silently she vowed to Rocky that she would do everything in her power to get them all out of this mess.

And Molly, Micky, and the flamingo children, like ducklings in a line, followed Wildgust through the sweltering crowds.

Back at the zoo, Petula was sitting with Lola, the dog-woman, in a hut by the water's edge.

The woman had floppy black ears and a wet black nose. Her skin was furry, and a tail stuck out of a hole in the back of her tunic.

"A good pampering is what you need," she said, eyeing Petula's dried-out muddy coat and her dirty claws. Gently she picked her up and carried her to a table overlooking the lake. Petula lay down and, sucking the stone she had picked up that morning, stared out at the water. She wondered where Molly was. Then the woman sponged her fur down and Petula shut her eyes as she was brushed and massaged. Petula sighed and let her mind wander. Soon she was running through the sweet-smelling fields of Briersville Park.

# Twenty-one

Wildgust led Molly and Micky along a path lined with rosebushes. Now back at the institute, they'd said good-bye to the flamingo children and were heading toward the water's edge where a small hut stood. Its flower-framed door opened and Tortillus emerged. He hobbled quickly toward them.

"Good to see you," he said warmly. "The guards have gone. Molly, will you please come with me? Wildgust, perhaps you could take Micky with you to the pingin enclosure. They're going to love those fresh fish," he added.

Micky hardly heard this, for Silver had landed on his arm and he was tentatively stroking the bird's head. "You're looking much better," Tortillus commented.

"Much stronger—and you've made a friend."

"Where's Petula?" Molly asked.

"She's quite happy," Tortillus replied, smiling. "She's in my room. Come."

And so for the first time since their arrival at the zoo, Molly and Micky parted.

Molly followed Tortillus through the wide, rush-weave door into a low room and at once Petula was upon her, jumping up at her knees.

"Oh, don't you look smart?" Molly said, giving her a massive hug. "You love having your claws polished, don't you?" Seeing her jumpsuit hanging on the back of the chair, all clean and bright white again, she took off the furry cat costume and changed.

In the corner was a bed laid with straw and dried leaves, and on the table was a large plate of lettuce. The walls were hung with paintings of snowy Alpine mountain scenes that at first seemed normal to Molly, but then, she realized, weren't. For they depicted life in *her* time.

"Those pictures must be five hundred years old!" she said.

"I like imagining what this mountain would have been like covered in snow, in the time when the world still had rain forests, and Africa still had rain," the old man said. "I'd *love* to have seen Mont Blanc white with snow," he marveled. "What a pity it melted. The meltwater made a lake that went on for miles and miles, you know. Over the years, with it being so hot now, it dried up. In twenty years there won't be any lake left *at all*."

"At all? What will happen to everyone when there's no water?" Molly asked.

"We will survive if pipes are built to bring water down here from the north. But if not, Lakeside will become a ghost town and the palace up there will be empty too."

"Do you think Princess Fang will build the pipes?"

"I don't know. If she is in control of other parts of the world by then, maybe she will simply up and move away, leaving everyone here behind to shrivel up in the sun and die of thirst."

Molly looked at the pictures longingly. The red tractor in one made her feel really homesick.

"You must miss your time," Tortillus said.

"Well"—Molly swallowed hard, holding back her tears—"yes, I do." She hadn't realized until now how much she had been affected by seeing hypnotized zombies all around her. "I miss my friends and my family." She paused. "Do you really believe me, Tortillus—that I'm from another time? You can't do; it sounds mad. You're just pretending to do."

The old man sat down in a rocking chair and lit his

long pipe. "I believe you," he said. "I know good hypnotists can stop time and time travel—as long as they have their crystals, of course." He put an electric lighting stick to the tobacco and blew out a cloud of bonfire-smelling smoke. "Sorry to separate you from your brother," he apologized, "but I have a sense that you are the person who has the courage that will be needed to overthrow the princess, not him. Am I right?"

Molly gulped. She saw that if Tortillus and she were going to work together, he would need to know the truth about Micky. "Okay." She nodded. "I'll tell you about him. But on the condition that you don't lock him up or do anything bad to him when you find out what he really is." Tortillus narrowed his eyes. "Because if you do, I won't help you," Molly finished.

Tortillus smiled. "Don't you worry," he assured her. "I already have an idea of my own."

"Well," Molly began, "put it like this: Micky is the one who hypnotized my friend Rocky."

"Mmm," mulled Tortillus. "My goodness! I see."

And so, explaining everything as quickly as she could, Molly told Tortillus about Micky's sad life. He listened attentively. "Poor, poor boy," he murmured when Molly finished.

"So . . . so you don't blame him?" Molly asked.

"How could I? That boy has been manipulated and

used all his life. From what you say, it sounds as though he is now coming around. It's impressive how quickly it's happening. He's like a plant that just needed the light to grow. He needed to see something of what he'd done—to see the truth about Princess Fang and Miss Cribbins. The blindfold has been lifted from his eyes at last."

Molly found herself relaxing. Now it was time to make an escape plan for them all. She had been ruminating on a few ideas on her way back from town.

"Is there any way you can get in touch with other countries, where the people aren't hypnotized?" she asked.

"Sadly not," Tortillus replied. "Princess Fang has created an invisible wall that stops any of our radio waves passing through. So we can't send radio signals or receive them. And of course there are no televisions in Mont Blancia now. No computers, e-mails, or phones either. I don't think people in other countries have any idea what is really happening here." He lay his pipe in a bowl on the table. "But now, Molly, we have to work out a way to get your skills back." Molly nodded. "You heard the announcement Fang made about the performance tomorrow up at the palace?" She nodded again. "The princess likes to give her foreign guests a good theatrical show. It is always a fairy-tale story acted out by the performers of Lakeside, with dancers, singers, acrobats, and light lasers to make it really spectacular. As head zookeeper, I have received an order that the Qingling animals from the zoological institute will participate. She calls that part 'The Greatest Circus Show on Earth.' Lots of flycopters will be carrying the relevant animals up. You and Micky will go too, disguised as animals, and *we will get you to that machine*."

Molly's heart leaped. "Fantastic!" She clapped her hands together. "Micky knows the combination for the machine room lock, so we can get in there!"

"Good. Good." Tortillus couldn't help chuckling. "So you agree?"

Molly grinned. "Of course I do." She laughed. "I mean—wow, Tortillus, it all sounds perfect."

As Molly laughed, Petula barked. It was lovely to see her mistress happy again.

"There are a few problems," continued Tortillus, more somber than Molly. "The first is the guards, of course. They will be very difficult to get around."

"True," said Molly. Then she stroked Petula and said, "But you know, Tortillus, it might not be such a big problem. Petula might be able to help. I've been thinking, you see. Petula has got hypnotism in her. Once she actually made time stand still. It was in a really extreme situation though, so I don't know if she could find the hypnotic part of her again, but if she could . . ." Molly leaned over Petula and picked her up. "If she could be smuggled into the palace with me and Micky, maybe we could work as a team. Maybe Petula could hypnotize the guards." She fingered Petula's velvety ears. "The only problem would be communicating with Petula to tell her who to hypnotize. I don't speak dog."

"No, but Silver does," said Tortillus, "and he can mind read too."

"Mind read? I thought so!" Molly exclaimed. "I thought he could because . . ." She stopped. She didn't want Tortillus to know that she was a mind-reader too. Tortillus continued.

"Yes, it is an amazing skill," he said, not noticing Molly's confusion. "It's some side effect of his genetic engineering. So if I *think* to Silver what we want Petula to do, he will be able to explain things to her. He can go with you to the palace tomorrow too." Tortillus opened the door of his hut and gave a low whistle. Silver fluttered down from the geranium trees nearby and landed on the ground before the tortoise-man, who invited the bird to hop onto his finger. Then Tortillus brought Silver inside, where he stared into the creature's blue eyes.

Silver looked at the weathered, reptilian face of the old man and gave a small chirrup. Then, sensing that he had been called for a reason, he summoned up a thought bubble over Tortillus's head. Inside it was a picture of the pug dog, Petula, with her mistress, traveling up to the palace in a zoo crate and then of them both trying to get into a room containing a giant jellyfish and a machine. In this picture, Petula had big, round, swirly, hypnotic eyes and looked as though she was hypnotizing first a guard, then a palace servant, and then the princess of the palace. Silver whistled. He understood what the old man was asking him to sort out.

"Chaaarrp! Naw prab-leem!" he squawked. He fluttered off Tortillus's bony finger and hopped toward Petula.

*Hello again. What's this all about?* Petula asked.

*They want you to go up to the palace tomorrow to help your mistress find the giant jellyfish. They want YOU to hypnotize people that need hypnotizing.* Petula looked flabbergasted. *Yes, I know it's an odd request,* Silver continued. *Like asking you to suddenly fly about the room or something, but I'm only the messenger, so don't blame me!*

Petula shook her head. *I can't hypnotize people. I've only ever hypnotized a bunch of sleepy mice and an American movie director once, and I'm not even sure I hypnotized him. It might have been my natural charm.*

*Well, whatever you call it,* Silver said, *hypnotism or charm, they want you to do it.*

Petula whined. *I'm not a hypnotist. Really. I tried to hypnotize a horrid pink cat-spider creature at the palace before and nothing happened at all.*

*Okay. I'll tell them.* Silver hopped in front of the old tortoise man. "Chaaaaarrrrpp! Dog *no* hyp-tize," he whistled. "Chaaarrrrp! Dog NO hyp-tize."

"She *knows* how to hypnotize! Brilliant!" said Tortillus, clapping his gnarled old hands.

"Chaaaarrrrpp! NO! NO!" Silver tried to explain. "Dog no hyp-tize."

"Yes, well done, Silver!" Tortillus said, completely misunderstanding the bird. "'Know! Know!'" he mimicked. "She know, she know! This is good news. Thank you, Silver! Well done, Petula!" He patted her on the head.

A red button on his lapel started to beep. Tortillus put his finger to his mouth, indicating for Molly and the animals to be quiet.

"Yes—sir?" he said in a hypnotized tone.

"Tortillus," came the young Professor Selkeem's high-pitched, overexcited voice, "the guards have gone now. Undig those children from wherever you have buried them and bring them here immediately. And don't eat them on the way!"

"Yes—sir," Tortillus replied. The red button stopped flashing. He smiled at Molly. "You have to go to him now," he said, putting a hand on her shoulder. "He will put you in a holding cell in his laboratory and lock you up. Don't eat anything he gives you. We will bring you food. And don't worry. Tomorrow we will travel up to the palace with the animals. With the help of your incredible dog, Molly, we will get your hypnotic knowledge back!"

Then suddenly, as if pouring water all over their rekindled hopes, something truly dreadful happened.

Molly heard a voice she recognized. For a moment she couldn't place it, for it was oddly distorted and amplified, booming out over the zoo. It was a lovely, velvety voice though, and the sound of it filled Molly with a warm feeling. Then she snapped to as she recognized who the voice belonged to and what it was doing. Quickly she slammed her hands over her ears and turned to Tortillus.

"That's Rocky," she explained, "my friend—the one Princess Fang took. He was hypnotized by Micky, but he can do voice-only hypnotism. He can't do any other sort, but if a person listens to him for a few minutes they'll fall under his power." Tortillus turned swiftly and opened a drawer, scrabbling around in it for something. He pulled out a lump of soft wax and pulled some tiny pieces off it.

"Here, I use this to polish my shell. Put it in your ears."

Then he opened the door of his hut. Rocky's melting voice washed over the zoo:

"Micky Minus and Molly Moon, I am so glad you're listening," he was saying. "I miss you and I hope you miss me. The palace seems empty without you and that is why you will come back because you want to be here again, more than anything . . ."

Tortillus moved quickly to find Micky, carefully checking that none of the hypnotized zoo visitors were about. Molly followed him. She had her ears blocked with wax and her hands were over them too, so Rocky's voice was muffled. They found Micky standing under a geranium tree.

Tortillus seized his shoulders. "Where's Wildgust?" he asked.

But Micky ignored him, merely staring up in awe at the zoo screen, half hidden by the leaves of the tree. "I—must—go—back," he said, pulling away.

Rocky was on the screen. His lips were moving but Molly couldn't hear him. It was lovely to see his face again but dreadful to watch him being used like this. To see him hypnotized himself and working for Princess Fang was horrible. Molly remembered how

Rocky had wished his hypnotic voice could be of more use. It was a cruel twist of fate that had made him useful to the palace people. She looked at Micky. His eyes were glazed. Already Rocky's words had worked on him.

Wildgust came walking around the corner.

"Where have you been, Wildgust?" Tortillus asked him. "Look, the boy's been hypnotized. Help us get him to my hut."

Molly felt really stupid. She should have realized Fang would discover that Rocky had hypnotizing powers. As they led Micky back to Tortillus's rooms he began to wail.

"I want—to go—baaaaack!—I must see—Rockeeeee."

Inside, they forced him to sit on a chair. Petula, scared by all the noise, slipped under the bed to hide. Outside, Rocky's voice had stopped. Molly removed her earplugs.

"He's going to have to be tied up and shut up," Wildgust said, finding some rope and tethering Micky's ankles, legs, and arms to the chair against the wall.

"Micky," Molly demanded, "what is the combination code for the mind-machine room? Please tell us now."

Micky shook his head wildly and yelled, "I must—see

him!" Above his head, all there were were images of Rocky's face.

"He's well and truly hypnotized," Tortillus lamented. Taking this as a cue, Wildgust put a cloth gag around Micky's mouth.

"Darn," Tortillus moaned. "Darn it."

Molly stood dumbstruck, shocked that things had turned so suddenly. Like a helium balloon with its mainstay broken, their wonderful escape plan was floating away. And she hated seeing her brother like this. He had been doing so well. Molly had begun to care about him. Now she'd lost him again. She felt really sorry for him, all trussed up like a chicken about to be roasted.

"Is there any way of reversing Rocky's effect on him?" Tortillus asked.

Molly shook her head. "Rocky didn't use a password to lock the hypnotism in, so it should gradually wear off, but it will take a while—four days or even four weeks." She watched with concern as Micky's face twisted into a grimace.

"Well," said Tortillus, "he's going to have to be lifted to Selkeem's tree house like this." Molly frowned. "But quick, we must move or the professor will wonder why we are taking so long." He eyed Petula, who was looking enquiringly up at everyone, her tail wagging. "And Petula should stay here. Goodness knows what might happen to her in his madhouse."

Molly nodded. "Definitely," she said, and she bent down to give her pug a hug.

They set off for the dognake-filled tree house. Wildgust carried Micky, who thrashed and complained from behind his gag. Molly hoped his noise wouldn't turn the professor's bad temper even more sour. She touched the tiny wax balls in her pocket. She would have to watch out for Rocky's voice and sleep with earplugs. His voice hypnosis might be aired again. She would have to be very vigilant.

# Twenty-two

"Good morning again!" said the professor, who had changed into a dirty red loincloth. Micky let out a muffled scream, and the boy registered his condition. "As I thought! The devil's got into you. So you took a sip of the hypnotism just now. I got a five-minute warning. The vixen allows me that."

"He is truly . . . danger-ous," Wildgust said in his best hypnotized tones.

"Well, lock him up then!" the professor replied. With Micky still struggling and shouting from behind his gag, Wildgust lifted him off toward a metal-barred cell at the very back of the room, near the other caged animals. The tree boy turned to Molly, looking up at her with his watery, mad eyes.

"Glad that my minions hid you well. Still got you

for myself. Lunchtime soon. You like pickled things?" Molly remembered the two-headed squirrels that she had seen on a shelf before. "And there's delicious roasted meerkatcat." As he said this he gave a horrid wonky smile, and Molly saw that each and every one of his teeth had black bits caught between them. She found herself wondering whether anyone had ever looked after him, whether anyone had ever taught him to brush his teeth. Probably not.

"A drink is what you need, isn't it?" Molly watched with growing disgust as the boy went to the side and took a goatskin sack from the wall. He tipped a brownish liquid into a glass. Seeing Molly recoil in alarm, he slunk back. "Or perhaps you'd prefer this." He pointed to the clear liquid that had been produced by the smoldering rocks earlier and began to pull the jar out from the experiment. Behind him, Wildgust shook his head and wiggled a bottle of water at Molly that he then hid in the cell.

"Er, no, no, don't worry," Molly said politely, even though deep down she was screaming, "Of course I won't drink that stuff. Are you mad?"

Then the boy launched into one of his strange two-way conversations.

"So go on then," the first voice urged. "Find out how much she knows. Don't want her ratting on you to the insects. Wouldn't be able to get the chemicals from the palace if she did. Chemiclies for experimenties. The door would be blocked off. Then what?"

"Oh darkness forever, forever," his other voice, the small one, moaned. The boy turned to Molly and with a crazy spark in his eye demanded, "Tell me what you know of the scorpion and its nest! Do you like scorpions? The scorpion's poison is everywhere." He moved close to her, until he was practically looking up her nose. His breath smelled of the moldy toast that he'd eaten for breakfast. "Do we want a scorpion with hypnotic eyes? And a world of people stung?"

Molly wondered what he was talking about, but seeing from the boy's face that she was expected to answer his question, she replied, "I've never seen a scorpion except at the zoo and on nature programs on TV."

"TV, TV, TV, TV, TV!" the boy shouted. "Mold from the past, it's true! And speaking of mold, perhaps I can interest you in a thousand-year-old egg for lunch. Of course, not *really* a thousand years old, there's poetic license there—more like a hundred days old!" Molly gulped. As the boy rushed to his grubby kitchen and began rummaging through his shelf of glass bottles, she dreaded to think what ghastly thing he was about to make her eat.

"Come here! Here's one, dug up yesterday. I put it in ash, salt, lime, and black tea and buried it. Left it for a hundred days. Delicious. Come here!" Molly reluctantly approached his work surface. The boy put a dirty-looking black egg in front of her and began scraping at its crusty shell. Molly could see that what he was saying about the egg was true. It had definitely not been in the fridge. She watched him as he enthusiastically polished the egg and then began to peel it. The egg was so old that instead of being shiny and white inside it was slimy and green. When he cut it in half, she saw that its yolk had turned into dark green ooze.

"Mmm! Delicious! Have it," he said, thrusting it in front of Molly's face. Its sulfurous stink wafted up her nose. It smelled of the worst fart she had ever smelled. "Tastes of avocado," he said, smiling madly.

"I'm very sorry," Molly lied, "but I'm allergic to eggs. They make me come up in a rash."

The boy hesitated. "Ah well!" he sighed. And with a greedy slobber, he gobbled up the rotten egg.

As he finished it, smacking his lips and wiping his mouth on his bare arm, Molly asked, "Have you been on the mind machine?"

This was not the right question to ask. As if stung by a bee, the boy began to hop about. "Of course I have! Can't you see? On, off, up, down! Yo, yo, yo. Back and forth. Pop! In a bubble. Pop! Out of a bubble. Pop, pop, pop. Rumble, tumble, scramble my mind. But there's still enough left to make the potion. To make the $H_2O$! Sit! Sit! HERE!" The boy pointed to a stool and began rushing about his laboratory. Two of his dognakes slithered in. They slipped across the floor and then coiled themselves up around Molly's stool. Resting their panting dog heads on their scaly bodies, they shut their eyes. Molly slowly pulled her foot out from under one of them. She remembered that dogs could always sense if a person was afraid of them, so she decided to try to pretend to be fond of the dognakes. "Good dognakes," she said quietly. "Good boys."

Meanwhile the professor fretted over his scientific instruments. "Time is running out!" he complained as he busied himself with potions and chemical mixtures. Molly saw the sweat building up on his forehead. He prodded and peered at the experiment projecting the muddy-colored rainbow. "If only the rock was *pure*!" he exclaimed. "Perhaps with a touch of X-ray it will be."

Molly knew that X-rays were dangerous. "Do you mind if I check that my brother's all right?" she asked hopefully.

The boy glared at her.

"Chicken, get in your cage," he said, and he whistled to the dognakes to uncurl themselves from Molly's stool. Then, still muttering, he opened the cell door and nudged her inside. "Are you a hippy?" he asked, prodding her through the metal bars.

"A hippy?"

"A hypnotist."

"I was," Molly replied nervously, hoping that he wasn't about to drag her out again.

"Did Fang put you in the microwave?" Molly was beginning to understand the boy's mad way of talking.

"You mean, did she put me on the mind machine?"

"Yes, did she put you in the washing machine and wash out your brain with soap and water?"

"Yes, she did," Molly replied. "She took all my hypnotic knowledge."

"Hmm . . ." Her answer seemed to appease the boy. He turned back to his experiments and didn't bother Molly for the whole afternoon.

As the hours ticked by, Molly stayed at Micky's side. Micky had given up fighting. He was no longer trying to break free from the ropes. Instead he lay curled up on the wooden floor, hugging his knees. His eyes were far away as though he could see through the wood of the tree house and was watching birds flying in the sky. And then he fell asleep. The boy professor bustled about in his laboratory. He fussed over the rocks in his light-making experiment as though his life depended on it. Then a smell of cooked meat filled the yurt. The boy brought Molly and Micky dirty plates with piles of meat that seemed to be roasted chicken.

"Roasted meerkatcat?" he inquired, hovering outside the cell.

"No, thanks, I had a big breakfast," Molly lied. Her stomach rumbled as though in disagreement.

After his meal, Molly saw the professor pull a bowl out from behind a chair. It was very like the bowl that Princess Fang had chosen a fortune cookie from a few nights before in the mountaintop dining room.

"Gypsy cookie?" the boy professor asked. "The royal guards brought them. Present from Fang-face for poking about in my hole."

Molly looked at the small red packages. They seemed clean enough and, since they were sealed and fresh and she was very hungry, she decided to have one.

"Thank you." She stretched her hand out and took two.

"Good curly whirly," the tree boy said, and he got back to his business.

Molly unwrapped her biscuit and Micky's too. She bit into hers. It was juicy and sweet and tasted of maple syrup. She put Micky's beside his leg, opening it for him so that she could poke it into his gagged mouth when he woke up. Then she read the white strips of paper that came with each cookie.

Micky's said, "As you sow, so you shall reap." Poor Micky. He certainly had reaped what he'd sown, Molly thought. He'd hypnotized Rocky and now Rocky had hypnotized *him*.

Her own fortune read, "When you want to test the depth of a stream, don't use both feet." She rolled the paper into a ball between her fingers. She'd remember that. If she did manage to get back to the palace, she would definitely tread very, very carefully.

Molly leaned against her cage and watched the mad boy professor as he fiddled with pipettes and powders, chatting away to himself all the while. She saw him feed a mouse with some concoction that he'd made, then swing a pendulum in front of its eyes.

"I could teach you!" he said to the mouse. "Teach you how to do it. Then there would be a way out of the hole."

Eventually exhausted by his mad ranting, Molly fell asleep.

That afternoon the Institute of Zoology was a hive of activity. Its gates were shut, and the zooeys began preparing selected animals for their journey up to the mountaintop for Princess Fang's big show. Vast cages and crates were wheeled out of a hangar near the waterfront and brought to the animals' pens, and everywhere animals were being washed and dried and brushed. The flamingo children visited various pens, taking Petula with them.

In the elethumper's cage, the beast was being hosed down and scrubbed with a broom. When it was dry, Belsha massaged its gray leathery skin with sunflower oil until it shone.

*Lakeside is in a flurry,* Silver explained to Petula. *The royal lunatic child has asked for a fairy tale called Hansel and Gretel to be performed. It's about two children who get lost in a wood. They meet a witch who lives in a gingerbread house. The performers have to do a dance of the woodland animals, and then of the woodland fairies. And you hear that sound?*

Petula cocked her ears and heard the distinct sound of trumpets on the air. *Yes,* she said.

"Well, that's the orchestra warming up," Silver continued. "You should see the costumes!"

At the bearunkeys' cage Petula watched as the ferocious beasts, a mix of brown bears and monkeys, were coaxed toward a crate containing bananas.

Wildgust stood in a small courtyard, washing the legs of a fat, red-breasted, eagle-sized robin. The lathery water splashed down its legs. Petula picked a stone up in her mouth and began to suck it nervously. *Silver?* she asked the black bird tentatively.

*Yes?*

*What will everyone do if I can't hypnotize anyone?*

"Craaaaarrk!" *Don't ask me,* Silver cawed, *but I will stay by your side. I can interpret what Molly says for you.*

Petula let the stone roll around in her mouth. She felt a little better, knowing that Silver would be there for her, but she was still very worried. For she now had a nasty feeling that when the time came for her to hypnotize people she would let Molly down.

As the stars started to appear in the night sky, as though some heavenly lamplighter was switching them on, Molly helped Micky, still tied in ropes, to get more comfortable, pulling a blanket over him.

"I'm sorry this has happened, Micky," she whispered, stroking his forehead. He blinked madly up at her. "Please relax. I'm going to try to sort everything out. Tomorrow I'm going back to the palace. I'm going to try to get my mind back."

# Twenty-three

The next morning, when the sun was already up, Molly felt a stick being prodded gently into her back. She turned to see Wildgust standing on a branch beside her prison. He put a finger to his mouth to indicate that she should be very, very quiet, and he pointed to the far end of the cage. Here, Molly saw, he'd pried the bars apart so that there was a slightly wider gap. Molly took out her earplugs and carefully crawled through to the outside of the tree house. Micky stirred but slept on, curling back up into a croissant shape.

Wildgust reached in and moved a pillow to where Molly's body had been, pulling the sheet up over it to make it look like she was still there. Then he bent the bars back into place before silently lifting Molly under his arm and flapping down to the ground.

When they arrived at Tortillus's hut, the old man was waiting with some toast and a cup of tea. Best of all, Petula was there to greet Molly.

"Oh Petula," she said, crouching down to give her a proper hug. Petula leaped up at her knees. Then Molly pulled herself upright and took the toast.

"Cor, I'm so hungry," she said. "You should have seen what the professor had on the menu." Wildgust settled down into a chair in the corner, saying nothing.

"Big day today," Tortillus said, smiling. Molly nodded, munching. "The crates of zoo animals will be airlifted this morning."

"So let's get going," said Molly, wiping her hands on her jumpsuit. "I'm ready. Which crate are we going to hide in?"

Tortillus turned and pulled some strange objects out of a bag. One was a hard, curved piece of yellow plastic. Then there were what looked like two black furry, floppy socks, and last, four yellow rubbery things that reminded Molly of washing-up gloves. "This is what Petula should wear. I don't think you've seen our quogs. They are dogs mixed with ducks. They don't bark—they quack. They're normally bigger than Petula, but I think with these long black ears and this elasticate beak and these webbed feet, she will look like a small quog. Do you think she will wear them?"

"She may need a bit of persuasion," Molly answered. Tortillus produced a brown furry body suit and a ratty mask. "And that's for me, I suppose?"

"Yes, I thought you could go as a sabrerat. Three other sabrerats will be going too but I won't put you in a cage with them as they aren't the friendliest of animals."

Molly raised her eyebrows and inspected the suit. "It's going to be hot," she said.

"The sabrerat cages are always air-conditioned and cool."

"And will my cage be near the quog cage?" Molly said, working the snaps on her furry suit.

"Near enough."

"I get it," Molly said. "So first, we get up to the palace. Second, Petula hypnotizes the guards. Third, we make our way to the mind-machine room—"

"I was thinking differently," Tortillus interrupted. "Petula could come onstage with the quogs. She can quietly make her way to Princess Fang's seat and, as soon as her eyes lock on to the princess's, hypnotize her."

"But if Fang spots Petula's not a quog," Molly pointed out, "then Petula will be caught. It's so dangerous. Because anyway, even if she manages to get to the princess to look her in the eyes, she may not be able to hypnotize her." Molly frowned. "If she can't, she's—she's dead!"

"You're right," Tortillus murmured. "We'll do it your way then." He rubbed his eyes. "Let's hope we get dealt some good cards."

Molly stroked Petula. She'd played lots of poker in the orphanage and remembered quite a few games where she'd been losing badly and then had had a run of luck. "Maybe Petula will be our ace in the hole," she said.

A short while later, Tortillus led a furry sabrerat and a small quog out of the hut. Petula waddled along slowly in her new flappy feet. She was very anxious.

*I can't do this, you know,* she confided to the mynah bird.

*You can only do your best,* her new friend replied.

And so Petula followed her mistress toward the loading area of the zoo. Once there, she looked into the quog crate and studied the animals suspiciously. They seemed peaceful. She sent polite greetings out to them, wondering whether they would understand dog and whether they would reply in a friendly way. Tortillus opened the cage door.

*Come on in,* came the thoughts of the biggest quog. *We're not going to eat you.*

Petula glanced across at Molly in her sabrerat cage. She took a deep breath, picked her feet up, and gingerly stepped inside.

The sky began to rattle with noise as big flycopters descended upon the zoo. Wildgust raised blue flags, indicating that the machines could prepare to lift the crates. Chains and heavy-duty canvas straps were lowered.

One by one, large and small crates were hooked up. As soon as each was ready the hawk-man waved a green flag and the crates were pulled up into the air. Petula's quog cage was one of the first to be hauled away. Her stomach lurched as though she was on a very fast-rising elevator. Through the metal grid she watched the zoo enclosures drop away, and the shimmering lake shrink. She watched the roofs of cottages and lawns of gardens become tinier and tinier until finally she was looking down a precipice of gray rocky mountain.

*Why are you dressed as a quog?* the biggest quog thought to her.

*I'm on a secret mission,* Petula explained. The quog's eyebrows jiggled as he digested this information. Petula wondered if he knew what a secret mission was. She looked at his gray scruffy fur and his *real* webbed feet and she hoped she would get away with her disguise.

The flycopters hovered over a flat, stony place. Petula peered out of her crate to see what lay below. To the right some very tall metal gates were open. Beyond these were huge passageways that led into the mountain to a showground inside the palace. Guards dressed as toy soldiers with ribbons in their helmets stood about, guiding the aircraft and their loads down. Petula wondered which one she ought to hypnotize first. *Hypnotize first?* Who was she kidding? Petula knew that her hypnotism was out to lunch. In fact it was out to tea, supper, and breakfast too. Any hypnotic skills she'd ever had had left town.

Tortillus opened Molly's cage, and attaching a lead to the collar around her neck, patted her fuzzy sabrerat head.

"Good sabrerat," he said loudly as a guard walked past. "Don't bite now!" He led Molly toward the cliff edge, where a score of iron rings were fixed to the ground, and he tied her lead to one. "Stay!" he commanded. He returned shortly with Petula.

"Good girl," Molly whispered to her, very impressed at her pet's acting. "I can see why that director put you in his movie." Molly was trying to lighten her mood, for her insides were bumping about with nerves. "It'll all be done soon, Petula. We'll do it—you just wait and see. Before you know it you'll be chasing rabbits in Briersville."

The guard by the rock turned and then began walking toward them. In the bubble above Petula's head Molly saw that she was thinking of nothing but the guard. All about him were swirls of silver light and his eyes were swirling too. Molly could see that Petula was preparing to hypnotize him.

*You can do it, Petula!* she encouraged her silently. The guard came closer.

And so, using all her doggy might, Petula summoned up the tingling electric feeling of hypnosis. Her legs and back became rigid with concentration. Her eyes stared up at the approaching guard's, daring him to stare back at her.

*Come on, come on!* Molly urged.

Petula could feel Molly's encouragement. When the burly man was finally near enough, Petula locked her black pupils on to his and willed him to be hypnotized.

But it was useless. The man was unmoved. Petula wasn't surprised—no whooshing fusion feeling had rushed though her body—so she knew that the hypnotism wasn't happening.

Petula collapsed on the floor in a heap. She had let everyone down.

"Zookeeper!" shouted the guard. At once Molly bristled with nerves. Had he seen through Petula's disguise? Tortillus quickly came over.

"That quog—is sick," said the guard. "Get rid—of it." He marched away.

"Petula can't do it," Molly whispered hoarsely, fighting back tears of exasperation. "She can't do it at all."

"Do you think she might have another go?" Tortillus asked. As he bent down to stroke Petula, Silver fluttered down by her side too.

*Oh, cat tails!* Petula moaned, with her head in her paws. *I've only ever hypnotized a bunch of sleepy mice. I wish they understood.*

*Don't worry,* Silver said. *I'll tell them how it is.* And flapping up to Tortillus's curved shoulder, he cawed, "IM . . . BOSSY . . . BELL. IM . . . BOSSY . . . BELL."

"Im bossy bell?" Molly asked Tortillus quietly. "What does that mean?"

"That, I'm afraid, means, 'impossible,'" Tortillus whispered back.

Molly found her insides being gripped by desperation. She had to come up with a good plan now, or she was as good as dead. And so her inventive mind began to whirr.

"Forget our first plan," she said, glancing across to Wildgust, who was holding a butterfly-winged mouse. "I think I've got a better one."

And as Tortillus stroked Petula's pretend beak,

Molly whispered her ideas to him.

Tortillus nodded. "So wait for the sign," he said and ambled away.

Molly sat down, trying to seem as sabreratty as possible. She looked out over the walled edge of the cliff and kept her eyes glued on the elethumpers. The hours stretched out as though time had taken a sleeping pill. When a palace servant passed, looking a little too interestedly at her, she growled at him, which sent him scurrying.

Then, from inside the mountain, Molly could hear that the show had begun. The sound of a distant brass band floated out of the giant palace passageway. She watched anxiously as the bearunkeys were shepherded into the tunnel and then ten minutes later returned. She saw the giant mice and the deer geese being taken in to perform.

Finally Tortillus said very loudly, "Elethumpers next!"

Molly edged her fingers up to her neck and surreptitiously undid her collar, placing it on the ground beside her. She took off Petula's lead too. And then the commotion that she'd been waiting for happened. Two enormous male elethumpers went crazy. One began kicking its back legs so furiously that it pushed its crate right up to the edge of the mountain, where it lay see-sawing, half on the mountain, half off. The other was bouncing on the spot, waving its trunk about, trumpeting aggressively at one of the guards. The hypnotized palace servants shrank back to the palace wall. Even Tortillus looked worried. Belsha stood behind the elethumpers, tickling their tails with a feathered stick, which wasn't helping; in fact, it was making things worse. She winked at Molly.

And then Molly heard a swishing in the air. Wildgust was swooping down on her. Molly felt like a field mouse being hunted by a bird of prey. She grabbed Petula and it was just in time too, for a split second later Wildgust's sharp talons were hooked under her arms, lifting her up. Instinctively, Molly put her right arm up to hold on extra tight to his leg. Then it felt as if they were falling off the mountain as Wildgust tipped his body and flew sideways and down. Molly looked below. Beneath her was a thousand-foot drop. Her stomach leaped. If Wildgust let go of her, she and Petula would be dead. Would he? Surely not. But Molly couldn't entirely trust the hawk-man. Quickly taking her mask off and holding it in her teeth, she gripped onto his leg even tighter.

Now Wildgust flew upward, around a shady part of the mountaintop city. His strong wings beat the air. Soon he was nearing the summit of the mountain.

Below, Molly saw colorful manicured gardens and the golden roofs of the fabulous mountaintop residences. It was completely deserted. Perhaps everyone was at the circus. Molly hoped so.

Higher and higher Wildgust flew, bringing them closer to Princess Fang's pinnacle palace. Molly recognized it at once. They were heading toward the large balcony where she had stood only days before.

As welcome as water to a netted fish, the ground met Molly's feet. Wildgust let go of her shoulders and deftly landed on the balcony wall. Before Molly could thank him, he took off again and was gone.

Down at the zoological institute, in the tree house, Micky was banging on the bars of his cage with his shoulder, shouting through his gag. Through the bars of his prison he could see Professor Selkeem's laboratory. Glass test tubes and dishes, the discards from the mad boy's night experiments, lay smashed on the floor.

"I'm coming, I'm coming," the professor said, finally rousing himself from his sleep. "What do you want?" he yawned.

"Uuugh, uuurgh," Micky grunted urgently, nodding with his head toward the empty cell. The young professor reached his arm through the bars and undid

Micky's gag. "Rockeee!" Micky yelled. "Molly's gone—to palace! Rockeee!—To the mind—machine. Rockeeeeee! Tortillus and Wildgust—are not—hypnotized!—Molly wants—to give them—their throne back!"

"What? Their high chairs back? Wildgust not hypnotized?! This is sewer-pit news!" The professor started twitching and looking to the left and the right of him in a flurry of panic. Then angrily he shouted, "Fang can't have them. We must get them! Wildgust must be stopped!"

"I must see . . . Rockeee!" Micky gasped, as though his life depended on it.

The professor opened the cage door and began dragging Micky along the floor toward the tree-house door.

"We will get them!" he snarled, gathering up a bag full of laboratory equipment as he went. "You will see Rocky. We must catch Wildgust before it's too late!" Then he gave a commanding whistle, and his four dog-nakes appeared. "Carry the boy. And follow me!" he shouted. "Head for the mountain tunnels!"

# Twenty-four

Molly breathed a sigh of relief. Poor Petula was in such a state of shock that her legs were shaking and she could barely stand. Molly knelt down and kissed her. Then a flapping of small wings overhead caught their attention. Silver hopped over to Petula and tapped his orange beak against her pretend quog one.

*That was terrifying,* Petula said with a whine.

*Lucky you weren't born a bird,* said Silver. *So, what are you going to do up here? This is a bad place.*

*My mistress will have something up her sleeve,* Petula said, trying to make herself comfortable in her yellow webbed feet. *She may not look like a champ, but she's quite good in tricky situations.*

Molly clutched her sabrerat mask and looked

around. The place was as quiet as a cemetery. She poked her head past the wall of the balcony to see whether anyone was watching. No one was about. But now Molly knew about the cameras and poisonous darts. She could see one camera now, attached to the pink brick wall ahead, and another that hung from the red-and-green branch of a strawberry tree. Rotating cameras were dotted about the grounds like security guards in a museum. Watching them swivel on their pivots, Molly saw there were black spots—moments when certain areas weren't covered. If they moved quickly, when the cameras had turned away, she and Petula would be invisible to the guards.

Straight ahead was the flower-decked passageway to the dining room. To the right of the balcony lay a garden and beyond this the courtyard where the mind-machine room was housed—it was tantalizingly close. Molly didn't know how to operate the machine, but, she thought, if she could just somehow get in, there was a chance that Princess Fang would come in at some point. If Molly could overpower her, maybe she could *force* her to give her back all her hypnotic knowledge. Even while Molly fantasized about this, she saw what a slim hope it was. For how could Molly trust the princess to program the machine to *return* her knowledge? She might program it to completely *empty* Molly's brain instead. Her excitement and hope were dampening, and despair was returning. She thought of her hippie friend, Forest, who always had good mental tricks up his sleeve. What would he say now to help her? she wondered. His laid-back voice filled her head.

*Cool it, Mrs. Foolit.*

*Always remember, it's not such big potatoes.*

*We're all only blips in the great big cosmic computer, Molly.*

*Think positive, and positive vibes will find ya!*

Molly smiled. "Okay, little potato," she said straightening Petula's quog ears and her webbed feet. "Let's turn Fang into mash!"

Putting on her sabrerat mask and waiting until the nearby camera had turned, she held Petula's collar tightly and led her out into the ornamental garden. Together they scurried down the flowered path toward the courtyard. Molly tried to make her movements as sabrerat-like as possible. When they got halfway across the grass, three cameras pirouetted toward them. Paralyzed by fear, Molly quickly lay down behind a bank of purple lilies, then, when the coast was clear, dashed forward. Finally, picking their way from a statue of Fang to a scented carrot bush, they made it to the mind machine room.

Molly gave the door a push. Not surprisingly it didn't budge. It was locked. She put her ear up close and listened. From inside came the *slush, slush* pumping noise of the jellyfish. It sounded as if the machine was on. Was someone having his brain interfered with right now? Perhaps Princess Fang was in there, stuffing her head with another victim's knowledge.

"Craaaarrrrk! Body coming, body coming!" Silver suddenly croaked from his lookout above.

Molly quickly found a large mossy rock and crouched behind it, half hidden in the shadows. Petula lay down in the sun in the long grass beside a bed of multicolored poppies. She eyed the archway ahead, wondering who was going to come through. To her horror, Taramasalata, the cat-spider, came scuttling into view. The last thing Petula wanted to do was meet her, but she couldn't risk Molly being discovered. And so, now acting as quoglike as she could, she gave a barky quack.

The cat-spider stopped in her tracks. She pricked up her ears and stood stiff and erect on her eight pink furry legs. Then her yellow eyes met Petula's. Immediately she sniffed the air and sent out an aggressive thought message: *This is private property. You don't belong here. Why are you trespassing?*

Petula sealed off the true thoughts in her head and sent back a quog message: *I'm lost. I come from the zoo, but an eagle picked me up and dropped me here. I want to go back to my pupplings—will you show me the way?*

Taramasalata blinked and then advanced. Soon she was a foot away from Petula, eyeing her rubbery webbed feet. She extended a pink leg and prodded Petula's beak. Petula quacked, aware that the cat-spider had smelled a rat, or worse, a pug. Petula began to feel desperate. If only she could remember how to hypnotize! All she needed was that warm, tingling sensation sparkling up from her paws. Then the cat-spider would be hers. Petula cast her mind back to when she'd watched Molly learning to hypnotize. She'd sensed then that Molly would peer into the inner feelings of her victims, and then echo the feelings back to them before she turned on the eye power. That was the method Petula had used to hypnotize the mice. It was worth another try, she thought. Deftly she delved into Taramasalata's mind.

Petula found whining, scratchy feelings mixed with smug purrings. She took a deep breath and, feeling as whiny and as scratchy and as smug as the cat-spider, she made herself purr back.

"Purrrrr, purrrrrr, purrrrrrrr." The creature in front of her paused. Petula purred again. Taramasalata tilted her head questioningly. Petula hoped this was a sign that it was working. And then she felt it. A tingling that was tickling the end of her claws now began trickling up her legs. She purred again and again. Now a fizz was creeping along her backbone. Three more purrs and it was humming like an electric halo around her head. Petula was thrilled. All she had to do now was bring this hypnotic energy into her eyes. Petula began to quiver with excitement as she brought her eyes level with the cat-spider's. But there it all went wrong.

Instead of lolling over, hypnotized, the nasty creature hissed, *You don't smell like a quog. Not enough duck smell in your odor. You smell too doggy. And your beak looks very odd.*

Petula gave a short quack. *Don't tease me. All quogs tease me. It's not my fault I smell more dog than quog.*

As Petula concentrated on acting the part of a bullied quog the tingling sensation died down in her. This was very frustrating. She couldn't let her efforts come to nothing! She simply must help Molly! So digging deep, she tried again.

Petula's tail now began to feel hot—hot as a hot sausage. Gritting her teeth and making the fizzy halo buzz about her head again, she drew up all the hypnotic power she could muster and, with a wallop of a stare, sent out what she hoped was enough hypnotism to sedate an elephant.

This time the cat-spider's thoughts halted. She looked into Petula's eyes. Petula glared deeply back. Taramasalata's yellow pupils were beginning to tremble. Spurred on, Petula intensified her look. The cat-spider's pupils were growing. Now they looked the size of cherries. And then the real fusion feeling rushed from Petula's tail, along her spine, over her forehead, and into her nose. It felt as if hot bubbling water was spouting through her veins. The cat-spider had fallen under her spell!

From behind her mossy rock, Molly watched Petula operate and was amazed. "YOU'RE BRILLIANT, PETULA!" she wanted to shout but didn't want to spoil her pet's work, so instead she kept quiet.

Immediately Petula sent instructions to the horrid animal. *Taramasalata, you are now under my power.*

The cat-spider nodded and twitched her whiskers.

*What is the code for the jellyfish room?* Petula asked.

*Do—not—know,* Taramasalata's hypnotized thoughts stammered.

Petula frowned. *Where is your mistress?* she asked.

*Co-ming.*

Petula darted a look toward the arch. *Coming where?* she said. Silver fluttered down to listen in on the conversation.

*Coming to—mind-ma-chine room,* thought the cat-spider. Petula looked at Silver worriedly.

Silver thought back, *Genius, Petula! Genius! Craaark! Crrreeerrk! Now get the cat-spider to let her mistress open the door, then get it to distract her long enough for us all to slip inside.* Petula nodded and gave a small bark.

"Hide!" Silver croaked, hopping toward the end of the wall near the balcony to indicate where Molly should go. Molly concentrated on the bird's thought bubbles and saw a crudely drawn person there. Who it was supposed to be, she wasn't sure. But the person in Silver's thought bubble was tapping numbers into the combination lock beside the mind-machine room door, then walking through it, followed, in the bubble, by a bird, a dog, and a girl. Molly got the idea. Dodging cameras, she hurried up the path to hide behind a pillar from where she could still see the mind-machine room door, while Silver flew into the branches of a nearby tree. Petula hid in the long grass again.

A minute later Miss Cribbins, powdered and rouged as ever, came marching through the garden archway. She was dressed in a black linen, box-shouldered suit. Her hair was now bronze, in a tall bottle-shaped style. Her heels clipped the ground as she walked with precise efficiency along the path.

As she approached the mind-machine room, her cat-spider sprang out onto the path in front of her. This made Miss Cribbins jump, but she simply sidestepped her pet and was soon at the control panel of the door, tapping in numbers.

It swooshed open. As it did, Taramasalata leaped

onto Miss Cribbins's back, scuttled up her mistress's suit, and pounced on her beehive hair. With all eight legs landing at once, she began tearing the hairstyle apart as if it was cotton candy.

"Taramasalata! *What are you doing?*" Miss Cribbins screeched, staggering backward. She grabbed at the animal's body and with some difficulty pulled it down from her head. But in doing so, since the cat-spider was attached to her tall hair, she tore that off too. Miss Cribbins was left bald as a boiled egg.

"You stupid creature! *What* has gotten into you?" Taramasalata let out a spraying hiss of spit that hit Miss Cribbins in the face. Then she bit her on the wrist. "Arrghhhhh!" the woman screamed. With surprising swiftness, dexterity, and strength, Cribbins plucked the cat-spider from her wig and flung the creature toward a rosebush.

"How dare you?" she shouted. Then, bronze-colored wig under her arm, she disappeared into the mind-machine room, the door slamming shut after her.

Molly was impressed by what she had just witnessed. She patiently waited in her hiding place. She knew that guards watching the camera monitors would have observed Miss Cribbins's squabble with her pet and she wanted to give them a few moments to lose interest in the screens before she came out. Then she patted her knees and Petula rushed over to her.

"That was *excellent*," she whispered to her, giving her a huge hug. "Well done!" In Petula's thought bubble, Molly saw the machine room door shutting again and again. "Oh, don't worry, Petula. You did absolutely brilliantly. It's just Cribbins who mucked it up."

Molly and Petula stared longingly at the door. It was galling to think how close they had just been to getting in. Then Silver hopped in front of them.

"Three, eight, six, five, four, one, three," he whistled. Molly looked at Petula and then back at him.

"Silver, you *superstar*!" she exclaimed. "Now this is the plan." And bending down to her animal friends, she began whispering to them.

Half a mile beneath them, the dognakes glided through the sinewy tunnels of the deep mountain. Riding on the creatures' backs, Micky and Professor Selkeem were propelled forward and upward. The professor clutched his laboratory bag as though it was his ticket to life itself.

"We'll put a stop to it!" he shouted again and again. "We'll stop it!"

"Get to Rockeeeee!" Micky screeched like some demented background singer. "Rockeee! Yeeeeeeah!"

# Twenty-five

In the palace security-control room, twenty screens blinked boringly because nothing was happening in the royal grounds. Everywhere was quiet. The action was concentrated instead on four monitors focused on Princess Fang's afternoon entertainment in the royal auditorium. Three guards watched numbly as the performance commenced and as a troupe of people dressed as woodland animals danced. Then "The Greatest Circus Show on Earth" began. The guards weren't that interested in the red-and-blue-spotted panthers or the tightrope-walking squirrel monkeys, but they were distracted by them. Every so often they would throw a cursory glance at another palace screen, only to find their eyes wandering back again to the strange zoo creatures. There was a little action on monitor sixteen when Miss Cribbins seemed to be having trouble with her pet, but this had sorted itself out and the woman had gone into the mind-machine room. So the guards' attention drifted back to the show.

Molly waited for the cameras to twist away before, with Silver perched on her wrist, she approached the mind-machine room's combination lock. There, using his beak, Silver tapped in the number 3,8,6,5,4,1,3, and the door slid effortlessly apart. Petula quietly padded in, followed by Molly with Silver. Before the door shut, the hypnotized Taramasalata scuttled in too.

Inside, a sea of blue light washed the room. Miss Cribbins, now in her blue, electromagnetic lab suit and with her disheveled bronze wig back on her head, saw a red light flash on the wall, indicating that someone had entered the laboratory. She left the side of the Chinindian scientist whose brain was being drained and went back past the giant jellyfish to one of the arches that led to the changing zone. She stood on its threshold, not wanting to step in, as she didn't want to be switched back into her ordinary clothes. To her surprise, a small bedraggled quog stood at the other side of the changing chamber, under an arch there.

"How did you get in?" Miss Cribbins said suspiciously. She stared at the animal, who had awfully big, pulsing eyes.

Feeling a little dizzy, Miss Cribbins put her hand

against the wall to steady herself. She hoped the injections she gave herself every day weren't making her feel queasy again.

Petula glared up at the beautiful spinster, beseeching her to look at her. Then the cat-spider appeared by her side.

"You!" Miss Cribbins exclaimed. "Taramasalata, my little munchkin! So you learned that combination code? You clever darling! Come to say sorry to mummy for biting her, have we?" Her pet stepped forward and was immediately given a blue electromagnetic suit, so that only the pink fur of her head was visible. The rest of her body was blue and shiny. Then Miss Cribbins heard Princess Fang's voice.

"Cwibbins!" she said. "Stand attention! Important visitor!"

"Yes, Your Highness," said Miss Cribbins, flustered. "Sorry, Your Highness, I assumed you weren't here." She hurriedly tried to pat her hair into place. Then she took her position, standing bolt upright with her hands behind her back.

That was when Molly pounced. She'd sneaked in under the other arch and was already in her buzzing electromagnetic suit. Realizing Petula's hypnotism had not properly worked, she leaped toward Cribbins. One swift movement with the supertape that had gagged *her* so effectively a few days before was all it took. She strapped and stuck Miss Cribbins's wrists tightly behind her back and wound tape around her ankles too. The woman yelped and tottered on the spot.

"You!" she cried out before Molly slapped a third piece of tape over her red-lipsticked mouth.

In the guards' room, all eyes were on the show. The elethumpers were still causing trouble. Two were hopping about, kicking their enormous back legs in the air, while another was on its hind legs, attempting to mount the auditorium walls. Two flamingolike young zooeys were trying to control them with long sticks that seemed to have fluffy feathers on the ends of them.

The guards watched with doleful interest. The audience laughed.

"Time to—inter-vene?" the first guard suggested.

"If they haven't—calmed down—in five minutes—yes," the other replied.

Neither noticed Miss Cribbins's silent yelp on screen twenty-six.

"You get an Oscar for that!" Molly whispered to Silver, who was now hopping about excitedly at her feet. "That was a *perfect* imitation of Fang." Silver bowed, his blue laboratory suit glinting in the pale light. Petula, whose quog disguise had been whipped off and who also now wore a laboratory suit, trotted over. "And you get the prize for Cleverest Dog in the World!" Molly whispered gratefully to her. "Don't we look blue?" she said, frisbeeing her sabrerat mask toward the surveillance camera so that it was covered. She hoped that the screen going blank in the guards' room wouldn't alert them. Then she pushed Miss Cribbins into the main part of the blue-lit laboratory, past the giant squelching jellyfish toward the platform where the unfortunate Chinindian scientist sat. Green sparks shot out of the metal skullcap on his head, and with every pulse the white bones of his skeleton were visible through his skin. Molly rushed over to him and undid the strap of the cap. She ripped it off his head and placed it on the floor.

"I hope that didn't hurt," she said apologetically. The scientist didn't reply. He was too dazed.

Behind her, Petula began snarling. Molly swiveled to see her nipping at Cribbins's heels. The woman was trying to hobble to the exit, but with Silver flapping about her wrecked wig, the cat-spider scuttling over her face, and her ankles bound, it was proving difficult.

Molly grabbed her arm. "Oh no, you don't," she whispered hoarsely. "You're needed here. You're going to tell me how this mind machine works." Miss

Cribbins shook her head defiantly. "Listen, Cribbins," Molly warned, "many of the most useful things I know are in that machine, *stolen* from me. I want them back and if you don't help me, I'll . . . I'll . . ."

Miss Cribbins smirked nastily behind her tape gag.

Molly snapped. "I'll put *you* on the machine now!"

On the floor by the scientist's foot, the skullcap lay flashing and sparking. Molly saw panic dash across the spinster's face.

"Mmmmh! Mmmmhh!" she frantically burbled. Molly put both her hands up to the woman's mouth, one to unpeel the gag slightly, the other to seal her mouth quickly again should she attempt to scream to alert the guards.

"I'm going to let you say something," Molly said firmly, "but you only have a few seconds. If you shout, I'll put that skullcap on you. Got it?" Miss Cribbins nodded, but Molly didn't trust her one jot. She let a tiny piece of tape off the corner of her mouth so that the woman could only just speak.

"Fang is ze only one who can program and operate ze machine," Miss Cribbins whistled though the side of her mouth. "I merely came in to turn it off as ze physicist was nearly cooked." Molly slapped her hand over the woman's red mouth and retaped it. Cribbins stared coldly at her, her eyes dark and sharp.

Molly read her thoughts. In the bubbles she saw pictures of guards and of Miss Cribbins standing obediently away from the mind-machine control panels as Princess Fang programmed it. This was enough for Molly. Miss Cribbins seemed to be telling the truth. Then the woman was imagining Molly sitting in a large birdcage that dangled from a mountain ledge. And of knives being sharpened.

"It's a pity your thoughts are so mean," Molly observed. "Bet you're picturing me caged up like a pet grasshopper. And what would you do with a sharp knife now, if your hands were free?"

The woman's eyebrows arched, but Molly ignored her reaction. Instead she pushed the skinny woman into one of the chairs at the side of the room and with more tape strapped her thighs to the seat. Miss Cribbins hardly struggled, which Molly took as a sign of her utmost confidence that the palace guards would soon arrive.

"Watch her, would you?" she asked Petula and Silver. Taramasalata made herself comfortable on Miss Cribbins's head, pawing at her wig and pulling her hair apart even more.

Molly quickly went to the control panel of the mind machine. Before her an array of unlabeled buttons winked expectantly. Molly looked at the now sparkless skullcap on the ground and then at the throbbing, watery jellyfish machine. There was no way she could experiment with the skullcap. If she did, the chances were she'd end up doing a lot of damage to herself. Waiting for Fang to arrive wasn't much of an option either. The last thing the princess would ever agree to do would be to put Molly's hypnotic know-how back, even if Molly threatened her with death. Anyway, Molly thought, she could never threaten to kill Fang. Killing wasn't one of her hobbies.

Molly stared at the mind machine in desperation. She wished she knew how it worked. She sank to her knees and put her head in her hands. She needed to keep calm. To think logically and clearly. She took a deep breath and tried to steady her nerves. Who had invented the great big artificial brain? Was there time to find them? Were they alive or had Fang used them to make the machine and then put *them* on it and sucked *their* brilliant minds out too? Their genius thoughts were probably bubbling about in the artificial brain right now. And then, as Molly imagined a white-haired scientist pottering about, inventing the incredible jellyfish, something struck her. The gelatinous machine was in fact a huge artificial brain. Maybe it behaved like a giant mind. Maybe, just maybe, Molly would be able to *read its thoughts*. The idea was so simple and so ludicrous that it made Molly gasp.

She thought of Forest. In Los Angeles he'd taught her how to meditate. This had helped make her mind stronger. A strong mind was what Molly definitely needed now. So, sitting cross-legged in her meditation position, she looked up at the jellyfish. If she just focused her mind and let thoughts of the world slip away, as Forest had taught her, perhaps she would be able to penetrate the jellyfish's blue slippery exterior and make it show her what it had inside. But would that be enough to get her precious hypnotic knowledge back? Molly took five deep breaths, breathing out very slowly each time.

Then she beamed up at the machine, *Show me your thoughts.*

Nothing happened. Molly's heart was pounding. She could imagine the guards running up the paths toward the jellyfish room right now, with Fang marching after them, her little feet angrily pounding the ground. Molly could hardly bear it. Like treasure lost at the bottom of the sea, her knowledge was before her but hidden out of reach. Molly shut her eyes and tried to calm down. In her mind she heard Forest's voice.

*Cool it, Molly. Just concentrate on your breathing and cool it. Imagine yourself a tiny thing on a huge planet. Zoom up into space and look down on yourself. Cool it.*

Molly found her breath steadying, and she cut off all fearful thoughts of people at the palace. She visualized herself on this mountaintop above the lake. This was good. She began to really feel how high up the palace was, and she imagined the land below the mountain too. It stretched away for hundreds of miles into the distance. And then her mind began to levitate above her body. Up and up she went, until the mountain with Molly Moon on it was a long, long way beneath her and the land around the mountain was the surface of the planet. Up and up Molly's spirit rose, until it was floating cross-legged *in space*. Now when she summoned the jellyfish, it was there too, floating in front of her. Black space was all about them, and then deep blue water. Molly felt like she was at the bottom of the ocean. The vibrations of the pulsing jellyfish lapped against her skin like waves and, knowing that the moment was perfect, Molly's thoughts reached out to it like wide, long tentacles.

*What are you thinking?* Her question flowed clear as a crystal spring toward the jellyfish.

And immediately a huge, misty bubble popped up. Molly opened her eyes and gave a whistle of amazement. An overwhelming number of images and numbers and pages of writing filled the bubble above the jellyfish. Its thoughts flicked by, thousands every second. Molly realized she would have to be more specific.

*Thank you.* Her hair felt as if it was standing straight up on her head, and her scalp was tingling as if a million ants were dancing on it. *Now please show me all the thoughts that come from Molly Moon,* she asked with her mind. *Thoughts on how to hypnotize, how to time travel, how to make time stand still. Show me all the thoughts that were taken from Molly Moon.*

The jellyfish bubbled and sparked, and Molly saw a multitude of images of herself and her life. Pictures of the hypnotism book and the pages in it . . . memories of the time she'd hypnotized Petula . . . memories of a clear crystal and the times that she'd made time stand still . . . memories of time traveling. She saw the white sievelike Bubble at the beginning of time that she'd traveled to, where the light restored a person's youth.

Molly desperately wanted these memories and lessons all properly back in her head. But she didn't have time to learn them all over again, one by one. Hoping that it was possible, and shifting her focus up a gear, she thought up to the jellyfish, *If it is possible, would you be able to please put all these thoughts, feelings, lessons, and memories—all this knowledge—BACK INTO MY HEAD?* As she launched the request, her earlobes began to burn. They felt so hot that Molly thought they might actually catch fire.

It was miraculous. Sparks hit the ceiling and others

arced toward Molly's head. She braced herself as a cloud of electricity surrounded her and as waves and waves of knowledge came home. They crashed into her brain, flooding it and filling the gaps where they had once lived, and quenching the fire in Molly's ears. She shut her eyes and let her mind be as open as possible. She wanted every last drop of what belonged to her. And then the crashing was reduced to splashing, until all that remained were the last ripples of her memories.

Molly opened her eyes. For a moment she thought she must be dreaming. At last she felt whole again. She got up and bowed respectfully to the machine.

*Thank you,* she thought to it. *Thank you. THANK YOU!* The machine gave a burp. Then, above it, a bubble with a shining sun in it exploded and disappeared.

Molly made her way to Miss Cribbins. She stood before her and stared at the nasty but beautiful woman. Molly felt as good a hypnotist as she had ever felt. With great satisfaction she directed a massive bolt of hypnotic power into the spinster's thickly lashed eyes. At once the fusion feeling blossomed in every part of Molly's body. She felt wonderful.

"Now, Miss Cribbins," Molly began, "you are completely under my power." Miss Cribbins nodded.

"Lean forward," Molly instructed. The woman did as she was told, so that the cat-spider and the wig nearly fell off her head. Molly undid the tape that held her arms.

"Lean back," she said. Taramasalata clung to Miss Cribbins's seesawing wig. Molly undid the tape that secured Cribbins's legs and her ankles, then she unpeeled the tape from her mouth.

"Where are my crystals?" she asked her.

"In a box in—Princess Fang's—bedroom," said Cribbins falteringly.

"Good," said Molly. "Now, acting completely normally, and telling no one that you are hypnotized or that you are under my power, you will go and get the box and bring it back here."

Miss Cribbins nodded and like a remote-control toy, and with Taramasalata perched on her shoulder, nibbling her ear lobe, she got up and walked toward the door.

# Twenty-Six

"What is your name?" Molly asked.

The witless-looking scientist said nothing. He was studying his thumb as though the answer to life lay in the creases of its knuckle.

"Name?" Molly repeated. "What is your name?" She felt really sorry for him. He must have been brilliant, but he'd been reduced to an idiot.

"Daksha Ashnu," he suddenly volunteered.

"Good. Now, Daksha, you must sit here and don't move. I'm going to help you get your memories back."

Moments later, a whirlwind of pictures and numbers were swirling above the pulsing, blue jellyfish. *If it's not too much trouble,* Molly asked the machine politely, *would you be able to send Daksha Ashnu's thoughts back to him, please?* She noticed her ears heating up again. And then the rebuilding of the scientist's mind began.

Molly swiftly removed the sabrerat mask from the surveillance camera and she and her animal friends left the laboratory. The electric-blue suits were sucked off them in the changing area. Molly, once dressed, took the sabrerat costume off so that she was in her original white jumpsuit again, and she helped Petula remove her webbed feet, fake ears, and beak.

It was cool in the mind-machine room. Molly had nothing to fear now and she wanted to sit in the sun so, stepping outside, she, Petula, and Silver waited in the courtyard for Miss Cribbins to return.

Success tasted very sweet. Molly lay back on the grass, shut her eyes, and smiled to herself. It felt absolutely blissful being complete again and, she had to admit, being powerful again too. Molly felt safe. She felt confident. All the knowledge about hypnotism washed like nutritious currents through her brain. Molly sighed with satisfaction. All she needed now was for Cribbins to hurry back with her crystals. Then she would easily sort everything out. She'd soon have Rocky free.

In the surveillance room a guard watching the show picked up a glass of water. As he sipped, his eyes fell on the figure of a girl lying on the lawn outside the royal machine room. Beside her lay a black pug and on its back perched a black bird. All were basking in the sun. Automatically the guard reached for the red button in front of him. Instantly the alarm was activated. Throughout the palace, workers saw the telltale flashing red lights. All knew what this meant—impostors in the palace. All the monitor room guards picked up their guns and at once set off for the mind-machine room.

Princess Fang sat in the golden royal box inside the auditorium, her pet turquoise grasshopper in its golden cage on her lap. On one side of her, Rocky sat staring straight ahead, dressed in a smart black suit and white shirt with a palm-tree-patterned bow tie. On Fang's other side, the president of Chinindia clapped delightedly as he watched the spectacular show. Behind, other foreign dignitaries laughed while various members of the royal household sat beside them, bored and stern. The children of the rich mountaintop families were there too, looking poker-faced. The only audience members having fun were the foreign guests and Nurse Meekles and her brood of little children, who sat close to the edge of the arena, having a whale of a time.

The seats sloped away in front of Princess Fang down to the sawdust-strewn stage, where Tortillus stood with two kangaraffes, and a microphone in his hand. In a monotone he was explaining how the beasts' pens were the largest in the zoo and, to illustrate why, he was getting the long-necked creatures to jump. As the kangaraffes bounced about, Princess Fang blew a pink gum bubble and sneered. She felt ill just looking at wrinkly old Tortillus in his long robe, with his huge tortoise-shell back. She loathed his ugliness. But seeing Tortillus's mutations also pleased her. For his lowliness reminded her of how she had removed him from his royal seat and taken the throne for herself. It had been like a grand game of musical chairs. Musical thrones. She would insist that he wear a hood and cloak to cover himself on future trips to the palace.

She fingered the many crystals that hung around her neck and wondered whether they would be bait bright enough to lure Molly Moon. Then she saw the red alarm light flashing on her dress. At once she sat straight as a nail. She popped her gum bubble and gave a childish giggle.

"Ah, so you've bitten, little fish! About time too."

"Sorry? Did you say something?" the Chinindian president asked.

"I've been bitten!" Princess Fang winced. "So please excuse me; I must get some ointment." She gathered up her pink taffeta dress, attached the grasshopper's cage to a sequined hook on her sleeve, slipped off her chair, and marched up the aisle toward the palace courtyards.

"Do not shoot de impostors!" she barked into a radio transmitter on her cuff. "I wepeat: Do not shoot de impostors!" She had already asked the palace guards to switch off the poisonous darts. Fang wanted Molly Moon and Micky Minus alive.

Petula gave a bark and Molly opened her eyes. At once she summoned Petula's thoughts. A bubble with images of palace guards in it appeared.

"Oh crumbs!" said Molly, jumping to her feet. Petula was barking to the left *and* to the right. "It's okay, Petula." Molly gave her a pat, trying to calm her, but she too was starting to feel distinctly nervous and foolish too for not being more alert. But the thing that made her feel most stupid was that she'd completely forgotten about Fang's and the guards' guns. Where had her mind been? What had she been thinking? She couldn't hypnotize bullets!

As two men in purple soldiers' uniforms appeared at the courtyard door she grew petrified. Then she walked bravely and briskly toward them. Why, Molly wondered, was Miss Cribbins taking so long? Doubts began to wriggle around in Molly's brain like hungry maggots. Perhaps Cribbins hadn't been hypnotized at all; maybe she'd been acting. Then Molly saw her approaching. She was clutching a red box, and two servants followed in her wake. Molly's imagination somersaulted. What if Cribbins wasn't hypnotized and the box had a gun in it or a deadly jack-in-the-box that would leap out at Molly when Cribbins opened the lid? But Molly couldn't be distracted now by Miss Cribbins. The pressing problem was the guards.

Molly walked toward the nearest one and fired a heavy hypnotic glare at him. Luckily his previous hypnotism couldn't have been locked in with a password, for at once he was overcome. The second guard was easy too. Adrenaline pumped through Molly as she breathed a small sigh of relief. She sent out thoughts to read Miss Cribbins's mind. It was blank except for a picture of Molly with a halo over her head. Molly relaxed and took the red leather box. As she undid its lock, more guards broke through the far door of the courtyard. Molly grappled to open the lid. It sprang open. Molly's heart rocketed and then sank. Inside the box was nothing, just its bare red velvet lining. Molly turned to see a dozen servants and guards bearing down on her and shrieked. Then, realizing that everything hung on this single moment, Molly pulled herself together.

"Help me, Petula!" she shouted.

Petula didn't need to be asked. They were in an emergency situation—any mongrel could see that. As Molly faced five soldiers who were marching, hands outstretched, toward her, Petula took on a small servant woman in an apron and peaked cap. With fear snapping at her very soul, Petula was determined her eyes would work instantly this time. And they did. The woman stopped dead in her tracks, as hypnotized as a chicken with a circle drawn around it. Petula barked angrily at her as if to say, "Now don't you DARE move," before tackling her next opponent.

Molly's eyes were like lasers. From her shoulder Silver watched as she turned on each servant and guard and in a second burned her hypnotic glare through to their will, binding each in a shacklelike trance. Within a minute they all stood ready to obey Molly's instructions. With adrenaline pumping through her and her hands sweating, she skidded around and looked about, hardly able to believe how quickly and easily the palace workers had been disarmed. Molly rubbed her fingers together impatiently.

"Come on, come on then," she said, convinced that more were about to burst through the door. But none did. Instead, Princess Fang appeared.

Seeing the stunned palace guards and servants, the

princess immediately assessed the situation.

"More guards! MORE GUARDS!" she screamed into her transmitter, her shrill voice ringing through the clear mountain air. Her eyes were murderous and accusing. Fang could see Molly had her skills back, and she was very puzzled as to how this had come about, but her primary feeling was of pure confidence—she had at last found Molly.

"So, Milly . . ." she said, not looking Molly in the eye, and moving toward the side of the courtyard.

*"Eeeny*
*Meeny,*
*Miny,*
*Moe."*

"Where's Minus?"

"Tied up," Molly said calmly, eyeing the crystals that hung heavily around the princess's neck—three green, three red, and three clear. Molly recognized her own, hanging on their string.

"You know you're totally twapped," the princess said, beginning to hurriedly climb a vine that hugged one of the cloister columns. "More guards are coming. Before you can weach me dey'll be here." Molly was amazed by how quickly Fang was clambering up onto the roof. "And when dey come," the princess shouted behind her, "I'll tell dem not to look in your eyes. Den you'll be powerless, Milly Moon. I'll have your pet pug fed to de bearunkeys and *you'll be incinerated*!" Her dress caught on the tiled roof and ripped as she scrambled up. "I'm de king of de castle," she jibed. "You're de dirty rascal!"

Molly stared longingly at the crystals bobbing around the princess's neck and she started to run toward the vine. Petula began barking. Then Molly heard the deliberate march of someone approaching the courtyard. She glanced over her shoulder and saw Rocky. She stopped. He walked into the courtyard like a mechanical zombie.

From her rooftop position, Fang cried, "Kill Molly Moon, Rocky! KILL HER! Whatever you do, *don't look at her eyes*!"

A second later Rocky registered Molly, and the princess's fatal instructions kicked in. A ghastly grimace crossed his face, his eyes flashed with hate, and, like a bull, he came charging across the grass. Molly was so shocked that she simply stood there and watched him hurtling toward her. Before she knew it, his hands were around her throat, trying to strangle her.

"Please, stop it! STOB IT!" Molly begged as he throttled her. She gasped and spluttered and then, rallying herself, kneed Rocky as hard as she could in the stomach. For a moment his grip loosened. Molly now punched him as brutally as she could. Her fist slammed into his neck. She hated to do this but saw this wasn't the *real* Rocky—this was a brainwashed Rocky, a killer.

Fury boiled inside Molly. She could have caught Fang—she *should* have caught her and hypnotized her—because now Rocky, of all people, had come to ruin everything. Tormented by this terrible thought, she swung her fist and lashed out again. This time Rocky thumped her in the face. She returned his blow, but did more damage to her fist than to him. His knuckles now came pounding into her nose, smashing it. At once blood began pouring out of it.

From her perch, like a Roman empress watching two gladiators fight, Princess Fang squealed and laughed. She clapped her hands and wiggled her bottom in a spontaneous little victory dance. So enthralled was she that she failed to notice the sound of wings beating behind her.

Like a black arrow, Silver dived toward Fang. His beak extended and, ready to snap, he aimed for the crystals that hung on a string around her neck. And then, for a split second, he landed on her shoulder. With a scissoring peck, he severed the string and took off again with his precious load. As fast as he could, he flew down to where Molly and Rocky tumbled, punching and kicking each other on the ground.

Silver dropped the crystals on the grass by Molly's hand and hopped onto her head. Molly at once saw her chance. With an enormous effort she rolled away from Rocky, ramming her heel into his knee as she did, and she grabbed her clear gem. Instantly, Molly froze time.

At once the world was cold and still.

The princess stood motionless on the cloister roof, her hands on her hips, staring angrily down. The guards and servants were frozen too. Everywhere was still. In the arena where the show was continuing, kangaraffes were suspended mid-hop and the foreign visitors were statuelike, their hands stiff in clapping positions. Rocky was set rigid, with a violent look on his face. Only Silver, because he was in contact with Molly, was still moving. He looked at the world and whistled.

# Twenty-Seven

For a few moments Molly lay exhausted on the grass. The pain in the bridge of her nose was so intense that for a while she could think of nothing else. Molly couldn't help crying. It had been the worse thing ever to fight like that with Rocky. Silver sat quietly on her head.

Then the throbbing in Molly's nose ebbed, and the blood in it clotted. Molly dried her eyes. Her face, she knew, was a tear-smeared mess of bruises, blood, and earth.

"Thank you, Silver," she whispered, catching her breath. Then she gave a shiver and looked about her at the frozen world. She glanced over to Rocky. His face was overcast with a vicious expression.

Molly knew that to hypnotize him she would have to

bring her eyes directly into his line of vision. She would have to touch him to send movement into him and, while the rest of the world was frozen, zap him with her eyes. And it had to work the first time, or the monster Rocky would be back.

The problem was that Rocky had originally been hypnotized by Micky and that hypnosis had been locked in. Molly cast her mind back to the picture that had bobbed over Micky's head when she'd asked him what his hypnotic password was. She'd seen a white meringue pudding on a dish. Was *meringue* the password? She could only find out by trying.

First Molly checked her eyes. Luckily Rocky hadn't managed to hit her there. Nothing was blurry—in fact, she could see well. So she summoned up a really powerful beam of hypnotism. It buzzed behind her eyeballs, making her sore nose tingle. Then Molly crawled over to Rocky and, looking straight at him, touched his shoulder. He came to life at once. Her eyes blazing, Molly let him have it, and in an instant Rocky was stunned.

"Now, Rocky," Molly said, "you are no longer under Micky's power. I unlock you with the password *meringue*." Rocky stared straight ahead as though he didn't understand. "Blast, it's not working," Molly muttered. Then she tried again. "With the password, *baked Alaska*. Still Rocky was unmoved. "With *meringuey pudding . . .*" Molly guessed. "With *yummy pudding*," she offered. Molly was starting to feel helpless. She thought of the whipped-up meringue she'd seen. Had it been ice cream? "With *ice cream*," she jabbed. But this didn't work either. What had the pudding looked like? Like a mountain of ice cream, she supposed. "With *ice-cream mountain*?" she asked. Molly was getting really desperate. At any moment Rocky might jolt out of his trance, if she didn't nail the password. "With *snowy mountain . . .*" she tried. Then, "With *MONT BLANC*." Molly threw this last guess into the air without any hope for it at all. But amazingly, it had the effect she wanted. At last Rocky nodded. "Is that the password?" Molly asked, dumbfounded. He nodded again. "Oh thank you!" Molly blew out a sigh of relief. "Now hold on, Rocky. All this will be over soon. So, just remember, when I bring you out of this trance you will be completely your old self, the real Rocky. You won't have any loyalty to Princess Fang. Okay? You will be as yourself as you were before we came to this place. Do you understand?"

Rocky nodded again.

"All right. In five seconds you will be free from all hypnotism, including mine. Five. Four. Three. Two. One. Now!" She clicked her fingers.

At once Rocky sat up. "Oh, Molly," he moaned, "*what*

*have I done?* I'm sorry, Molly. Oh no. Oh NO! Look at your nose . . . your face!"

Molly smiled. She felt like life was suddenly filled to the brim with joy.

"Thank goodness you're back," she said and flung her arms around her best friend's shoulders.

For a while the two friends sat embracing in the still, cold, suspended world. Then Molly gave Rocky a quick briefing on what had been happening. Princess Fang stood on the cloister roof, puce with fury, and the palace workers stood rigid as if they were made of wood. Petula was frozen in the position of barking at Rocky, her body curved, her mouth snarling.

"Poor Petula," said Rocky. "She'll never trust me again."

"She'll understand," Molly said. "Don't worry. Right, let's get Her Horribleness up there sorted out."

At once Molly allowed the world to move. Petula resumed her barking, but then stopped and stood confused. She put her head to one side and sniffed at Rocky. He had lost his angry metallic smell, and Molly looked happy.

On the cloister roof Princess Fang was equally muddled. Then, seeing Molly tie the string of gems around her neck, she understood immediately what had happened.

"GUARDS!" she screamed, stamping her foot. She began backing up the sloped roof, looking at the wall between the courtyards and wondering whether she might cross it. Desperately she scanned the gate below, hoping for assistance, but as every batch of muscly men entered, time seemed to skip a beat and the next moment the very same guards were sitting on the ground quiet as roosting pheasants. Moon was freezing time to hypnotize the guards. And there was absolutely nothing that she, Princess Fang, could do about it. She could hardly bear it! If the Moon girl got the better of all the guards, there would be *nothing* to stop her. And then all would be lost. The kingdom . . . the empire! She would never be Queen of the World. Princess Fang would be finished! Then she heard a heavy beating behind her. It sounded as though a huge kite with leathery flapping wings was coming toward them.

Princess Fang turned. Turned to see that the flying thing in the air at the side of the mountain was brown and furry with four legs. Its hooves dangled beneath it, and its strong wings beat the air. It was a cow flapper and it was coming straight for her.

With one arm Princess Fang shielded her eyes from the bright sun. Then, seeing that the creature was dive-bombing her, she dropped to her knees. In the next moment, there was a bubbling noise and the princess saw something falling though the air toward her.

"UUURRGHHH!" she screamed, but it was too late. The ripe and juicy cowpat hit her square on. Cow poo splattered all over her sophisticated angular hair and sprayed the shoulders of her pink taffeta dress. It trickled down her forehead, her cheeks, and her back.

*Bull's eye!* Silver thought up to the cow flapper. *Thank you!*

*My pleasure,* the strange creature thought back to him, mooing as it flew. *That will teach her to take potshots at cow flappers!* And it gave the mynah bird a broad wink before tipping its body sideways to fly up and away.

Neither Molly nor Rocky could stop laughing. Then, eventually, seeing that the princess was attempting to escape over the high courtyard wall, Molly pulled herself together and froze the world again.

Silver was on her shoulder. Together they scaled the vine to the cloister roof. Molly almost felt sorry for the princess. The little girl was petrified, but Molly had no sympathy for her. She knew that behind the frightened eyes lurked a hard-hearted dictator.

"Craaaaarkkk!" croaked Silver. "Nasty!" Molly gathered her hypnotic strength and let the power build up behind her eyes. Finding a part of Princess Fang that wasn't covered in cow poo, she reached out and touched her. Immediately the princess was animated, even though the rest of the world was still as a picture.

Molly let her have it. A hot beam of hyperconcentrated hypnotism shot out of her eyes and hit home. As the force exploded into her, the horrid child jerked backward. Then she stood still, now totally entranced by Molly.

"You, Fang," Molly began, "are now completely under my power and will be until I tell you otherwise. I lock this instruction in with the words—"

"Spoiled brat," sang Silver.

"With the words *spoiled brat,*" Molly agreed, and she let the world move.

Fang nodded obediently.

"YES!" shouted Rocky from below, punching the air. Petula barked enthusiastically, and Molly turned and curtsied.

"FANTABULOUS!" She laughed.

"You can say that again!"

"FAN-TAB-U-LOUS!" cawed Silver.

Now down from the roof, the princess stood beside Molly and Rocky like a quiet, respectful kid, fresh out of kindergarten. Her imprisoned turquoise grasshopper, on the other hand, chirruped madly from its tiny prison on her sleeve.

"I know how he feels," Rocky said, and he opened the little latch on its cage door. With a grateful spring the grasshopper leaped out onto Rocky's shoulder. Then it hopped down to the ground and went away. Petula and Silver watched it go.

Leaning over Fang, Molly removed the other gem necklaces and put them around her own neck.

"Right, let's get things going," she said. "To start with, let's leave the foreign visitors to have their fun."

"Yes," Rocky agreed. "Get Miss Smelly here to wash her hands and face and change into a clean outfit, and she can go and see them off."

"Good idea, and while she's changing I can hypnotize all the other royal children and the rest of Fang's crew."

"Nice."

So that's exactly what Molly did.

In the palace auditorium, Tortillus and the animals were now off the stage. The Lakeside choristers, dressed as mermaids, were performing their last song—a ballad about how lovely life was by the water. Dancers leaped and turned before the audience, trailing long blue riverlike ribbons.

Switching the world on and off as though she had a pause button for it, Molly brought all Fang's horrid playmates and advisers under her spell. And the finale continued as if nothing had happened. As the singers hit high notes and made harmonies that echoed through the mountain, the foreign guests and Nurse Meekles, with her children, listened and watched. They were completely oblivious to the fact that everyone in the auditorium apart from them was now hypnotized.

After the show was over, Princess Fang did exactly as she'd been told and went to bid her guests good-bye. She was dressed handsomely in a violet feathered dress, but although her face and hands were spotlessly clean, her hair looked as though it had mud in it. What was more, the Chinindian president could smell a distinct farmyardy pong when he bent low to bow his good-bye.

"It was a pleasure meeting you," he said, trying not to breathe in.

As they were airlifted off the mountain, the visitors all commented on their marvelous trip.

"What a happy country!" they agreed.

They had no idea how close some of them had come to losing their minds.

The scientist Molly had saved from the mind machine sat with a computer open on his lap. He was taking notes about his interesting trip, convinced that he had spent the day studying new forms of oxygen-making jellyfish.

Professor Selkeem's dognakes had brought him and Micky to the palace laundry room in the depths of the building. They had entered through the secret hatch near the ceiling, and the dognakes were now gliding down the metal laundry machines' sorting arms. They deposited the two boys on the floor.

Professor Selkeem immediately went for the door but found it locked.

"Damn!" he cried. "You're a lychee!" he shouted at Micky. "We're both lychees in a tin! And who's got the tin opener?! Will Ai Mu come and open the door? No, she won't come here today!"

Micky ran to the door and, frothing at the mouth, began to bang on it.

"Rockeee!" he shouted.

"No ears there," the professor said, sitting down on a pile of sheets and frantically opening his laboratory bag. "Too deep in the building. Must try to open it." His dognakes curled up protectively about him. He pulled out a black object and, getting up, advanced toward the door. "Crack the door locks. Just find the weakness in the code and manipulate it with the magnet." He began passing the black object in his hand over the doorframe. "Don't stir your noodles, little chili head. We'll get their blood."

# Twenty-eight

Wildgust, Tortillus, Belsha, and the flamingo family were on the rocky outcrop, overseeing the crating up of the zoo animals. It was very strange. There were no guards marching around giving them orders, but, knowing about the palace cameras, they behaved as though they were under surveillance. They had no idea what had happened to Fang. Hearing nothing, they'd assumed that Molly's attempts to get her hypnotic powers back had failed. Now, desperately worried, they got on with their work.

Then a powerful beating of wings in the air above their heads caught their attention. A brown cow flapper and Silver landed on the mountain ridge. Silver hopped toward Tortillus and Wildgust and broke the news.

"Craaaaark! Fang gone! Palace . . . safe. SAFE. SAFE. Craaaaark! Come!"

"I don't believe it!" Tortillus said, startled and quite overcome with astonishment. "That girl has done it. She's been brilliant. BRILLIANT!" he shouted. He paused, then said to Belsha in awe, "She's made it possible for us to start *living*!" He clasped his wife's hands. "Mont Blancia will be ours again! The people will be free once more—"

Wildgust interrupted him. "What are we waiting for?" he said darkly. "Let's go now."

And so Tortillus led his family back home.

They found Molly and Rocky in an extrapretty garden with a fountain bubbling in its center. Petula lay on the warm grass, sucking a stone, while Silver pecked at tasty insects that crawled about in the dirt. Molly and Rocky had cleaned themselves up, and were enjoying a picnic tea. Miss Cribbins and Princess Fang were quiet, sitting cross-legged with the other members of the royal court making daisy chains under a shady tree.

"So you got Silver's message!" said Molly, getting up and beaming at him.

"You've been through the wars," said Tortillus worriedly, touching her bruised cheek.

"I'm fine," Molly assured him. "It doesn't really

hurt." Then she added excitedly, "We sent a couple of guards to fetch the professor and Micky. Rocky's going to sort Micky out."

Tortillus shook his head. "You are amazing."

Molly shrugged. "I couldn't have done it without Silver and Petula."

"And that cow flapper put the cherry on the cake," said Rocky with a smile.

Molly introduced Rocky to Tortillus and his family, and they all sat down to help themselves to the delicious picnic.

"Now," Molly said, when every cake and sandwich had been finished, "I've got an idea that you might all like. Let's take Princess Fang to her broadcasting studio. She's got one last royal appointment that she can't miss."

Soon they were all crowded inside a small white transmission room with the princess poised in front of a camera operated by a now dehypnotized engineer.

"Come to—the screen," the hypnotized princess beckoned, staring into the camera's eye. "Everyone must—come and watch—your near-est screen."

In the valley below, thousands of people, all dressed in their fairy-tale costumes, stood to attention, their eyes and ears honed in on the giant hypnotic loudspeakers and screens. They watched as Princess Fang's small mouth moved and listened as the child spoke.

"People of Lakeside," the princess declared, "you are all now—under Molly Moon's—power. You will no longer—be under my power."

Molly's face now smiled down from the screen. Her green eyes were huge and pulsating. "Lake people," she said, "very soon you will be free of the hypnotism that has held you captive for so long. Before I unlock it, I want to let you know that Klaucus will again be your king. I hope you will all make this place, Mont Blancia, one of the happiest and best places in the world. Now with the words that you have been trapped by, *Mont Blanc*, I release you."

"It's funny how simple it all is with the help of a bit of hypnotism," Molly said to Tortillus as they returned to the palace garden again.

Tortillus smiled, the lines of his face creasing like small concertinas. He looked up at the sky. "I can't believe I'm up here again." He patted Molly fondly on the shoulder. "Now you, I expect, when you have your brother back, will be making a beeline for your time and your home."

Molly nodded. "I think we will," she said with a smile. Then, fingering her green crystal, she added, "I know how much you, Tortillus, would have loved to have seen this mountain covered in snow. Before we go, if you want, I'll show you." Molly glanced at the small badgelike watch that was fastened to Tortillus's tunic. "I can have you back before four o'clock."

"But that's in five minutes!" The old man's hand shook. "Are you serious, Molly?"

"Yes. Fancy it?"

"Can Wildgust come too?"

"Of course."

So, leaving Rocky with Petula, Silver, and the royal family, Molly took Tortillus and Wildgust to a quiet area beside a jasmine bush. The two hunched men held hands as Molly had instructed them. She clutched her green crystal in her palm, and taking herself into a semi-trance, bid its boomerang-shaped scar open. At once it became an eye-shaped swirl spiraling into itself, all green and airy.

"We're ready," Molly said. She gripped Tortillus's hand. "Whatever you do, keep hold of each other's hands. As long as we're in contact, you will travel with me." She looked at Wildgust's wide, apprehensive eyes. "And don't worry, Wildgust. You're going to love it."

Molly shut her eyes to concentrate, and Tortillus and Wildgust followed suit. None of them saw the dognake slither toward them with the professor on its back. None was aware that the dognake had clamped its jaws around the hem of Wildgust's cloak. So when they took off none knew that Professor Selkeem and his dognake were traveling back in time with them.

The sky above flashed day and night, so fast that it became blur of dawn and dusk light. The mountaintop palace soon disappeared and there was rock all around them. Suddenly, even behind their closed eyelids, they were dazzled by a white light that became brighter and brighter. Molly wanted Tortillus and Wildgust to see Mont Blanc in its full glory—completely covered with snow. Watching the sky, she slowed down and selected a day when the sky was azure blue. And then they stopped. Quick as mercury, the dognake slithered off, hiding the boy professor behind a rock.

The mountain and valleys around were coated in snow. Fresh, powdery spring snow as white as the cleanest cloud. It peaked on the rocky mountains like whipped egg whites—like meringue.

"Heavens above!" Tortillus gasped. Wildgust squinted and cupped his leathery hand over his eyes.

"So bright," he murmured. Then he threw off his silk cloak. "I have to fly," he said. "What bird could resist flying here?"

"Go for it," Molly said, smiling.

And so extending his wings and shaking them out, Wildgust took off. He circled about Molly and Tortillus, laughing as he flew. Then he dived down the side of the ridge and disappeared. A few minutes later he reappeared, spiraling the thermals farther down the mountain.

"This is a truly wonderful experience," Tortillus said to Molly. "Thank you, and again thank you for everything you have done for our people. Whenever you want, Molly, please come back and visit us. You will always be our most honored guest."

"Thanks," said Molly, grinning, stamping her feet, and slapping her sides with her arms to keep warm. "Before I go, I want you to make a snowman! I'll get some stones for its eyes and nose."

Behind the rock, the little professor's flesh was turning blue from the cold. He shivered in his loincloth.

"I am watching you," he said coldly, observing Wildgust swooping below. He saw Molly walking farther up the mountain, away from Tortillus, kicking the snow as she went. Tortillus stood alone on the bare white ridge.

"N-nasty, I know," the professor stammered through chattering teeth, "to be all alone." Molly had disappeared behind a snowy rock farther up. And

Wildgust was now ascending through the air, approaching Tortillus. "I'll get you," the professor hissed and he prepared to move.

Wildgust landed. "Stupendous!" he said, his feathers ruffled by the wind. "I suppose there are some advantages to having been mutated into a bird-person." Exhilarated and breathless, his hawk eyes didn't see the brown dognake, its tail wrapped around a rock, making its way toward Tortillus's ankles. Wildgust took a step toward his brother, putting a hand out to touch his back.

And then the most unexpected thing happened. Wildgust gave Tortillus an almighty push. Tortillus teetered for a split second on the brink of the cliff edge—and then fell.

But not so fast that he wasn't able to take hold of Wildgust's arm and pull him with him.

And not so fast that the dognake wasn't able to firmly curl its upper body about Tortillus's ankle and hold him fast. From higher up the slope Molly saw them fall, and she saw the dognake around Tortillus's ankle. Then she saw the boy professor emerge from behind his rock.

"NO!" she shouted. "Leave them alone! *Leave them alone!*" and she began to run down the snowy slope.

Wildgust fell lower and harder than Tortillus, but

he flapped his wings and was at once airborne. He grabbed at Tortillus's arm and began tugging it, trying to pull his own brother down to his death.

"WHY?" Tortillus shouted.

"*I* will be king, not you," Wildgust cried, his wings beating furiously.

Molly sprinted down the slope, skidding on the ice at the bottom, and nearly falling over the ledge herself.

"You're demented! YOU'RE EVIL!" she shouted at Selkeem.

"Schnapps is *saving* him," the professor replied. "Do you need a magnifying glass? And what are you waiting for? Use your crystal!" Molly instantly felt stupid for not thinking of that herself. Now she froze the world.

At once everything was still and Molly saw the situation in its true light. Wildgust was tugging at Tortillus, his huge wings spread-eagled, trying to pull him to his death. Tortillus hung upside down. And the dognake was clinging on to the rock, half slipping as he tried to stop the old man from falling. On the snow beside her, the professor looked completely out of place in his Tarzan-like loincloth.

Molly reached forward and touched the dognake, carefully directing movement into only him. Schnapps came to life and at once saw the situation. Summoning all their strength, he and Molly pulled. They pulled as hard as they could, and slowly but surely, like a bucket from a well, Tortillus began to move up through the still air toward them.

"Eeeerrrghhhh," Molly groaned as she wrenched him up. As soon as his body was on the cliff edge she was able to reach Wildgust. Concentrating very hard, taking great care not to let any movement pass into him, she undid his hands from around Tortillus's arm.

Molly lay on the ground panting, with the frozen people about her on the spring snow, and Wildgust hanging in the air like an angel from hell.

She crawled over to the rock and unwound the dog-nake's body from it.

It was now that she let the world move.

Wildgust plummeted away. The professor and Tortillus looked completely bewildered.

"Quick!" Molly cried, grappling for her red crystal. "Join hands. Grab Schnapps, Selkeem! We've got to leave. *NOW!*"

Wildgust flapped his wings and began soaring up high above them. Now he could see the ledge. Molly, Professor Selkeem, Tortillus, and the dognake were huddled there in a circle.

"I'll get you," Wildgust roared furiously. But as he shot toward them, he saw that he had lost. He suddenly realized why they were all so close together. It wasn't from fear. It was a necessity for time travel. They were going to leave him. And, with a BOOM, they were gone.

# Twenty-nine

As they whizzed forward through time, the professor gripped Molly's shoulder and cried out, "Blissful to be the rider, so nice not to be the horse for once!" Molly had no idea what he was talking about, but since Selkeem always spoke in riddles she didn't worry. What *did* worry her was how wrongly she had read him. She'd thought he was bad to the core, but he'd proved that he wasn't. And she was very concerned about Micky.

"Is Micky still at the institute?" she asked, her hair flicking about her face in the time winds.

"The Mickster is not a trickster. He's okay. I left him to find his rock to stand on."

"You left him to find Rocky?" The boy professor nodded.

Tortillus held Molly's other arm. He was staring straight ahead with a sad look in his eyes. To have your own brother try to kill you was deeply shocking. Molly had been upset by the incident with Wildgust. Tortillus must be a thousand times more traumatized.

Molly brought them into a time hover and then she slotted them precisely back into where they'd come from.

As they materialized, a worried-looking crowd hurried around and greeted them.

"Professor Selkeem and his dognake are fine," Molly explained at once, seeing their confusion. "They helped us. It was Wildgust. He . . ." She faltered, not wanting to be the one to break the horrible news.

"He tried to kill me," Tortillus said, embracing Belsha. "He hadn't changed like we'd hoped. He's jealous as he ever was. He must have been hiding his hatred of me all these years." He bowed his head. "We . . . we left him behind."

Everyone fell silent.

"One day you can go back and find him," Molly said. "I can take you back. And if you think he's changed, I'll help you to bring him back home again."

"That's kind of you, Molly."

Then the professor piped up, He's completely moldy. Gone off. Past his sell-by date. Never be good again."

"You might be right," Tortillus agreed sadly.

Molly ran her eyes around the gathering. She was impatient to find out what had happened to *her* brother. To her great relief she saw Micky sitting cross-legged on the grass by the fishpond, watching them.

"Have you dehypnotized him?" she whispered to Rocky.

"Yes. He's all back to normal."

Molly walked across to her brother and stood over him with crossed arms. "Are you all right?" she asked, smiling down.

"Yes, I'm fine now," Micky said. He squinted slightly as the sunlight hit his eyes. "But being under someone else's power is really bad. I know that now, Molly. I felt like my body was a robot that I was trapped inside." And then, getting to his feet, he did something that Molly had never thought he would do. "Thanks, Molly," he said. "You're a great sister." And he gave her a hug. Molly hugged him back. It was strange, she thought, how such bad things and such good things could happen on the same day.

The bell over the palace nursery entrance rang out to the tune of "Hickory Dickory Dock" and the door slid apart, revealing Nurse Meekles's garden. A gaggle of children ran around a big green ball, shouting and playing. Three more dug in a sandpit, two dangled on swings, and two others rode futuristic-looking hover trikes around the paths. Alerted by the bell, the old nurse came out of the house to see who'd arrived.

"Can I help?" she asked, her eyes darting from Tortillus to Belsha. She spotted Molly but didn't react. Micky, hanging back in the shadows, was too indistinct for her to see clearly. She registered Miss Cribbins's lopsided wig, but her eyes rested on Princess Fang. "Can—can I do anything, Your Highness?" Princess Fang stared dumbly at her. Nurse Meekles came closer, looking nervous.

"Tell her that you will do anything that she asks of you," Molly instructed the princess.

"I will—do anything—you ask—of me," Fang repeated mechanically.

"Sorry, I didn't catch that." Nurse Meekles hesitated, convinced that her ears were failing her.

"Do some cartwheels," Molly ordered. "Do some cartwheels now and tell Nurse Meekles that you are her servant." Immediately the princess did as she was told. Her feathered dress was soon rolling with her inside it, like a great big, wrapped-up birthday present, toward Nurse Meekles.

"I am your servant," she exclaimed, arriving at the Chinese woman's feet.

Nurse Meekles looked perplexed and then worried. "Is this some sort of joke?" she said.

Molly stepped up to the old woman. "No, Nurse Meekles. But Princess Fang *will* be your servant from now on and so will Miss Cribbins. Thanks to your help, everything's been sorted out. Look, here are King Klaucus, and Queen Belsha.

Nurse Meekles gasped. "Your Majesty, is that really you? I—I didn't recognize you. What's happened to you? Oh my goodness!"

"It's good to see you, Ai Mu," Tortillus said.

"I don't believe it!" Nurse Meekles shook her head.

"And this is my friend Rocky, back to his normal self," said Molly. "And"—she grinned—"here's Micky."

"Micky, my plum pudding dumpling! It *is* you!" Nurse Meekles clapped her hands with delight. Micky rushed toward his old nanny and threw his arms around her.

"Thank you," he said. "And Molly's right—we're all free because you helped. Thank you for knowing what was right."

Nurse Meekles fell on him like a parent reunited with a lost child. "I knew you were still good at heart, Micky. I knew it. You're a good boy, my honey cracker, always were." Then she nudged him away to look at him. "And how well you look!" she exclaimed.

Micky blushed. "You know I was brainwashed by those people, Nurse Meekles. I'm—I'm so sorry I became what I did. They made me feel that I was useless—that I was nothing without them. Miss Cribbins told me I only had a few years to live. Even the name they gave me was to make sure I felt bad about myself. I mean, Micky *Minus*! Who wants to be a minus? Not me."

"What are you going to call yourself now?" Nurse Meekles asked, laughing, "Micky Plus?" She hugged him again.

"Well, I don't know if I'd be allowed"—Micky turned to Molly—"but I wondered whether Molly would let me take on the same name as her."

"That would be brilliant!" said Molly happily. "Micky Moon! It sounds perfect!"

"Yes, it is perfect," said Nurse Meekles, giving him yet another hug. "So Micky Moon it is."

Then the smile drained from her face as she noticed Professor Selkeem, standing half hidden behind a bush. Without saying anything, she walked toward him. And to everyone's astonishment, she knelt down and embraced him too. They began to talk quietly and earnestly. Nurse Meekles, Molly thought, must have looked after the professor when he'd been younger as well.

That night at the palace, the shallow pool in the center of the dining room table was lit up so that it glowed purple. Candles were floated on it. Shiny spoons and silver chopsticks reflected their light. Glasses glittered full of different-colored liquids—concentrated orange squash for Molly; something bright yellow for Micky; exotic fruit juices for Rocky and Professor Selkeem; and delicate pink wines for Nurse Meekles, Tortillus, and his family. Petula and Silver were given places of honor at the head of the table. Petula ate rare fillet steak, while Silver was given the best seed in the house. The food was delicious—spicy meats and creamy potatoes, freshly picked vegetables and salads. Molly was reminded of the weird dinner she had been to with Princess Fang and her bratty companions. She looked outside to the spray-fountain courtyard. There were Fang and her friends now, sitting on the steps eating millet porridge. She turned to Micky.

"Did you ever muck about with those friends of Princess Fang's?"

"I wasn't allowed," said Micky, eating a tiny, bright tomato. "Cribbins said I'd catch something. Anyway, I never really wanted to—they weren't like the kids I'd known from Nurse Meekles nursery. They couldn't play properly."

"Princess Fang wasn't really like a child at all," said

Molly. "I mean, when I had supper with her here she was drinking wine and smoking—and the books she read! She was learning about astrophysics!"

"She's a genius, I suppose," said Rocky. He pointed at the professor, who, now dressed in a blue jumpsuit, was also in the courtyard, where he had constructed a makeshift outdoor laboratory, "Just like Selkeem. Except it seems, from what he did to save you, Tortillus, he's a mad *good* genius, whereas Fang was a mad bad genius. I'm surprised her brain didn't explode from all the knowledge she tried to cram into it. And whoever heard of a six-year-old wanting to take over the world? Wow! That six-year-old was beyond any child ever!" Everyone around the table nodded, except Nurse Meekles.

"Fang *was* beyond any child ever," she suddenly volunteered, "because—and this is going to be news to you all—because that person sitting out there, whom you call Princess Fang, *isn't a child*."

Around the table, mouths fell open, conversation stopped, and chopsticks and spoons were laid down. All eyes fell inquiringly on Nurse Meekles.

"Isn't a child?" Tortillus exclaimed. "But of course she's a child. Just look at her."

Everyone glanced outside at Fang, who sat on the step looking at her belly button. Her podgy little legs were sticking out straight in front of her. Her small arms and little hands, her big eyes and full face were completely childlike.

"Yes, look at her," said Nurse Meekles. "That, my friends, is *Queen* Fang."

Tortillus's shell rose up his back in surprise. "But how can that be? The old queen would be about sixty years old by now."

Nurse Meekles nodded. "It's a long story—an incredible story. I'll try to put it in a nutshell for you." A murmur went around the table, and the old woman began.

"Once upon a time there were two royal hypnotists—a bad one called Redhorn—he's the one who snatched you, Micky—and a good one, a much more talented one, called Axel. Axel was my husband. Both knew how to time travel with hypnotism and they knew about a place at the beginning of time, a Bubble with marvelous properties. If a person goes there and bathes in its light he becomes *younger*."

"That's true." Molly nodded. "I've been there."

Nurse Meekles smiled. "Well, Redhorn told the old Queen Fang about that place and she was very, *very* interested in it. You see, Queen Fang loathed everything ugly and everything old, and this included herself. She hated looking at herself in the mirror. Every year she spent months in and out of the operating theater, having surgery to make herself look younger. And every day beauticians spent hours treating her face with oils and creams to make her look more youthful. She took medicines to stop herself from aging; she even injected herself with chemical concoctions at every mealtime. She used every scientific trick in the book to keep herself young. But the wrinkles kept coming. And so she became obsessed with the Bubble at the beginning of time. She wanted to be made *as young as a child again,* since she thought that the youth of a child is more beautiful than anything else."

Nurse Meekles took a sip of her wine and then, with a faraway look in her eyes, continued. "The old Queen Fang desperately wanted to go to the Bubble, but Redhorn couldn't do it. He couldn't get the colored crystals to move him backward in time fast enough. Then one day, using hidden microphones that he'd sneakily set up, he overheard my husband, Axel, talking to me about how he'd been there. That was it. Queen Fang, of course, had to have Axel take *her* there. Axel refused. So the queen told him that if he didn't take her, *I* would be killed. This time he agreed, and he took her back in time. When she came back she looked *four years old*." She shook her head in wonder. "Although she looked like a child, her mind was still an adult's—or nearly all of it was. A small part of it had become childish again. The queen became more bouncy and full of energy like a child. She spoiled herself. She had her fancy playrooms built and had every toy she wanted. She dressed in the way she thought a child who had everything should dress." The old nurse shut her eyes and tutted. "And the hypnotized people of Lakeside became her toys. She had the houses built so they looked like cottages out of a fairy tale and had the people dress in nursery-rhyme-style costumes. Then she decided that the rest of her court should also be made to look young again. They all leaped at the chance. See those ten children outside? They are all really adults. Axel was forced to take them *all* to the Bubble of Light. My poor Axel went backward and forward through time. And of course he became very young himself as he had to spend so much time in the Bubble. It was awful. There were other side effects too. His brain started to scramble. Sometimes I could hardly make sense of what he was saying. Luckily he worked out a way of putting Queen Fang's people in the Bubble and hovering outside it so that he didn't turn into a baby or disappear entirely. But even so, his skin grew rough and rhinoceroslike from all the time travel. He tried to fix it in the Bubble of Light but it didn't work. And though he could still time travel, he lost all his hypnotic powers." She shook her head and fiddled with her napkin. "Redhorn died of course."

The room was so quiet you could have heard an ant hiccup.

"Amazing." Tortillus sighed. Everyone looked at the children outside.

"Whereas Miss Cribbins," continued Nurse Meekles, "she was too nervous to take the trip back, so the princess, the *queen*, made her have plastic surgery. Now the woman has to take all sorts of medicines and give herself an injection six times a day. If she doesn't do that, her beautiful, youthful face will start to fall apart."

"I think *you* have a beautiful face, Ai Mu." Professor Selkeem had come into the dining room. "Tell them," he added. And so Nurse Meekles let last the bomb drop.

"Three years ago was Axel's last trip. My husband came back the size of a three-year-old, so he now looks six." She paused. "Yes, you may be guessing it as I speak. This, this boy here, this boy you know as Professor Selkeem, the tree boy—well, *he is Axel*."

Now everyone around the table was well and truly silenced. Molly and Micky stared at each other.

"Yes, that's me," the boy said, "a shrunken, shriveled thing. I'm a prune. I talk in riddles and am all back to front, so I'm Professor Meekles backward. Professor S-E-L-K-E-E-M. See?"

"That's amazing," Molly said. Bending her head, she unfastened one of the gem necklaces that hung there. "In that case, professor, these belong to you."

"Lovely jubbly!" the professor replied, enthusiastically taking the string of crystals. "Welcome home, little bulbs!" Then he turned to the waiter and in a more high-pitched voice asked, "We'd love some burned cabbage. Can you make me that?"

"Like you and your family, Tortillus," Nurse Meekles explained, "Fang banished him to the Institute of Zoology, where she could keep him until she needed to travel to the Bubble of Light again. She put him away there like some broken toy. She let him have his tree-house laboratory, for she saw his work as crazy and harmless. But his experiments weren't crazy at all. He was researching water storage in animal body cells. It gets so hot here, as you know, and water is precious. If animals could live on less water, it would help."

"Always nice to the animals though," Axel piped up. "Never hurt them."

"But you had their hearts dried and strung up in your kitchen!" Molly couldn't help blurting out. "And you drank their blood!"

"Oh tosh!" the professor replied, giving a mad little laugh. "Sun-dried tomatoes and tomato juice! I do think you need a magnifying glass!"

"But what about that dead meerkat thing?"

"Died of old-age pensioning," Axel replied. "Waste not, want not. And look, missy—right now you are eating dead pig." Molly looked down at her bowl of pork dumplings.

"So," asked Micky, "did Axel build the secret door into the laundry room?"

"Yes, my little chili pepper," Nurse Meekles replied. "It was for me to visit him, but I never could get up to that trapdoor, and he never visited me. Thought it might endanger my life if he did. I wanted to tell him that Tortillus and Wildgust were King Klaucus and the prince. I so wanted to tell him about Micky, but I could never get to him."

"Ahem!" Axel coughed loudly so that everyone turned toward him. "And now, ladles and gentle-spoons, boils and stirls, listen here! Please put down your chopsticks and whatnots and come with me, for I have a watery firework display for you!"

Everyone got up from the table and followed the professor outside. Petula padded along, keeping close behind Molly with an eye on the professor's dognakes. Silver hopped by her side.

*He's a bit of a walnut, isn't he?* Petula commented to her avian friend.

*Truly a pecan!* Silver agreed.

Axel stood proudly in front of his temporary laboratory, with its labyrinth of test tubes, pipes, and glass spheres. His dognakes curled up on the ground by his feet.

"This doesn't look like bobble squeak, I know," the professor declared as he took a large, glass-lidded vat, "but I think that if my calculations are right, you are about to witness something fantabulous. See my colored time-travel crystals and my clear time-stopping stone?" Axel held them up for everyone to see, then put them into the vat and began to heat it from underneath. "I used to do this with impure crystals," he explained. "It never bob-diddlied."

Molly bit her lip and watched as the precious crystals grew hot. A puff of sky-blue smoke drifted up the glass tube in the lid of the vat into the transparent doughnutlike container above it. Here the smoke was sucked through the sponge there, from where it emerged as a clear liquid. This solution trickled down a pipe until it became a big drip that plopped out.

"Let there be . . . !" the professor shouted, and taking a small, very powerful pocket flashlight he shone its beam onto the drip. There was an explosion of light. A huge bubble of rainbow-colored light filled the courtyard. It engulfed everyone so that for a moment they were all in a dreamy, bright rainbow, surrounded by all the colors of the spectrum. Reds, oranges, yellows, blues, greens, and purples flashed about them and then disappeared.

Everyone was astounded. They all clapped and hollered their appreciation.

Axel now picked up the crystals from the hot vat.

"They're cold," he said. "Completely undoodled by the heat. Could be used for eternity and they wouldn't fall a-party with crackers and cake. My best invention ever. You see"—he took the pipette and licked the end of it—"this is pure water— $H_2O$! This is how to make water out of air!"

"That is marvelous, Axel," Tortillus said. "Could this be the answer to our water problems?"

"Could be, could bee, could wasp," Axel replied.

Molly felt like a fool. She saw now that the mad professor had harbored good intentions all along. She patted Schnapps on the head.

"I'm sorry I misunderstood you, Axel," she said.

"Easy mistake to missmake, miss. The words come out in a fuddle, you see. Tongue connected to the muddle, not the noodle."

"Yes," Molly said, thinking she knew what he meant. Then she took the professor's grubby hand. "I'm really sorry. I can see that you are a great scientist, and you were obviously a brilliant hypnotist too. And you look the way you do because you were protecting Ai Mu. If you hadn't taken Fang to the Bubble, she would have had Nurse Meekles killed. You're a hero, Axel. You really are."

The professor nodded and smiled a snaggle-toothed grin and then curtsied. "Thank you. Nice of you to say so. Not so cowardy custard yourself. Now, if you don't mind, I'll be getting back to my brewing." With that he swiveled, did a small hop, and began tapping at one of his glass test tubes.

Molly turned to Micky.

"Now, Micky, *you* and *I* have a very important appointment. Let's go to see Mr. Jellyfish."

# Thirty

The next morning Molly woke fresh and clearheaded. She stretched in her bed. Her crystals clicked together around her neck. She felt great. Everything felt complete. Except for one thing. Would Micky come home with her?

Leaving him and Rocky still asleep, she slipped on some new clothes: a red cotton jumpsuit and twenty-sixth-century sneakers that had superconcentrated pockets of helium in their soles. Then, with Petula by her side, she walked on air to the courtyard.

Tortillus was already up, sitting outside his room under trellised arches covered in lemon blossom. A black bird with an orange beak sat among the blooms.

"Hello, Petula. Good morning, Molly," he said, offering her a cup. "Do you want some coffee?"

"No, thanks. Concentrated orange squash is my preferred wake-up drink. Anyway, I'm not really thirsty or hungry yet."

Tortillus smiled. "Well, join me at least. I am having a lovely time, Molly. Life hasn't been this good in years." Molly chose a cushioned stool and sat down.

"I've been thinking. That mind machine is going to be very useful," Tortillus continued. "For instance, very old people can have their memories downloaded on to it for others to enjoy. And instead of it being used *by* criminals, it can be used *on* criminals—no one will be able to lie and get away with it."

"Yes," said Molly, smiling, "this place could become Mind Mountain. People will come here from all over the world."

"And with the money we make, we'll be able to pay for pipelines to bring water from the north to keep the lake filled. What with this and Axel's inventions, we should be able to live here always."

"Well, Fang and her crew are all hypnotized to obey you, Tortillus. I locked their instructions in with passwords and they will be like that until you choose to release them."

"Good. Very good," the old man said, chuckling. Molly reached for the blue grapes in a bowl on the table and twisted one off its stalk.

"It's time for me to go home now. Either with or without Micky."

"I know. You'll come back and visit us, I hope."

"Of course I will."

Tortillus tapped his cup with a gnarled brown nail.

"You're really very good at this time-travel business, aren't you?" he said.

"Not bad," Molly agreed, nodding.

"And hypnotizing."

"Yup."

"I've seen your other skill too, you know," Tortillus said. "You give off the same glow as Silver when he mind reads. But you're right not to tell people about it."

"Oh. Yes." Molly smiled.

"Hmmm."

For a moment they both sat there quietly. Molly wondered whether the old man knew what she could do. He'd picked up on Micky's trouble, and he knew that Silver could mind read. Then it suddenly occurred to her that Tortillus might think her some sort of show-off, so she added, "but there are ten tons of things that I'm really bad at. I'm useless at sports and I never was any good at schoolwork and I'm not tidy at all. And I'm clumsy. I mean, I may have all these weird skills, but at ordinary things I'm not talented at all!"

"Nobody can be good at everything," Tortillus

replied. Then he put his hands up to Molly's head and shut his eyes. "Hmm," he hummed. "You have more still inside you, Molly. There are more talents there that haven't germinated yet, but you just wait. Something very strong is lying dormant in you. I think it will be out soon."

"What do you mean?" Molly asked. But before Tortillus had time to elaborate she heard people coming. It was Micky and Rocky, with Silver hopping on the ground after them.

"Morning, Micky and Rocky and Silver," Tortillus said. "You're up early."

"He had a dream," Rocky said.

"A good one?"

"Yes," Micky replied. He turned to Molly. "I dreamed . . . dreamed I came back to your time with you." He stumbled over his words. "It felt really good to meet Primo and Lucy. And—and then I got thinking. Molly, you got me my hypnotic skills back from the machine last night. Would you teach me how to time-travel so that I can come back here when I want to? I don't know if that's possible."

"Sure it's possible," said Molly, grinning. "That is exactly what I see you doing!"

"Excellent!" said Tortillus. "In that case it is time for good-bye presents." He reached into his pocket and pulled out a box, which he handed to Rocky. "I know you have asthma, Rocky. It's a horrid thing, and something that's been cured now. Take this pill and your asthma will never bother you again."

Rocky's mouth dropped open. "In-incredible," he managed to say. "That's amazing! Thank you."

"My pleasure," Tortillus replied. Then he gave a sharp whistle and with eight springy hops and a flutter of wings Silver was standing on the table. "Silver would like to come with you, Micky." Tortillus explained. "He knows that he was the first friend you made here."

"Phooowheeek! What a boy!" whistled Silver.

"And for you, Molly and Rocky, here is . . ." He gave another whistle.

The black bird that had been sitting in the lemon blossom now flew down and perched on Tortillus's finger.

"This is Silver's son," he explained. "His name is Mercury. He is good at mind reading but not at talking, not yet. But that will come. He's quite a character."

"How *lovely*!" Molly exclaimed. She stroked the bird's small head. "But are you sure he wants to come?"

"Definitely. Mercury's a very adventurous bird. He likes to be around children. Silver told me that he would like to come."

"Well, we'd love to have him," said Molly.

"What an amazing present!" Rocky agreed, touching the bird's feathery breast. "Hello, Mercury."

By nine o'clock everyone had assembled on the mountaintop landing pad to watch Molly and Micky and Rocky leave.

Micky was the last one to get into the large white flycopter. He spent a long time saying good-bye to Nurse Meekles. So long that Molly thought that he might change his mind about coming.

But eventually he climbed the steps and was soon sitting behind Molly, doing up his belt. Petula sat beside her, sucking a stone, and Silver and Mercury were perched on the seat beside Rocky. The door slid shut.

Molly smiled at the hostess as she brought her a drink of orange-squash concentrate and thought how nice it was not to have to be hiding all huddled up at the back. Then the aircraft catapulted off, tipped back, and extended its wings. With a clunk the helicopterlike propellers snapped into the top of the machine and at the same time a loud expulsion of supersonic exhaust sent the plane shooting upward. Soon they were thousands of feet up in the sky and the jet leveled off. They sped through the sky with the greatest of ease.

Lunch was served on gleaming trays. It was triangular pasta with a seaweed salad followed by a white meringue pudding called Mont Blanc. As a finishing touch there were fortune cookies. Molly unwrapped hers and read the white strip of paper that had fallen on her napkin.

"You've got to risk it for a biscuit," it said. *You certainly have,* Molly thought. She slipped her shoes off, wriggled her toes, and settled down for a well-earned snooze.

When Molly woke up, she looked out of the window. The landscape below had changed. It was much greener and it looked colder.

As Tortillus had promised, they were brought as close to the Briersville of 2500 as air-traffic control would allow. The plane dived down, morphed into its flycopter form, and landed on the icy runway of the local airport. They all put on their coats.

Outside, on the tarmac, Molly got everyone to hold hands. She hugged Petula tightly, while Silver and Mercury sat on Micky's left shoulder. Then Molly gazed into the heart of her green crystal and with a sonic BOOM they were gone. Cool time winds brushed past them and the world was a blur.

Molly focused her mind with all her might. She was really excited to be going home and to be bringing

Micky back. She didn't want anything to go wrong now.

They stopped. The landscape had changed again. It was wintry, but the trees were different. Instead of the ferns and conifers that had surrounded the twenty-sixth-century airport, there were the leafless oaks and beech trees of Molly's own time. Some even bore a few flapping yellow leaves that the autumn winds had missed. The airport had gone. Instead there was a field. A town stood nearby.

"I think that's Ricksford," said Rocky to Micky. "It's the next-door town to Briersville. We could get a bus back from here."

"Let's get a cab," said Molly. So they walked on to the road.

Micky's eyes were wide as he soaked up the sights and sounds of his new home.

"Stone Age!" he said. "The cars look like the ones in history books!"

"That," said Molly as a sleek silver sports car drove past, "is considered very cool and modern. Wait till you see your new home. It really *is* old."

Soon they were motoring up the long winding drive past scores of animal-shaped bushes to Briersville Park. The llamas looked up, clouds of steamy breath puffing from their noses in the cold morning air.

Then the house came into view, white and majestic—

a beautiful stately home. The cab pulled up on the gravel.

"We'll pay you in a second," Molly said to the driver. "Our parents have the money."

She got out of the car and leaped up the stairs. She rang the bell and kept ringing it while Rocky, Micky, Petula, and the birds assembled on the steps.

The huge door creaked open. There stood Primo Cell and Lucy Logan. Everyone stared at one another. It was a perfect moment. Molly put her hand on Micky's shoulder and proudly proclaimed: "Lucy and Primo, meet Micky."

"Micky Moon," Micky added shyly, not looking up from the ground.

"Micky Moon," agreed Molly. "Your son."

# Thirty-one

That afternoon everyone was in the kitchen. Forest, with his long white dreadlocks tied in a ponytail and with a chef's hat that read GET IN THE COOKING GROOVE, was preparing a bean-sprout salad. Ojas was kneading dough for naan bread; Molly and Micky were making sandwiches; and Primo, Lucy, and Rocky were sitting at the table drinking tea. Silver and Mercury were perched up high on a saucepan shelf, and Petula was curled up asleep in her basket.

"I don't know how you can eat those sprout things," Rocky said.

"I agree," Lucy joined in. "It's a bit like eating grass with the seed still stuck on the end."

"Don't tell 'em, don't tell 'em," Forest whispered

into the bean sprout packet. "If they knew how good you were, there'd be none left for me."

"And ketchup sandwiches sound revolting," Micky told Molly.

"Well, to an unsophisticated person that might be true," Molly replied, slapping butter onto a slice of white bread, "but to a connoisseur like me they are the best thing to eat on earth."

"What about on the moon?" Primo asked. "What's the best thing there?"

"Moon's marshmallows, of course."

Micky eyed the cupboards above the work surface.

"What are you going to put in your sandwich, then?" Molly asked.

"Don't suppose you've got any meerkat and mustard?" Micky smiled. "No, what I really want is some . . . I don't know if you have it in this time."

"We might do. Give it a try."

"Well, it's very Chinese."

"So what is it?"

"Soy sauce."

Everyone laughed.

"'Course we've got soy sauce," Molly teased him. "What did you think this was? The Stone Age?"

"Well . . ."

"So is that your favorite thing to have in sandwiches, then?" Molly asked.

"Favorite thing to eat, full stop," Micky admitted. "And you won't believe this, but my best drink is undiluted aprimango cordial."

"Apri-what?!" Forest exclaimed.

"You're peas in a pod," said Ojas, pummeling his dough.

"But don't you *dare* forget Miss Cribbins's instructions," said Rocky, sternly impersonating her voice. "EAT NUTRITIOUS, NOT GREEDY. KEEP KITCHENSIDE TIDY!"

"Eat nutritious, not greed. Kaap kitchenside tady," Silver chirped from beside a large copper pan.

"Et nootreeshash—naat graady—kaap katchen tady," Merlin echoed at his side.

And high over the white ridges of Mont Blanc a large bird circled.

Three children out on a morning ski came to a halt and pointed up at it.

"It's *huge*!" the girl said, rubbing her mittened hands together.

"That's not a bird—it's a vampire!" the boy beside her observed darkly.

"Vampires don't exist," laughed his older brother.

Then the enormous creature began flying toward them. As it approached, its great brown wings cupping the air, it became quite obvious that this was no ordinary bird. For it had human legs, was wearing orange trousers, and seemed to have a man's face.

"It's a wizard!" the little girl screamed.

"Let's get out of here!" the small boy cried.

"Ski as fast as you've ever skied in your life!" yelled his brother.

And turning their skis about, the three of them pushed off.

Wildgust trod air and let his wings beat so that he hovered above the children.

"I mean no harm!" he called down. "I just want something to eat!"

But below him, the colorful shapes of the skiing children shot down the slopes of spring snow and were gone.